Blood on the Mother Road

No Place to Hide

An Oklahoma Mystery
(Book 2)

Blood on the Mother Road

No Place to Hide

An Oklahoma Mystery
(Book 2)

Mary Coley

Blood on the Mother Road: No Place to Hide. An Oklahoma Mystery

Published by Mary Coley/Moonglow Books through Amazon Direct Publishing. P.O. Box 2517, Tulsa, OK 74101 USA

www.marycoley.com

ISBN: 13: 9798741054024
ISBN: 10: 8741054024

Dedication:

I want to thank my family and my friends for patiently waiting as I created this book. The COVID-19 epidemic was devastating to many people. Lives and livelihoods were lost.

Everyone suffered during quarantines as the necessary precautions were taken in an attempt to hinder the progression of this life-changing virus. In many ways, our lives will never be the same.

Creativity also suffered in this time of upended lives. Many days, I felt as if my writing muse had taken a vacation without me.

She returned, and here is the result.

To my friends and family: enjoy another Oklahoma adventure! Thank you for your support.

Chapter 1 - TUESDAY
Claire

Claire Northcutt woke from the dream soaked in sweat. She rolled out of bed, charged across her moonlit bedroom to the window and pulled the curtain open to the late October night sky. The moon, high above and waxing toward full, cast shadows from the trees on the wide lawn of her five acres outside Stillwater, Oklahoma. Shadows reached toward the dark house on the neighboring plot of land. Holt's house.

A week had passed since he'd been home. She didn't know where he was. She hadn't asked where he was going. Claire pushed her dark hair out of her eyes and took a shaky breath. Holt was probably safe. It was only another bad dream.

It was more than that. Her memories had pieced together a nightmare quilt. Two guns. A scythe. A pitchfork. And blood—everywhere. Two men dead, two gravely wounded. She drew evil men to her. But for two years, she'd been safe.

The back of Claire's eyes ached. The all-too-frequent headaches came when Holt was out of town, doing whatever it was he did for weeks at a time. In the years she'd known him, he'd never told her where his work trips took him. Two years ago—after she'd shot someone—she'd asked him why he'd had a pair of handcuffs in his pocket, ready to secure the man who had orchestrated one murder and nearly killed her. He'd responded with the cliché, "I'll have to shoot you if I tell you."

She took that to mean he was in some type of law enforcement or espionage. Now he was gone again.

Her already too-short fingernails touched her lips. Claire dropped her hand and fingered the hem of her pajama shirt.

Holt was a handsome, intelligent man. But every time she thought about taking their relationship to the next stage, nightmare memories closed in.

The most recent memories were of events two years earlier. The first event happened in the small barn on her property, where the stalker lay on his back with a pitchfork driven into his leg. The second was of a wounded man on an idyllic tiled patio overlooking the tree-covered banks of the Cimarron River.

Another image replaced those gruesome scenes. Five years ago, an image of the naked stranger she'd shot in her apartment after he'd crawled into her bed.

Claire closed her eyes to the moonlit yard. More images came, memories of arguments with her ex-husband. Hands raised to strike; angry eyes narrowed. Broken dishes, broken photographs. Her broken heart.

Holt couldn't shoulder his way through those images. Couldn't slip into her shattered heart or smile his way into her wary being.

It had to be enough to be friends. She was nearing forty, with an eighteen-year-old son. It was too late to start life over again. She had to salvage what she could of this life and stop obsessing about the past. She had to focus on work, like Holt all to obviously did.

Her suitcase was open on the end of her bed, half filled with clothing for a five-day stay in Persimmon, Oklahoma. Part business, part pleasure, the trip was a welcome get away. She intended to enjoy it. She hoped to start a new chapter in her journalism career.

A cloud covered the moon and what had been only shadows became a vast darkness. One edge of the darkness reached toward her house. The vivid nightmare came back as Claire watched the shadow wax and wane like the frothy tide on a beach.

Her heartrate and her breathing quickened. The pulsating shadow couldn't be real.

The moon returned, the shadow retreated.

But it had been there.

What did it mean?

Chapter 2 - WEDNESDAY
Rhonda

"She was dead," the man told his companions in a low, gravelly voice. "Yes, I'm sure."

Rhonda's head jerked up, her green eyes wide. She hadn't seen the man before, but today was only her third day on the job, her third day in Persimmon, Oklahoma, her third day in the life of Rhonda the Waitress. Her former life as Dr. Renee Trammel was history for now. She had never seen any of the customers in Tiny's Route 66 Diner before.

Her legs moved her away from the raspy voice at Table 14, but her thoughts froze. The man's words, like a winter wind laced with ice, stunned her.

"Hey, doll, can I have more ketchup for my fries?" The leering, middle-aged bozo tugged at the hem of her pink tunic as she passed Table 3. He handed her an empty ketchup bottle when she paused. His look appraised her up and down. She wanted to slap him. Instead, she glanced back at Table 14 as she brushed her auburn hair away from her face. Plates clattered, and the aroma of grilled burgers, fried onion rings and potatoes swirled in the air.

The man she'd overheard was around forty with thin brown hair, pudgy cheeks, and a dimpled chin. A pot belly bulged beneath a lime green golf shirt. Beads of sweat clung to his forehead.

Rhonda headed for the wait station.

"Order up, *mesa cinco*," Eduardo, the short-order cook, called from the kitchen.

Rhonda grabbed a ketchup bottle from the wait station at the end of the line of tables and took it to Table 3, averting her eyes as the customer upended the ketchup bottle and poured the blood-red sauce over his French fries. She glanced at the table by the swinging door.

Two men sat across from the lime green shirt, the greasy remains of their lunch platters pushed to one side. One of them was skinny with a goatee like some parody of the 60s. The edges of a blue and green tattoo reached from the collar of his shirt toward his Adam's apple. He tilted his chair away from the table and stared at the ceiling. Gray strands streaked the hair on the third man's temples, and a white scar paralleled the line of one eyebrow. He peered at the sweating man across the table.

"Um, Rhonda? More water, please?" An elderly lady in a nearby booth read the name stitched in red thread on the pocket of her uniform.

"Sure thing." Rhonda returned to the service stand and grabbed a pitcher. Water slopped on the table as she tried to refill the woman's glass a few seconds later.

The customer glanced at Rhonda's shaking hands. "You okay?"

"Um, yeah. Sure." She set the pitcher down on the table and smiled, tucking her hands into the pockets of her uniform's skirt, willing them to be still. She glanced through the big plate glass window at the front of the café.

Orange and red leaves trembled in a gust of wind. Some of them fluttered down from the tree and raced along the ground. Diffused light swirled, gilding everything with gold.

Fall had been Renee's favorite time of year. Now, as Rhonda, she hated it.

Who was dead?

She forced the thought out of her head. It was none of her concern. Her only business had to be staying alive until the trial. Draw no attention. Then maybe she'd see her children and her parents again. Maybe, she could return to her life.

Rhonda passed Table 14. The men sat, eyes down and silent.

She pushed through the swinging door into the kitchen. Instantly, the overwhelming odor of fried liver and onions slammed her. She staggered to the pick-up counter.

Her appetite hadn't returned since the massacre at her vet clinic a week ago. She needed to eat, but she wasn't hungry. How could she think about food?

Why had she let them talk her into Witness Protection, and into this job?

After pulling in a few deep breaths and centering her mind on the current moment, Rhonda carried the partially prepared dinner plates to the prep counter and added garnishes. Parsley here, a dill pickle spear there. She loaded a tray and headed for the dining room.

The men were gone.

Her shoulders dropped. Her shaking hands stilled.

Thank God. I don't have to do anything. I can't get involved.

But Rhonda still wondered who was dead —and why. Lance, the busboy, stepped up to Table 14 and piled the dirty plates onto his dish tray.

* * *

"You're catching on, Rhonda," Vivian said. The experienced older waitress smiled, showing coffee-stained teeth, and pushed her empty dinner plate—she'd had the Daily Special like Rhonda—to one side before she leaned over the table. "I know you've never waitressed before. Don't know if Lloyd will see it. He notices hair and eyes, but mostly tits. Don't matter to him if you keep up with your orders or get 'em right. He can't hear half of what you say anyway. You beautify the place."

Vivian pulled a red lipstick out of her apron pocket and coated her mouth, looking at her lips in the little square mirror attached to the top of the lipstick tube's cap. She smacked her lips together, opened her mouth and checked her teeth for lipstick smears. Her eyes narrowed. "Lloyd don't care. He's too focused on that car club and driving his rust bucket to every rally in the region. He may not care, but I do. You gotta carry your weight. No excuses just because you're older. Get it?"

Rhonda pushed her half-eaten plate of meat loaf aside. She wasn't the youngest waitress, but she wasn't the oldest, either. Fifty was still five years away, and she suspected that both Vivian and Jean—another hard-working waitress at the café—had reached that milestone. "Vivian, I really need this job. I'll get the hang of it. And I'll carry my weight."

The thing was, she *didn't* need this job, but the program insisted she work in the community where she lived. She supposed it made her appear less suspicious, gave credence to the story that she'd recently moved to Persimmon, Oklahoma, near Tulsa on old Route 66.

Vivian dumped the lipstick into her pocket, fluffed her short brown hair, and stretched a hair net over it. "You already get more tips than Jean and Lynnie combined. Why should I help you?" The corners of the woman's ample lips turned down. "You're too smart. Too good lookin' with your green eyes and red hair. Too quiet. And you're married. What are you doing here, anyway?"

How many times in the last three days had Rhonda asked herself that same question? She didn't want anyone to remind her of the answer, didn't want to dredge it all up again. It was bad enough that she relived it in her dreams every night. She rubbed her wedding ring and fought back tears.

"I need a job."

Vivian snorted. "You'll get a better one. And I'm telling you, we're all going to be mad if you walk out of here without giving Lloyd notice like Tatia did. He was supposed to be in Texas at some rally. Instead, he had to cover the front and work the counter. It's prime tourist time on Route 66. Those bikers are always hungry. Not to mention the RV crowd. Truth is, when you showed up, Lloyd needed you as much as you say you need this job."

"I won't let you down, Vivian." Rhonda forced a smile. Her future was anyone's guess. Who knew if she would still be waitressing at Tiny's Diner in another month? It all hinged on the trial of a murderous drug dealer.

She carried her plate to the big dishwashing sink, scraped the scraps into the trash can and slid the dish and utensils into the water.

God, help me. Surely, I won't still be here in a month, or worse yet, a year.

But what if she was? She scrutinized the suds as she scoured the plate with the bristly brush and tried to ignore the sting of the soapy water on the five-day old cuts which were healing on her hands and lower arms.

Just a week ago, life outside of Austin had grown routine, she and Daniel working at their vet clinic, empty nesters. They passed the days caring for the animals of their community. The troubled waters of life had receded; they lived on a plateau where the only ominous sounds were the buzz of the bumblebees in their garden. She hadn't suspected that the evenness of life, the absence of troubles, meant there was a tsunami on the horizon.

When the water had begun to swell, she hadn't noticed. The dog arrived at the vet clinic in the arms of a grumbling misogynist neighbor. In that instant, when the man deposited the dog in her arms and told her how he'd found it and how it wouldn't eat, the water began to rise around the clinic. She had not seen the foam swirling around her ankles, hadn't seen how the drug wars she had dismissed as happening somewhere else had crept closer to her life.

If she'd looked out the clinic windows, would she have perceived the drug wars as they were, like an immense wave of water poised on the horizon, sucking energy in from the depths of the sea, energy that would sweep away life as she knew it?

Instead, she'd focused on her mission, her sworn profession to care for animals large and small. To relieve pain and suffering. To heal.

An image from television footage of the Indonesian tsunami tumbled into her head, people running as the gigantic wall of water rushed toward them like a hungry snake, mouth wide, unhinged jaw ready to devour everything in front of it.

Now she was lost in her own immense sea of despair. *Don't think about it. Don't imagine that wave of water, don't remember the lives lost that day, the family destroyed, the business gone forever. Don't remember.*

"Breathe, Rhonda. You're white as mayonnaise. What are you doing? You don't have to wash your plate.

There are customers waiting to be served. Go," Vivian growled.

But the room fogged around her and in her mind, she kicked up through twenty feet of lake water, frantically swimming for the surface after driving her SUV over a cliff. She'd tried not to gasp for air despite the ache in her chest. Brown water would fill her lungs. And if she didn't get back to the surface, she couldn't return to the clinic with help for her wounded husband. Wouldn't know for sure if Daniel were dead. She had to —

Rhonda jerked her mind back into the diner's kitchen, gingerly patted her hands dry on a paper towel and hustled toward the dining room.

Chapter 3
Claire

Claire Northcutt glanced at the movie-star-handsome man behind the truck's steering wheel. Around the eyes, Holt Braden looked a little like George Clooney, but the resemblance ended there, despite his prematurely graying hair. He was every bit as good-looking as Clooney. *Those dimples.* Claire turned toward the window to hide the blush in her cheeks.

Was it more than coincidence that her news assignment had brought her here to Persimmon where he was on assignment? She couldn't deny the butterflies in her stomach. And something was happening in her heart. Claire forgot the dark shadow of foreboding she'd felt the night before as she prepared to work on her latest news story for AP, a celebration of the many miles of world-famous Route 66 that stretched through Oklahoma.

For weeks, she'd talked the idea over with Manny Juarez, her editor at the Stillwater News Press. In between news pieces with time constraints, she'd researched this idea, and when she'd brought it up at a staff meeting, Manny had considered it. Despite Casey Stinson, a fellow reporter, insisting there wouldn't be enough interesting information, Claire had convinced Manny to let her try.

She'd selected a few towns on Route 66 in eastern Oklahoma to research. A lucky coincidence brought Persimmon to the top of her research list. A barrel racing competition was scheduled at a nearby round-up club, and Claire had entered her horse, Blaze. Her son Cade's girlfriend, Neve, had been practicing the barrels with Blaze. Under her nephew Denver's tutelage, Neve and Blaze had been able to reduce the time of each run around the barrels to an acceptable 20 seconds. If they could shave off a little more time, Neve might be a contender for the First-Place ribbon.

The bright October sun beamed through the sheltering branches of the trees along streets lined with century-old buildings and storefronts with tall, wide windows. Many of the stores in Persimmon advertised antiques or consignment clothing. Mom-and-pop cafés occupied several buildings. Others small businesses, including Pay Day loan companies, laundromats, craft stores, and quilt shops offering alternations shared the street with empty buildings. She could be in any small town in two dozen states. It was easy to forget that Oklahoma's second largest city, Tulsa, was a few miles up the turnpike from Persimmon.

Last night, Claire had stared at Holt Braden's dark house in the middle of the moonlit night, feeling that her neighbor/boyfriend had cast her aside. It was time to get on with her life. This morning, she'd confirmed her arrival for late morning at a bed and breakfast inn she'd found on the internet.

She'd left Holt a phone message: "I'll be gone for a few days to the Tulsa area. I've registered Blaze in the Persimmon Round-up Club's barrel racing competition. Not sure where you are or when you'll be back. Just letting you know."

She'd made the call just in case he returned home and wondered where she was. Not that he cared.

He returned her call five minutes later. From Tulsa. They made plans for a quick lunch in Persimmon before she began interviews for the news article. She and Cade checked into the Bed and Breakfast Inn, and Holt picked them up not long after. Minutes ago, they'd dropped Cade at the Round-up Club arena on the outskirts of town.

Now, she couldn't keep from smiling. *Those dimples.*

"Let's make a fresh start of it, sweetheart. I've left you alone for weeks," Holt said.

The resignation in his voice surprised her, softened her. They'd been dancing around an on-again off-again relationship for five years. She'd always been the one to pull back, to send the relationship back to plutonic.

He reached across the seat for her hand, blue-gray eyes sparkling. Air from the truck's heater vent blew his musky aftershave across the truck's cab. Her stomach reacted with a pleasant twist.

"Don't feel like you have to join us at the barrel racing competition. Cade will be hanging around with Neve at the arena. You're busy, and I have a lot of work to do. I need to finish my research on Persimmon for this article, *The Mother Road, 100 Years and Counting*, before we head back to Stillwater Sunday night. If I don't find details unique to this town, I can't include it."

Holt cleared his throat. "I get it, you're busy. I am too. My work in the Tulsa area could last a couple of months. You noticed I wasn't home last week, or the week before, didn't you?"

"I did. But since you never tell me where you're going or when you'll be back, I didn't think much of it." She heard the accusation that edged her voice and wished she could take it back. He was simply abiding by the rules she'd set for their 'no expectations' relationship.

"Nature of my job, honey." He glanced at her as he stopped at a red light. "How's the B&B?"

"Cute place. Four suites, each with double queen bedrooms. I think the owners are sisters. They were arguing when we checked in this morning. Something about a bakery skimping on the order. The place is clean. Very homey. And our suite is nice. In addition to the beds, we have a sitting area and a full *en-suite* bath. They offer a continental breakfast on weekdays and full breakfast on the weekends."

"Good." He frowned at the road. "I'm glad you're here for a few days, but it may not be easy to find time to spend together. Honestly, I'm afraid I may not get home to Stillwater for several weeks. Maybe even months."

Claire felt a tug on her heart, but at the same time, her jaw clenched. She'd struggled with these conflicting feelings for years. Part of her was always relieved when Holt was gone for a few weeks. He sometimes annoyed her and intruded on her personal space. Yet, when he wasn't next door, she felt off-center, ready to jump at any sound. When he was around, he made her laugh. He made her feel wanted. And safe.

Not to mention how helpful he was. Her horse-trainer nephew Denver couldn't manage some of the chores on her five acres, even with Cade's help. Between Denver's leg injury and the PTSD resulting from his years of service in Afghanistan, some days were a challenge. Denver's marriage to Jenny two years ago eased some of his occasional melancholy, but he often withdrew from personal contacts. Holt willingly stepped in when he could.

"Does your lack of response mean you'll miss me, or that you won't?" Holt intruded into her thoughts.

"Sorry. My mind is on other things. I have an interview at two with the town mayor. Where are you taking me for lunch?" She had to divert this conversation. She didn't want another relationship discussion now.

"Little place right up the street. On old Route 66. Tiny's Diner. Flash back to the 50s. Always lots of vintage cars there if you like that sort of thing."

"Sounds great as long as they have good burgers. I haven't had one in months." How long had it been since she'd had a juicy third-pounder? Holt's grin probably meant their burgers were top notch.

He navigated a corner under her watchful gaze. His confidence and intelligence both intrigued and repelled her. Handsome, intelligent men had burned her before; they'd stalked her and come close to killing her.

Holt was a man she barely knew, even after years of friendship. He was private about so many things, unwilling to share, unwilling to let her into the workings of his life.

Not that different from the way she was, was he? But she had an excuse. More than one. Previous experiences. What reason did he have?

The neon sign flashed, advertising the diner in brilliant colors even though it was midday. A half dozen vintage automobiles from the Sixties and Fifties were parked in the diner's lot, sunlight glistening on paint in the most popular colors of the time, turquoise, greens, and blues.

* * *

The burger was good, juicy, and flavorful, and so were the onion rings, battered by hand and deep-fried to perfection. Cade would love this place, and Claire could easily see making a habit of eating here during the few days they'd be in town. The café was a throwback to the post-World War II years with black and white tile floors and red furniture accents. Movie posters and car photographs decorated the diner's white walls. The soda fountain/counter area in the front room featured photographs of Oklahoma's best known eastern Oklahoma Route 66 attractions. The photographs framed a wide mirror behind the display of flavored powders and malts next to three milk shake blenders.

After they were seated, Holt scanned the diner. He drummed his fingers on the table and cleared his throat.

"What's up? You're nervous about something," Claire observed.

"Nervous? Not really." His laugh sounded fake.

He was keeping something from her. Again. She didn't know why he was here, and he wouldn't tell her. She bit into another crunchy onion ring. Silence ballooned around them as she chewed. It was one perfect onion ring. Homemade batter. Lightly fried. Claire studied the other customers: casually dressed couples at tables, businessmen at the counter, a booth of noisy teenagers.

She peeked at him over the rim of her iced tea glass. "So, you're working in the Tulsa area for a while. Anything you can tell me about, or is the job top secret?" Claire was sure he was in some branch of law enforcement, not the day trader he'd claimed to be when he first moved in next door.

His job could be dangerous. Someday he might not return. The thought opened a hollow in her chest.

He cleared his throat again, pushed back into the red Naugahyde booth, and grinned. Matching dimples caved in his cheeks, but his eyes were wary.

He wouldn't tell her anything. Nothing new. She supposed they'd have to be married before he'd tell her anything about his work.

Marriage? The short fingernails of her left hand grazed her lip. She'd tried marriage once and look what she had ended up with. Her considerate, loving fiancé had gone psycho control freak as soon as the ring was on her finger. She'd stuck it out for seven years before their divorce. The blessing she'd gotten from the fiasco was Cade. She vowed all those years ago, never again. Her nearly fatal encounters with handsome criminals reinforced her determination.

"Why don't you tell me about this news story you're working on. An interview with the mayor. What kind of questions do you have lined up?" He crossed his arms and leaned toward her across the table of the booth.

Diversion. Always diversion. Claire smirked and nodded. "That's okay. Change the subject. I'm not surprised." She sipped her tea, and leaned in. She lowered her voice. "Question One for the mayor: Where are the bodies buried?"

Chapter 4
Rhonda

Rhonda surveyed the dining room to make sure that the three men she'd overheard earlier had not returned. Only two new customers had come in during her late thirty-minute lunch break, and they weren't seated in her section.

The couple sipped their drinks as they talked. She knew the man. Holt. He'd never mentioned a girlfriend. Rhonda debated whether to saunter by and say hello but decided that might be awkward for him. Would he feel the need to explain who she was? What if the woman had no idea he was with the DEA? He was undercover, wasn't he?

The bell on the front door jingled and she moved through the maze of chairs and tables toward it, hurrying to seat the group of men. The fall air followed them in and beckoned her outside. Unlike her life last week, she couldn't cancel her appointments and take the afternoon off.

She glanced again at the couple in the far booth. If Holt wanted to talk to her, he'd motion her over. Otherwise, she'd stay away. She didn't know the protocol, and she didn't want to damage the tenuous relationship she was building with her 'keeper.' He was staying somewhere close enough to bring her food, and to check on her daily. He was only a phone call away, and other undercover agents were also watching out for her. Some of them could be here now.

Rhonda hoped that the drug gang believed she was dead. After driving her car into a lake five days ago, she should be. Instead, she was in Witness Protection, hiding, and one day she'd testify in court to help put the drug dealers away for a long time.

It wasn't healthy to dwell on it. Nothing would change and she couldn't bring Daniel back. She needed distractions.

The conversation she'd overheard this morning had been a distraction.

Rhonda wanted to get Holt's take on it, but it would have to wait until he checked in with her tonight.

"Order up!" Eduardo, the cook, called from the kitchen. Startled, she almost dropped the water pitcher she'd been returning to the wait station. Her hands shook.

The order was probably for Table 10. She was learning the amount of time it took to make various dishes. Orders were usually delivered within five to ten minutes, depending on how many changes the customer made to the menu listing. All the daily specials were prepared either early that morning or the night before by the owner's wife, Nancy. Eduardo, the short order cook, whipped up the other food orders in the café's well-planned kitchen.

The bell over the door jingled again, and she glanced at the newcomers. A pair of Mother Road pilgrims paused in the doorway to get their bearings. Locals always walked right by the sign that said, 'please wait to be seated.' Tourists gawked at the walls, the men focusing on the muscle car photographs while the women grinned at the movie posters.

Rhonda considered every customer who walked in the door. Could they be a member of the drug gang? Were they troublemakers? Rhonda found answers in their clothing, their grooming, and their eyes. If their eyes made her fidget, she avoided conversation, served them, and got them out of the café pronto.

The hackles on the back of her neck rose when the next customers came through the door. She approached them slowly. "Table for three?" she asked the men.

They looked at one another. "*Si. Tres personas.* Three," one of them responded.

Rhonda pinched her eyes closed for a second. It was unreasonable to associate any group of people with what had happened at her clinic. But it was recent, and horrible.

She nodded and forced a smile. Many of her clients in Texas spoke Spanish. "*Una mesa para tres personas. Alli,*" she responded.

They followed her to a table in the corner.

* * *

Rhonda plodded up the cracked cement steps to the narrow board porch that someone had added onto the front of the rundown bungalow where she'd spent the last three nights. Overgrown bushes crowded the outer walls of the clapboard house, and long-neglected gold chrysanthemum blooms with long straggly stems hung over the crumbling sidewalk.

Her feet ached. Since Monday, she'd covered a regular six-hour shift and two long ten-hour shifts at the diner, hours of walking back and forth across a hard linoleum floor carrying heavy food trays. It was only Wednesday. This ache in her legs wouldn't go away until she could find and relax in a steamy tub of hot water.

The front door wobbled as she unlocked it. She stepped inside, and pushed it shut behind her. Low beams of sunlight filtered through the grimy side window and the opaque cotton curtain fluttered in a breeze that huffed in through the quarter-inch crack at the bottom. The place smelled musty.

In the bedroom at the back of the house, across from the doorway, a mattress rested on a low bed frame. Next to it, a painted wooden apple crate served as a nightstand. A small battery-powered camp lantern supplied light to read by. She'd stacked her two suitcases, full of newly purchased clothes, in the corner beyond the crate.

The yellowed floor crackled as she crossed to the corner kitchen. She laid her purse down on the aluminum table—vintage Sixties with a yellow plastic top and one matching chair with a padded yellow seat—then pulled a glass bottle of tea from the small white refrigerator and grabbed a cookie from the jar on the green and black linoleum counter.

The bathroom door next to the refrigerator stood open. She entered the small space, eyed the shower, and wished for a bathtub to soak in. A large bottle of ibuprofen sat on the bottom shelf of the mirrored medicine cabinet above the sink. Rhonda tossed three caplets onto her tongue and washed them down with a gulp of tea.

Home sweet home. If someone had told her a month ago that her life would become this nightmare, she would have called them crazy. A waitress. Who had suggested that? Holt Braden? And then he had the nerve to bring a girlfriend there for lunch? She steamed. The man might have a slew of women at every location where he had an assignment. She didn't care. She thought about her husband Daniel, and her lower lip quivered.

Rhonda unbuttoned the front of the pink tunic and stepped out of it. As she pitched it onto the table, the embroidered name on the pocket caught a stray ray of the dropping sun through the dirty west window. *Rhonda.* Her new name.

She sank into the only other chair in the room—a well-used ladder back with a sunken cane seat—then reached down and rubbed her calves, avoiding the scabbed-over scratches she'd received the previous weekend.

A quick rap came at the door, and before she could stand up, the door swung open.

Holt Braden slipped inside. "Why isn't the door locked?" He growled, then glanced at her long enough to register the bra and matching bikini panties before he turned his back. "Sorry."

"Damn!" Rhonda bolted out of the chair, shot to the suitcases in the bedroom, pitched one onto the mattress, then rummaged through the contents for an oversized t-shirt. She slipped it over her head and took a few deep breaths as she smoothed it down over her body. She pulled on a pair of sweatpants and then returned to the kitchen; her arms crossed over her chest. "You can't barge in here like that."

When Holt turned, his blue-gray eyes focused on her face. "I'm sorry. I just found out that your new house will be ready this weekend. Thought you'd want to know."

She shrugged, still shaken at the unexpected intrusion. "Meanwhile, I'm living in this roach hotel." She scanned the room. The filtered light passing through the filthy windows shimmered on floating dust particles. "I've never lived like this, not even during vet school." The apartment she'd lived in with Daniel had been a small studio with a Murphy bed, but it had been clean, freshly painted, and full of light. There was no comparison to this dump.

"It's temporary, remember. We had to move you quickly. By Sunday, you'll have a decent place to live for as long as it takes to get the rest of Mendosa's gang."

Her dry, scratchy eyes suddenly stung with unshed tears, and her throat clogged. "I don't think I can do this. I want to go back." The words caught in her throat.

"Think about that, Rhonda." He emphasized her new name. "Remember."

Her saliva evaporated. "I can't forget. I'm terrified. This place is *not* secure. Even the three little pigs who live across the street could make their way in here in the dead of night, forget about the big bad wolf."

"You are safe. It's only for a few more days. If they're looking for you, they'll check every B&B and hotel in all neighboring states, not rat hole rent houses. You've only been gone five days." His stare was intense.

She lifted her head, straightened her back. Five days. Five days in living hell. Every day since she'd watched them shoot her husband Daniel.

Chapter 5
Claire

Late Wednesday afternoon, after she'd interviewed the mayor, Claire stepped into the Persimmon Round-up Club arena. A practicing barrel racer urged her horse across the dirt expanse toward a triangle of widely spaced wooden barrels at the far end. Then, she leaned toward the first barrel, forcing the horse into a tight turn around it. She charged the animal toward the next barrel, and then to the third, racing in a clover-leaf pattern through the barrels before galloping back to the far end of the arena where she had started.

A man with a stopwatch threw up his hand as the rider pulled the horse to a stop. The animal tossed its head and reared up on its hind legs. The man barked out, "22 seconds." The girl's face fell. Determination hardened her jaw. She lined the horse up to give it another try, wanting to lessen the time it took to race around the barrels. Claire imagined she could be one of the competitors in Neve Bright's class.

Claire scanned the oval arena and the bleachers looking for Cade and his girlfriend Neve.

A passageway connected the barns to the arena, and Claire headed toward it. She had paid to board Blaze at the club stables during the event. Neve was probably with the horse, waiting for her turn to practice. She guessed Cade was there, too.

The acrid scent of horse manure, dirt and straw tickled her nose as she reached the barn. Inside, horses snorted, stomped, and kicked the boards of their stalls. The sounds and smells were familiar. Her own little barn only housed Smoky, her burro, and Blaze, the mustang that her nephew Denver had trained for her. Dozens of horses filled the stalls in this barn. A murmur of voices cut through the neighs and whinnies.

As Claire neared the loudest voices, someone shouted.

Claire stepped up to a nearby stall and peered inside. Neve and Cade stood close together, but as she watched, the girl pushed her son. He stumbled, glared, and lifted a fist.

"Cade?" Claire asked sharply. "What's going on?"

The startled teenagers glanced up.

Neve's face flushed. "We were just … talking." The girl's look darted from Claire to Cade and back again. Her brown eyes glistened with moisture. She flicked her long dark ponytail over her shoulder.

Cade scowled, his eyes squinting with anger.

Whatever the pair had been arguing about, it wasn't any of her business, but his action was. She knew Cade had a temper, but she rarely saw it. Most of the time he was well mannered and helpful, unlike some of her friends' teenagers. But now, he glared at his mother.

Claire froze in her tracks. Her mouth had gone dry. This was a different Cade. She'd interrupted something. "Neve, how's practice going?" She cleared her throat.

The girl's creased brow smoothed and her face relaxed. She swiped at her eyes. "Good. Blaze likes a challenge. I think we'll do okay." She chewed at her lip and glanced at Cade as she inched across the stall toward Claire. "Um, some of us girls are going out to eat. We need a break from the arena. See you tomorrow, Cade. Okay? Later." Neve dashed past Claire, her ponytail swishing from side to side as she moved. "'Bye."

Claire's mind filled with questions as she watched the teenager hurry away. When she turned back to Cade, he crossed his arms.

Remain calm, Claire told herself. *The way to learn what you want to know is to speak calmly. And never accuse.* "What was that about? Looked like you were going to hit her."

"Mom. Seriously? I wouldn't hit Neve. Or any girl. I was mad, but I wouldn't hit her." He rubbed the top of his head, spiking the brown hair that usually hung over his forehead.

"Were you threatening her?"

"No. Neve knows I'd never hurt her."

"Does she? She left awfully fast after I interrupted." She waited for an answer.

He shrugged. "She's stubborn. And she won't listen to me. There's nothing more I can do. Whatever happens … well, that's on her. Can we go?" He crossed the stall and moved past her.

Claire grasped his arm. "We'll go when I'm finished talking to you. You know better than to raise your hand to anyone without good reason. I get that you're upset about something, but that's no excuse to lose your temper. I do NOT want to hear that anything like that has happened again."

He glared. "Sometimes, you have to get physical to get what you want." His chin jutted up.

In that instant, Cade resembled her ex-husband. Her stomach clenched. "Who told you that? Not your father, I hope."

"Dad looks at things differently." He tilted his head.

Claire chilled. "And that could be the wrong way, Cade. We've talked about this." She'd always been open with Cade about what had happened between her and Tom. And she'd tried as hard as she could to keep things friendly with her ex. Lately, it had gotten harder.

"Yeah, we've talked about it. Dad has a different story about why your marriage ended. He has different opinions about a lot of things."

She didn't want to hear this and she didn't want to argue in the arena barn. Her son had spent every other weekend and half the summer vacation with his father since the divorce when he was five. For many years, each time he came back to her house it took days to bring back the playful, happy boy she cherished. Things had improved after his cousin Denver came to live with them. They developed a relationship, but now … this discussion of violence was new. What had Tom been telling Cade?

She couldn't think about that now.

"Where is Neve staying?" Claire asked.

"Her grandmother lives here. She's staying with her. Why?"

"I'm curious. She's your girlfriend. I'd like to have something to talk to her about besides Blaze and barrel racing."

"We've been going out for months. Why the sudden interest?"

Claire sighed. "I've always been interested, Cade, but you aren't willing to share anything. You're shutting me out. If you don't ask her to stay for dinner after practice with Blaze, how can I get to know her?" Even as Claire spoke, she knew the answer. For the past few years, she'd been building her career, free-lancing when she could, and doubling down on her articles for the Stillwater News Press. She had rarely been home early enough in the evening to make dinner or plan far enough ahead to invite Neve to stay.

"Don't think you're going to get to know her now. She's competing, Mom. She's focused on that, and some family stuff. She doesn't care about anything—or anyone—else, apparently."

Neve had seemed secretive, but so did Cade. What was going on with these two?

Maybe she'd made the wrong decision to ask Cade to come with her. Maybe he should have gone to stay with his father in Stillwater for the weekend. But he'd insisted on coming, and, only a week past his eighteenth birthday, what little hold she still had over him as a parent would end when he left for college next year. He was too old for her to discipline like when he was younger, but what she said or did, especially in front of his friends, could still sway him.

It was only words, and she had to make sure the words she chose were the right ones.

"Things could be different tomorrow, son. Let's go back to the B&B and figure out what we're having for supper. Okay?"

"Yeah. And aren't there supposed to be some cookies for us in the dining room? I need something to hold me over until we eat."

Claire smiled. Some things never changed.

Chapter 6
Rhonda

Rhonda's hand shook as she rubbed her eyebrows. Her throat tightened. Memories overwhelmed her. Why had she and Daniel agreed to operate on that dog last Saturday when he didn't belong to a client?

Holt took a step closer. "You okay?"

She shook her head, chewed at her lip, and moved away from him. She thought about Michael and Erin, both juniors at Oklahoma University in Norman. Or were they? Had they gone back to school? She didn't know when Daniel's funeral was scheduled, or if the feds would schedule a fake memorial service for her.

Holt had delivered one letter from the twins. The FBI agreed it was cruel to let her children believe they'd lost both parents. They knew she was in hiding for an undetermined length of time. Holt assured her they were under constant surveillance for their own protection.

Her heart twisted.

When Holt cleared his throat, she shifted her focus from her misery to his face. He had a tiny scar below his left eye. A childhood injury?

Before she'd known Daniel, Holt might have seemed attractive. Curly hair, prematurely gray, big blue-gray eyes, full lips, and—this late in the day—a five o'clock shadow covering his cheeks and jaw. He was several years younger than she was, but if she were looking for romance, the difference in age wouldn't matter. She wasn't looking, didn't intend to look for love again. The lump in her throat ached.

"How'd the job go today? Better?" His brows lifted, and the edge to his voice disappeared.

"Could be worse. The diner's clean, food's good, I'm busy. No time to have a pity party. Nobody has time to get nosy." She would always be honest with Holt. She couldn't be truthful with anyone else. "But it's only Wednesday. Getting through each day is hard."

"This isn't a bad temporary gig. I've waited tables while undercover. You meet interesting people and overhear crazy conversations." He shrugged.

He didn't understand. She wasn't talking about waitressing being hard. She was talking about living.

She was dead, I'm sure.

Rhonda closed her eyes and shook the memory away. "It's like the wait staff is invisible. The diner catches lots of truckers, bikers and RV vacationers crossing the country on Route 66. One woman wanted to talk about the Blue Whale."

"In Catoosa, right? Have you seen it?"

"Mom took us on a 'see Oklahoma first' vacation when I was a kid. Me, from wheat country, had no idea what eastern Oklahoma looked like." She vividly remembered the trip, surprised by what she saw as they drove the old station wagon along the curving roads. Forested hills, sapphire-blue lakes sparkling under brilliant skies. She'd learned about Will Rogers, the Cherokee people and their language, Belle Star the outlaw, and the ancient people of the Spiro Burial Mounds.

"Where else did you go?"

"The round barn in Arcadia, Big Splash and Casa Bonita in Tulsa, and then some state parks in the Oklahoma Ozarks—Natural Falls, I think—and Robber's Cave." Her memories tumbled like marbles in her mind. She remembered family trips and how her dad had taught her not only how to read a road map, but how to refold it.

"I still don't think you should have been placed in a state you've lived in."

She'd insisted on Oklahoma, wanting to be somewhere that would offer some solace, someplace that might ground her rather than make her feel severed from everything she loved and cherished. "These are my people, and it's been thirty years. I sound like they do, look like they do. There'd be just as much of a chance of me running into distant family or acquaintances in half a dozen other southern states. And I don't stand out." It was the same argument she'd used five days ago as the DEA debated where to hide her in plain sight.

He squinted and rubbed his eyebrow. "We can't protect you if you make contact with anyone who knows you as Renee."

Pain shot into her heart. "My parents, my brother and his family—they all think I'm dead."

"You have to stay dead for now. Mendosa's gang may wonder if you survived that dive into the lake. Without a body, they're bound to wonder. Meanwhile, we're building our case on the drugs—and what happened at the clinic. A few more weeks, hopefully no longer."

The quiver began in her stomach and shimmied down to her knees. She leaned over the table and rested her head on her folded arms.

"You'll see your family again."

She wanted to believe him. But mostly, she was terrified by the thought that she wouldn't see her children again or meet *their* children. She feared that her mom and dad would die believing they had lost their only daughter and son-in-law on the same awful day when a devil came out of a Texas hell hole. A physical ache carved a valley into her chest.

"I, uh, brought something for you," Holt said in a low voice.

"Yeah? A real bed? A television? An Echo?" She sat up.

"Be right back." His footsteps sounded across the room and then the narrow board porch. Rhonda hurried to the sink and splashed water on her face. Hot tears burned her eyes.

Holt clomped back inside. Something whimpered. When she turned, the animal he held in his arms whined.

Rhonda closed her eyes. The pitch of the animal's whine grew higher. The dog yipped.

With trembling hands, she reached for the dog, stroked its brown head, and ruffled its ears. "Look at you," she whispered to the wriggling animal. "I've missed you, Samson."

Rhonda squatted and put the animal on the floor. She petted his long, hairy ears. His tongue darted out and licked her chin. She scratched his favorite places.

Holt touched her shoulder. "I thought you'd like some company. Your kids couldn't take him to college. They told the rest of the family that the dog ran off. Are you okay with this?"

She wanted to be. The dog had been the family pet for more than six years. The question was, could she take care of another being when her spirit had drained away in the aftermath of her personal tragedy?

"There's another reason you should keep the dog."

Rhonda gathered the beagle/shepherd mix into her arms and stood. "And that is?" The dog's long tongue licked her ear.

"It's normal for a person who owns a dog to know a lot about them. He'll help your cover."

Holt was right. After nearly twenty years as a veterinarian, it would be hard for her to stop diagnosing health and behavioral problems in people's pets, and she couldn't resist interacting with animals. She'd already had one close encounter with the woman next door, Mrs. Petrovsky, and her Basset hound, Harry.

"The more excuses you have for what you know, the better. Samson's his name. Right?"

"Yes. Look at those big eyes and those long silky ears. It's a perfect name."

Holt moved toward the door.

"Thank you." It might have been right to give him a hug, but the heaviness in her heart, her awareness that her husband Daniel was dead, was too new.

The dog squirmed in her arms, and she released him. He sniffed the floor, crisscrossing the room, following scents. She hoped he wasn't following the trail of a mouse.

As Holt went through the doorway, he called, "Lock the door," and closed it behind him.

Rhonda looked at the dog through misty eyes. For the first time in nearly a week, she felt a tiny flare of hope. Then, the memory flashed.

Daniel pulled away from the surgery table, glanced up. She looked down and saw what he had seen, the bloody bag in the terrier's stomach, blocking the pyloric valve at the entrance to the duodenum. She pulled it out with the forceps.

Samson whined. Rhonda sucked in her breath and squatted, reaching for the shivering dog, needing to pull him close. "It's going to be okay, Samson. Really, it is."

Her words sounded hollow.

Chapter 7
Claire

Claire stretched out her legs in the B&B's patio lounge chair and reviewed the notes from her afternoon meeting with Mayor Martinson. There wasn't much there. The man was skilled at taking a question and turning it into something he wanted to say on a totally different subject. It wasn't the first time she'd noticed a politician using that strategy. What she didn't understand was why the mayor of Persimmon would do that when asked about Route 66 history. She'd learned about the Route 66 Car Museum and vintage car rallies held all over this part of the U.S., but nothing more specific about his town.

Cade sat staring at his phone, hunched over in another lounge chair on the other side of the backyard patio, eating the last bite of a chocolate chip cookie. Leaves skipped across the lawn. An empty soda pop can rolled among them, nudged by the wind into the adjacent alleyway, where it clattered against a chain link fence.

A horn honked on the nearby street. Cade typed a text message into his phone. He did not look happy.

He wasn't a kid anymore. She should treat him like a man and talk to him like a man. Maybe it was time for an adult conversation about divorce, and a frank discussion of what she believed to be true about how men and women should behave in a relationship.

An unexpected shiver raced down her spine. She closed her eyes. In past years, she'd been stalked by two men who wanted to possess her. One of them had died by her hand, and the other was in prison for attempted rape. Cade knew about both episodes. She hoped the violence of her experiences had not led him to conclude that it was okay to use violence to get what he wanted.

Another honking car brought her thoughts back to the present. She glanced down at her notes.

The mayor had not been forthright with her. He'd given her little to add to what she already knew. Before she left Stillwater, she'd gone online to Wikipedia, and to Oklahoma's tourism department website to learn about Persimmon. Claire had also rooted through archived articles from area newspapers, searching for anything related to the famous road. She'd searched for murders or crimes with a connection to the highway in eastern Oklahoma and come up empty.

It bothered her that Mayor Martinson was evasive. He recommended the Creek County museum and referred her to an old timer who might remember the road realignment in 1952. The mayor thought the man could tell her his personal experiences at an old drive-in movie theater and Dixieland Amusement Park, with its roller rink and swimming pool off Route 66.

She'd made an appointment to talk to the elderly man tomorrow, Thursday. Hopefully, he'd have something interesting to say. Otherwise, Persimmon might not make it into her article. From what she'd seen, it was a nice town. And it could use some good publicity.

Claire reminded herself of the goal of the article. She wrote it across the top of the notebook page: *an update on how the Mother Road's presence changed a community for the good or the bad in the ninety-plus years of its existence.* The Road had made an enormous difference when it was the primary paved route for travelers crossing the country from Chicago to LA and Santa Monica. For more than twenty years, millions of travelers drove that two-lane highway, until the days of turnpikes began in the 1950s with the Eisenhower administration. In Oklahoma, the Will Rogers Turnpike and the Turner Turnpike caused travelers to abandon the Mother Road and its host cities for the sake of faster travel, unhindered by stop signs and stoplights as it passed through Oklahoma's towns and cities.

She glanced again at her list of questions, and then flicked on the pocket recorder she'd used as a backup to her iPhone.

A lifelong resident of Persimmon, Martinson had graduated from high school forty years ago. Two years ago, he'd been elected mayor. Pleasant but condescending, he'd talked about his high school football career, his years as an insurance agent and realtor, and his lifelong car collecting hobby. Smiling, his black snake-eyes seldom wavered from her face.

He was hiding behind his suave answers.

Claire shifted in the lounge chair, a prickly feeling between her shoulder blades. She could be stirring up a snake. Her mind flashed back to the Cimarron Valley Ranch, and the story she had written two years ago, lauding J.B. Floren, owner of the mustang rescue ranch. What a fiasco that had turned into. The man had secretly been selling mustangs not to caring animal rescuers but to a slaughterhouse. She'd praised him, and then, after someone murdered him, she'd found out the truth, but not before her nephew had been arrested, two people close to her were hospitalized, and she was nearly killed.

Since then, she'd avoided controversial topics, had gone from an investigative reporter to a local newshound, specializing in unusual history, and regional activities. She was treading water.

Claire needed to get out in the real world again, to cover stories that made a difference. With an important anniversary of Route 66 approaching, this new piece was timely, if she uncovered interesting facts. Cade would go to college soon, and this was the perfect time to expand her career.

Cade got up from his lounge chair.

"When are we going to eat? I'm starving." He rubbed his hands on his thighs.

"I'll check online for nearby restaurants. You hungry for anything special?"

He shook his head. "Whatever." He snatched up the room key beside her phone on the concrete slab and sidled away.

Claire watched him go. Her easy-going little boy was gone. The teenage years had changed him. Hormones. They rarely talked without him glaring at her over something she'd said. He'd pull the silent treatment or stalk out of the room when the conversation wasn't over. She'd ground him, take away privileges, iPhone, or iPad. He'd straighten up for a while.

How could she get inside his head? Questions didn't work. He rarely stayed in the same room with her for long. Whatever it was she wanted to know about her son, she wouldn't hear it from Cade.

As Claire gathered up her things, someone called her name. She turned toward the woman's voice.

"Glad you're taking time to enjoy this wonderful fall weather. Is your suite satisfactory? Do you need anything?" Betsy Spoon, the co-owner of the B&B, walked toward the patio.

"Everything's fine, Mrs. Spoon. Are you having a good day?"

"Oh yes. I brought some chocolate chip cookies for you and your son. Remember, complimentary cookies each day in the dining room."

"Cade already grabbed some. I hope they improve his mood. Girlfriend issues." Claire gestured toward their suite.

"That's hard. I raised two boys, so I remember about girlfriends."

"Thanks for the cookies, Mrs. Spoon." Claire took the napkin-wrapped cookies and set them beside her as she shoved her laptop into her work satchel.

Chapter 8 – THURSDAY
Rhonda

At 5:20 a.m. Thursday, Rhonda filled Samson's water bowl and told him good-bye.

It was still dark as she rushed down the rickety porch steps and cracked sidewalk to the driveway where she'd parked her white, loaner Camry (200K miles with balding tires). A cool, wet breeze tousled her dark red hair. Rain in the forecast? Without a television or radio, it was hard to know. The cell phone they'd given her—programmed only to call Holt—had no internet connectivity. It was as if she'd time traveled back to the Eighties, to the days before everyone became connected to the rest of the world through their iPhones and Androids.

Now she was disconnected, unaware, uneducated. And she couldn't reach out to her family to let them know she was alive, or where she was.

Pink and red neon lights outlined the roof of the diner. Two semis sat, motors rumbling, in the side parking lot, their drivers in the cabs waiting for the café's blue neon 'open' sign to flash on. Rhonda parked in the designated employee section. Lloyd had parked his turquoise and white 55 Chevy in his usual space near the door.

The scents of cinnamon and yeasty bread rushed past as she opened the back door. "Good morning!"

"Good morning yourself." Jean, a fifty-something veteran waitress and the oldest of the café staff, was unloading the dishwasher. "What's your excuse for being so cheerful? I hate morning people."

Jean was no cheerier in the evening, no matter what she said about morning people. Rhonda had worked with her each of the past three days. With nothing else to do— nothing else she *could* do—why not pretend to be cheerful? These people and this job kept her from going insane with loneliness and the horror of what had happened to her life. At least now she had Samson with her.

Rhonda carried a tray of mixed silverware from the dishwasher to the back table and began to wrap place settings in square paper napkins. She glanced at the clock. Twenty minutes until the café opened. They'd need at least fifty sets to get through the morning rush. She worked quickly.

"*Buenos dias, mis amigas!*" Eduardo, the short order cook, charged through the door.

Rhonda cringed. Eduardo's voice was a dead ringer for the drug dealer who had marched into her vet clinic and altered her world forever. She heard this voice every day and his accent chilled her blood. Eduardo checked the ice machine as he ambled toward his grill.

"Senora, are you okay?" Eduardo asked under his breath as he passed her.

She forced a smile and glanced into his brown eyes.

The back door opened again, and Lynnie blasted through. "Geez, did you guys hear the news? My neighbor, Sheila Biggs, is dead! Someone murdered her." She covered her face with her hands. Her chest heaved.

A spoon clattered onto the table and bounced to the floor at Rhonda's feet.

"Where'd you hear that?" Jean scoffed.

"Channel 6 out of Tulsa, as I left the house. I went to church with Sheila last Sunday night." Her voice broke. Lynnie wrapped her arms around herself, pulling her white sweater tight across her shoulders. "I don't feel safe here anymore."

"It's as safe here as any place else. Loonies are everywhere." Jean sprayed disinfectant on the setup counter and swiped it with a cloth.

"Lynnie, that's awful. I'm so sorry." Rhonda stooped to pick up the dropped utensil. Her mind whirled. A woman dead. "What did she look like? How old was she?"

Lynnie stared at her in horror. "She's my age, and she was my friend. What does it matter what she looked like? They found her face down in the grass in her front yard."

Rhonda remembered Daniel's bloody knees after bullets had blasted them. Bile rose in her throat. She swallowed and focused on Lynnie's pale face. "Someone shot her?"

"Stabbed her over and over." Lynnie clutched her stomach.

Rhonda grabbed the side of a counter, her legs suddenly weak. Her thoughts jumped. Would the criminals who were after her use a knife to kill her instead of a gun?

"They said that on television?" Jean's hands rested on her hips.

"I was in school with her since kindergarten." Lynnie sniffed.

"So, you need the day off to grieve or what?" Jean asked, wiping the counter again.

"You're mean. You don't have any friends, so how would you know what it's like to have one die?" Lynnie's voice hitched.

The two women glared at each other. Lynnie dabbed her eyes with a wadded tissue.

She was dead, I'm sure. Rhonda grasped the counter tighter and took several deep breaths. Yesterday's customer had known this long before the newscaster reported it on the TV.

Did the café's customer kill Sheila Biggs?

* * *

"Holt, I overheard something yesterday. I should have told you last night." Rhonda spoke quietly into her cell phone while she stood at the café's back door. The sun was nearing the horizon, brightening the October sky. Birds twittered in the trees. A trio of quacking ducks flapped over. A red Chevelle pulled into the parking lot.

"I wasn't sure if it was important at the time, but I overheard a customer at the diner saying, 'she was dead.' And then this morning, Lynnie said she heard on the news that a woman was murdered."

Holt was silent.

"Holt? Should I tell the police?"

She heard the clicking of computer keyboard strokes through the phone.

"I'm checking." The clicking continued. "Yep, here's the report. Woman, late-twenties. Teacher. What did you overhear?"

"The customer said, 'she was dead, I tell you.' That's it.

"The guy could have been talking about a hamster or a goldfish."

Rhonda snorted. "I doubt this guy would care about a hamster or a goldfish. He was scared. Sweating."

"Maybe the temp in your diner was too hot for him. Or the food too spicy."

Holt wasn't taking her seriously. "It's not a joke." She chewed at a fingernail and then tucked her hand in her pocket. It was a nasty habit. Why was she doing it again? She'd conquered nail chewing years ago in middle school.

"Okay. Write down a description of the men and what they said. I'll turn it in as an anonymous tip if it seems relevant."

"I'll have my descriptions for you tonight." She tucked her cell phone into her pocket with her order pad and went inside.

* * *

"Where you been all my life, Rhonda?"

The silver-haired man flirted. He'd been in for breakfast every day since she started work at the diner, showing up mid-morning and sitting at Table 6 in her section. And it was the fourth day in a row he'd ordered a hard-boiled egg, a side of bacon, and white toast with grape jelly. She tucked his totaled meal check under the shallow bowl of single servings of creamer.

"Thanks for coming in." Rhonda tried to make her smile reach her eyes.

"You're welcome, sugar. I come in every day, you know. We'll be getting to know one another well. Howard Noble's my name. Where you from?"

"Kansas City." She rattled off the autobiography spiel she'd memorized. "Spent most of my life up there. You lived here long?"

"More than seventy years." He winked. "Grew up here. Worked in the oil business 'til I retired two years ago. Cancer took my wife Claudia this past summer, so I'm here every morning, having the same meal she fixed me every day while we were married."

Rhonda smiled sympathetically. On her right, another customer sat down in her section.

"Excuse me, Howard. Enjoy your breakfast, and I'll see you tomorrow morning."

"You can count on that."

Noble lingered over his second cup of coffee.

Outside the front window, a tour bus chugged into the parking lot. Two dozen older ladies with gray or white hair, two dyed redheads, and a half-dozen balding men stepped carefully down from the bus and navigated to the front door.

It took all the wait staff to get the group seated and take their orders. Jean pulled on an apron to help Eduardo cook their breakfasts.

"It sure is beautiful over here, honey," one of the redheads said to Rhonda. "The leaves are turning so pretty." Circles of color on her cheeks matched her hair.

Rhonda remembered the town west of Oklahoma City on I-40. "Beautiful day for it."

The woman's smile beamed. "You're a native Okie, aren't you? I hear it in your voice."

Oops. Rhonda moved down the table, filling coffee cups. She wasn't supposed to give away anything about her past, wasn't supposed to engage anybody in conversation, not even octogenarians who appeared harmless.

The woman waved one hand toward Rhonda and called, "it's good to travel, honey. You get out there when you can. Keep an eye out for tornadoes. Of course, you know all about that."

Lynnie started taking orders at the far end of the table, and Rhonda filled coffee cups. She glanced out the front window at the clear sky.

One white-haired lady reminded Rhonda of her grandmother, then her thoughts rushed on to her mother.

Guilt dropped over her—her mother believed her only daughter was dead.

Blinded by sudden tears, Rhonda poured out the last serving of coffee in her pot and took refuge in the kitchen.

Chapter 9
Claire

"Will you take me out to the Round-up Club, Mom? Otherwise, I'll hitch a ride." Cade stood near the outside door of their suite in the B&B, shifting his weight from one foot to the other.

"Cade, you'll do no such thing. Wait a minute, will you?" Claire threw back the bedspread and got out of bed. "I didn't hear you get up. It's early." Dim light outlined the drapes on the room's large window.

He shrugged. "Nothing to do here."

"Just give me a second. Please, wait, Cade." Claire stepped into the bathroom and closed the door. Cade's mood hadn't improved. There wasn't anything she could do to help him, except give him the pep talk. Other fish in the sea, and so on. It hadn't helped much when she was a teen, she didn't imagine it would help Cade either. As she brushed her teeth, she recalled the previous night.

They'd gone to dinner at a pizza place a few blocks away. She'd tried to have a normal conversation with her son, but he'd been sullen and uncommunicative. When she asked him about his relationship with Neve, he got up from the table and went outside. It was likely that every time she tried to talk with him about his girlfriend he would walk away. How could she stop him? He was six inches taller than she was and outweighed her by sixty pounds. Someday—she hoped it would be sooner rather than later—he would be a reasonable human being again.

She dabbed on makeup and stroked on eyeliner, then slipped into slacks and a lightweight sweater before returning to the sitting area. Cade was gone. She smoothed her dark hair and tucked it behind her ears.

Claire muttered as she grabbed her purse and left the room. She needed to talk to someone about Cade. Certainly not his father. Tom was likely a big part of the problem. Holt had offered advice at times, but he'd never raised a teenager. He had, however, been one once.

She pulled out her keys and started for the SUV. Cade was leaning against the passenger door, eating something. Her anxiety eased. He wasn't hitchhiking to the Round-up Club.

"Thanks for waiting, son. Is that breakfast, or do you want to swing through McD's and get something bigger?" Claire unlocked the SUV's doors.

"Yeah. This cinnamon roll won't last long. I should have grabbed five more." He slid into the front seat, and then handed her something wrapped in a napkin.

She unwrapped it and smiled at the coiled pastry. Gooey brown sugar/butter mixture had crusted on the top, beneath cream cheese frosting. She took a bite as she started the car. "Thanks. I think I saw a McDonald's on the way out to the arena." Her shoulders relaxed. She wanted the day to get off to a good start. She took a bite of the yeasty bun, savoring the sweet flavors.

Claire turned a corner and continued to drive down the busy street. Cade gazed out the window. Suddenly, his slumped shoulders straightened.

"Hey, turn in here."

It was the diner she'd eaten at with Holt yesterday. If she wasn't mistaken, one of the cars parked in front, between a vintage Ford Thunderbird and an El Camino circa Seventies, was Neve's white Honda.

Claire wrapped the remains of the bun in the napkin and led the way into the diner. She stopped, attracted to the photographs of Route 66 attractions that surrounded the mirror behind the soda fountain. One striking night exposure photo featured the iconic neon soda pop bottle at Pops restaurant near Oklahoma City.

When she looked for Cade, he'd passed the hand-printed sign that said, *please wait to be seated*, and headed for a table near the front window where two young women were eating breakfast. One of them was Neve. She glanced up as they approached.

"Is it okay if my mom and I sit with you?" Cade's voice had deepened, and his eyes had softened. His transformation to an intelligent, polite young man was nothing short of miraculous.

Neve's look shifted to her table companion. "Sure. The waitress will be back in a minute. She's great about keeping our coffee cups full."

"How are you? I meant to ask you yesterday, how's Blaze taking to the arena?" Claire slung her purse over the back of the chair and slipped into the seat.

"I'm good, and Blaze is getting used to it. We're on the schedule for 9:00." She glanced at her sports watch.

"Did you have fun last night?" Cade leaned towards her.

Neve took a long swallow of coffee. "We hung out at an arcade. There was a kid's birthday party going on." She rubbed the edge of her coffee cup with her finger.

"Thought you were going to find a bar?" He frowned.

"Janelle doesn't have an ID." Her low voice was hard for Claire to hear. Neve turned to her. "Mrs. Northcutt, Cade said you're researching a news story. How's that going?"

The air hung heavy around the table. An entirely different conversation might be going on if she hadn't been sitting there. Fake IDs? A bar?

"The article is about Route 66, the highway we're on. It used to be the major road–"

"We studied it in school, Mom. She knows," Cade quipped.

Neve nodded. "We did. Cyrus Avery was the Tulsa man on the Highway Commission who made sure it passed through Tulsa and Oklahoma City."

A waitress placed two glasses of water in front of them. Tall, with beautiful auburn hair and tired green eyes, she didn't smile. "Good morning. What can I get you two?"

"Pancakes," Cade said. "With a side of sausage. And coffee."

Claire had never seen Cade drink coffee. But Neve was drinking it.

"And what can I get you, ma'am?" The waitress looked at Claire.

"I'll have a Denver omelet, salsa on the side. And coffee." The waitress could be the same age as she was, or possibly a few years older. With her dark red hair pulled back in a low ponytail, it was hard to tell. She was attractive, clean cut and poised.

"You got it. I'll be right back with that coffee. My name's Rhonda if you need anything."

As the waitress walked away, Claire turned back to Neve. "Route 66 was one of the first important paved highways across the United States, long before interstate highways or turnpikes. That was nearly 100 years ago. I could get good play on an anniversary article."

"What are you trying to find out?"

"When the Route was first constructed, towns all along the Road boomed. Motels, souvenir shops, and gas stations catered to travelers during the 40s and 50s. But everything changed on Route 66 when the Interstates and Turnpikes were built in the 60s and later. Lots of small family businesses, motor courts, and diners, went out of business in towns like Persimmon."

"Has this diner been around that long?" Neve looked at the Naugahyde upholstery in the booths, and the chrome and plastic dining tables and chairs. "It looks pretty good in here if this place is that old."

"The furniture is reproductions, I'd guess. I bet many of their customers are people driving old Route 66, including bus tours and motorcycle clubs."

Cade leaned back into the booth. "I'd do that. Ride a motorcycle all the way from Chicago to LA on the Mother Road." He nodded at Neve. "Would you?"

"Maybe. Depends."

"On what?"

"Time of year. Summer's too hot. Winter's too cold. How long would it take?" Neve peered around the room and then her look rested on Cade.

The waitress set coffee cups in front of them and poured the steaming brew from a pot. Cade grabbed two sugars and two creamers from the bowl on the table and doctored his cup. "You could make it take as long as you want. Maybe two weeks."

"Two weeks. That's a long time on a motorcycle." Neve sounded skeptical.

"It would be amazing. Freedom. Drive if you want. Stop when you want. Eat when you want. Nobody telling you what to do."

Claire recognized typical teenage angst in her son's words. It wasn't unexpected, but what she really wanted to know was what had brought it on so strongly, right now.

Chapter 10
Rhonda

The lunchtime regulars began to push through the front door at 11:30.

Right upfront at the soda counter sat Josh Richards, a banker. Sharing the row of stools were two men she didn't know, and Cab Martinson, Mayor of Persimmon. Lloyd was jawing with them, laughing.

Local business owners often sat at the counter. Most of them drove the few blocks from their Main Street stores and offices to enjoy the café's home-style cooking. Other small groups of travelers stopped to eat while passing through town on Route 66. By 1:30, they had finished their lunches and left.

The aroma of chicken and noodles and home-made yeast rolls, the Thursday Special, had overtaken the smell of cinnamon in the café. It swirled in the air, propelled around the room by the box fans Lloyd had set in every corner. Several windows were open, letting in the autumn air.

When Rhonda's section had cleared of customers, she did whatever was needed, refilling drinks, and suggesting desserts. The homemade pastries and pies were fresh, daily. Lloyd stood at the blenders, making milk shakes for two of the Mayor's friends.

Whenever she passed near the group of men, they lowered their voices or stopped talking. As Rhonda approached from behind Martinson, she paused at the bakery case for a piece of lemon meringue pie. The mayor said, "The sooner that damned reporter's out of town, the better."

She set the dessert plate on the counter in front of the case to wipe away a stray glob of whipped cream.

"You're crazy. We've nothing to do with the Road. She's not going to be here long enough to find out anything," another man said.

"But she could. And if she happens to get hold of that old Indian woman …"

"Shhh," someone cautioned.

Rhonda shut the pastry case and picked up the plate. Lloyd was at the sink, rinsing the glass container he'd used to mix the milk shakes. She stepped away to deliver the pie.

* * *

About 2:45, Rhonda counted her tips and went to Lloyd's office to turn in her order tablet.

"You're getting the hang of it, aren't ya?" Lloyd sat behind his desk in the corner office, reading glasses askew on the tip of his bulbous nose. Tall and lanky, with graying hair and sagging yellow skin on his neck and face, the man was often out of breath.

"Enjoy your evening." He peered at the chart on his computer screen. "And I'm sure you know people are a lot of bluster. All talk. Take anything you overhear with more than a grain of salt. A saltshaker full." He grinned and flicked his hand her way.

"I do." Was he referring to the conversation at the counter she'd overheard? He'd been standing there, too, but the water had been running. And Jean had told her he didn't hear well. She thought about what Vivian had said about Lloyd noticing her body. The man was quiet and well-mannered. Holt had assured her that Lloyd, a retired Navy Seal, would tell no one Rhonda was in the Witness Protection Program. He'd apparently sheltered others in need of protection in the years he'd owned the café.

In the kitchen, Lloyd's wife, Nancy, scraped out the dregs of the big pot of chicken and noodles she'd brought in mid-morning for the lunch special. Today, the 'special' was gone by 1 p.m.

"I scraped the pot and got a small serving, Rhonda. Want to take it home?"

She peeked into the pot. "No, but thanks anyway. It was delicious."

"Got a date tonight? Going out for dinner, maybe dancing? Thursday night pre-weekend parties used to be a big deal."

Rhonda shook her head.

"I'm surprised. Men notice you. Pretty, not too fat, or too skinny. And no tattoos that I can see." Nancy giggled, and her aging face lost years as her eyes sparkled.

"Not even any that you can't see," Rhonda confessed. Her daughter, Erin, had come home from college the month after she turned 19 sporting a butterfly tattoo on one shoulder blade. Daniel had freaked, but what could you do after the fact? Besides, as Erin said, everyone WAS getting them.

Back in the dining room, Rhonda made sure her tables were clean before she left for the day. It was habit. She and Daniel had always cleaned up the vet clinic before leaving for the day.

Only two tables remained to be cleared, and Lance, the bus boy, was at work on one of them. They weren't her tables, but she wasn't in any hurry to get home to her beautiful bungalow. She grabbed a spray bottle of cleaner and a roll of paper towels and went over to help.

Lance had jammed his earbuds into his ears and was humming. Rhonda wiped the table after he'd cleared.

Two guys sat on stools at the counter, drinking coffee. At a booth, another man was reading today's Tulsa World newspaper.

Jean sauntered over. "Schedule says you're pulling another double Saturday. Holiday weekend. Tourists driving the Road." She tucked her pencil behind her ear and played with one dangly silver earring. "We'll be swamped. And don't count on Lynnie to show up on time. She's still scared because that neighbor of hers got killed."

Rhonda grabbed the spray bottle and paper towels and moved to another table. "Any suspects yet? Haven't heard the news." She wanted to know details. What did the victim look like? Did she do drugs? Was she in the wrong place at the wrong time?

"No news to hear. Cops are investigating." Jean shrugged then headed for the kitchen while Rhonda wiped the cloth over the table in continuous circles. It was almost 3 p.m. Lynnie would soon return to finish her split shift. When she did, Rhonda would go to her temporary home. A murderer was loose in the town.

The bell jingled on the front door. Two men wound their way through the tables to a window booth in her area. Both men peered at her.

Her heart stilled. The men had been at Table 14 yesterday with the man who mentioned the dead woman. They settled into the booth. One scowled.

Hands shaking, Rhonda shoved the kitchen door open and hurried across it to her locker in the back-storage area.

She grabbed her cell phone and stepped outside on rubbery legs. Holt answered on the second ring.

"Two of those men are back. Should I call the police?"

"Did they speak to you?"

"No. I ducked into the kitchen. But they sat in my area. One of them glared at me."

"Feign a stomachache and go home. I called my police contact. They've had a lot of tips about that murder and are following up on each one. The woman had recently complained to the city about odors. They'll be in touch with you soon at work. Tomorrow, most likely. I told them you don't have a cell phone."

Rhonda was relieved that Holt had passed on the tip about the men. But her body wouldn't stop quivering. "Holt, could you ..."

"Thought I'd bring a pizza over later. What kind do you like?"

Her tension eased. She had not been looking forward to another evening alone in that little house. "Supreme—or any mix with lots of cheese and garlic ..."

"I'll see what I can find. Be there about 5:30."

She glanced over her shoulder as she raced to her car. Even though Holt had passed on the tip about the men, he hadn't seemed concerned. Rhonda couldn't dismiss it so easily. She could supply descriptions. The one with the goatee was tall with sandy-brown hair, deep-set, wide dark eyes, and thin to the point of being gaunt. Then there was that snake tattoo.

The other was older, not as tall but still more than six feet—graying hair, steely-blue eyes, and a scar down one cheek. His mottled skin could be from a splotchy sunburn.

Both men wore denim work shirts and jeans. She could ID them in a line up.

They'd had a good look at her, too. And they knew where to find her. Right here, at the diner.

Chapter 11
Claire

Thursday afternoon, Claire rang the doorbell of the stone ranch-style home and stepped back from the glass storm door. Howard Noble, the man the mayor had recommended that she interview, was a longtime resident of Persimmon. The home was well kept, and the yard was immaculate. He either enjoyed doing yardwork himself or had a yard man. Either way, he cared about appearances.

Claire had made their appointment for 2 p.m., and it was straight up two o'clock. She pressed the doorbell again, remembering a rancher who'd once been late for an interview. Minutes later, she'd found him brutally murdered. She shook off the morbid memory and peered through the square window in the oak door. Nothing moved inside.

No autumn leaves had piled around the door frame despite the forty-foot-tall sycamore trees towering over the house. Keeping the porch leaf free would take diligence. Faced with orchard stone, a blonde sandstone, the house featured long windows and a hip roof with low eaves, typical of many built in the 1950s or 60s. Ample flower beds beneath the windows were still bursting with blooming rose bushes. Noble could be a gardener, or at least his wife had been.

Two wrought iron chairs and a small table with a glass top occupied the far end of the porch. A coffee cup and a saucer sat on the table. In the yard, leaves dropped from the trees and ran from the westerly wind.

"Hello," a deep but raspy voice called from the corner of the house. In the yard beyond the man, a separate garage or workshop stood, painted green with white trim.

Claire studied the older man as he stepped spryly across the lawn toward the porch. He might be close to eighty, but he had a spring in his step. His evenly trimmed silver hair was still thick. He wore a blue cardigan that looked new.

"I'm Howard Noble, and you must be Ms. Northcutt. Thanks for making an appointment with me. My days can get busy, despite my being 'retired.' I volunteer for Meals on Wheels, the Food Pantry, and anything that has to do with Route 66. Tours, car shows, memorabilia, the Mother Road collection … The mayor said you needed information about our community. How can I help?" His look took in her wavy brown, shoulder-length hair and her clothes.

"I'm writing an article. Do you mind if I record our conversation?"

Noble shrugged. She pressed the record button on the cell phone in her hand.

"It's nearly been 100 years since the Mother Road was paved through here. I'd like to talk about what kind of changes the community has seen over that time because of the highway. Any outstanding events? Good or bad?"

Noble chuckled. "I may look a hundred, but I'm not there quite yet." He cleared his throat.

"I didn't mean to insinuate that, sir, but you've lived here a long time and seen a good deal. Right?"

"Yes, born in 1945. Dad survived the war and came home to his bride to find a baby on the way. Me. Nothing scandalous there. He'd been on leave a few months before."

Claire wasn't sure what to say that wasn't trite or cliché. "I bet things were hopping around here after the war with people traveling Route 66."

"They were. My Dad got a loan and built a motor court right on 66. Did fairly good 'til the turnpikes went in. Still, he ran it into the 80s. After that, it wasn't much more than a weekly rental place for people who couldn't afford to stay any place else." He scratched his head and cleared his throat again. "Shame on me. Can I offer you a drink? Would you like to come in and sit down? If Claudie was still living, she'd have had us both settled on the sofa with a glass of tea and a cookie."

He pulled the storm door open and led the way inside the house. The house smelled slightly musty. Bookcases lined every wall. Photos cluttered many shelves; hardback and paperback books filled others. Light from the open drapes brightened the otherwise drab upholstery of two sofas and several armchairs.

Claire followed him through the long living room and into the kitchen, where he pulled two glasses from a cabinet. With shaking hands, he filled them with iced tea from the refrigerator. Maybe he wasn't as healthy as he'd seemed at first glance. That, or the memory of his wife's death upset him.

"Let's sit here. If you don't mind." He eased into a chair at the small dinette table in one corner of the kitchen. Outside the curtained window, a flat wooden bird feeder swung from a wire attached to the roof eave. Sunflower seeds and millet covered the flat surface.

She glanced around the kitchen. A saucepan, dirty plates and glasses filled the sink. If he had a housekeeper, she hadn't been in to work today.

Noble touched his forehead, then rubbed at his left eyebrow. "What exactly was it you wanted to know?" He folded his hands, but the shaking didn't stop.

"I'm talking to people about how the Route changed their town, and what happened after the interstates diverted traffic. Businesses died, and main streets emptied when the stream of cars stopped passing through. But what else happened? The mayor seemed to think you might have something useful I could add."

The man rubbed the condensation off his glass with one finger. "Folks got mad; I can tell you that. Disbelief, first. The government didn't ask them before they built those interstates. No one said, how about if we build a new road that bypasses your town, so no one comes there anymore? We saw the writing on the wall. People lost hope. Some moved away. Some found other ways to make money." His expression hardened. He glanced out the window; sparrows foraged on the nearby bird feeder.

She'd hit a nerve. Claire took a sip of tea, hoping he'd want to fill the awkward silence, but he didn't. He stared outside.

"Tell me about your dad's motel." She needed to get him talking again.

"Auto court. Pretty little place. A string of ten cabins, and three duplexes, all air-conditioned. Even a swimming pool. Big sign out front with a moving neon arrow. He was so proud of that place." Noble's voice dropped. He stared vacantly at the table.

"Do you think it would have survived if the traffic hadn't been diverted?"

"I was counting on taking over the place when dad retired. Had me a good job in the oil fields at Glenpool, taking care of my own little family. But I always believed I'd end up with that motor court. I was looking forward to it, too."

Claire sipped her tea and wondered why the mayor had sent her to talk to Howard Noble. The man was bitter. Had the mayor sent her here to discourage her from focusing on Persimmon?

"But then, he got—cancer. It was all about over by then. We closed the doors. Could've taken in boarders, monthly rentals, but then someone would have had to clean the place, and take care of maintenance, all that. Claudie and me tried for a year. Not our cup of tea. People can be disgusting. So, there it sits. No doubt there's squatters in there now. Not to mention rats and maybe bats. Haven't checked on it for a while. Used to drive by every week, pick up the litter, make sure no one had broken in. Not much point now. Too much work anyhow." Noble's empty glass slammed into the table.

"Mr. Noble, I'm sorry about the motor court. Can you think of anything else that happened because of Route 66? Or even after the traffic no longer came through town?"

He rubbed his eyebrow again. "Lost our stores, our movie theater, and the drive-in. Then, years later, people started remembering the Road. There was a big hoopla. Books, photo displays, museums filled with memorabilia. Everyone started talking about it again. A revival. Bus tours, motorcycle rallies, car shows. Celebrating the times."

"That was a good thing, right? It brought businesses back. And started new ones."

His expression hardened again.

"What else happened? Something you didn't like?"

"Some people changed their way of doing business. Started taking short cuts to save bucks."

"Can you give me some examples?" She hadn't been looking for dirt on the townspeople but if Noble wanted to talk about them, she wasn't going to stop him.

Howard Noble slid his empty glass in a circle and then glanced at the electric clock plugged into an outlet above the nearby linoleum counter. He pushed his chair back and stood.

"Nope. Just an old man grousing. I wasn't much help to you. Sorry."

Claire took a final swallow of tea and followed him to the front door. She glanced into an open doorway off the hallway. Car photographs covered the walls, and a collection of antique hood ornaments filled several shelves.

Noble waited for her at the storm door, holding it open.

Why had the Mayor suggested she talk to him? Maybe it wasn't because of what he knew, but because of what he wouldn't say.

If she had another source, she might be able to return to Howard Noble with specific questions. She needed a more balanced witness, not someone recommended by the mayor. What about the two sisters at the B&B? Would they willingly answer her questions?

Meanwhile, Cade was at the Round-up Club. She should check on him.

Chapter 12
Rhonda

Late Thursday afternoon Rhonda drove away from the café and turned down Persimmon's main street. Skeletons and flying black bats decorated the windows of Main Street businesses. Someone had stretched fuzzy string or yarn in a web pattern across the store front; a giant black spider hung in the center.

Corn shocks held a sign advertising the corn maze outside of town.

She had no energy to love Fall anymore, not even a beautiful—nearly perfect—day. Rhonda pulled the car into the driveway of her old bungalow and trudged to the porch. She unlocked the door.

Samson barked and leaped, trying to reach her face with his tongue.

"I'm glad to see you, too. Let me take off this uniform and then we'll take a walk."

The dog sat by the door, quivering with eagerness. She tied her tennis shoes and hooked on his leash. He pulled her out of the house and across the front yard.

"Rhonda? Rhonda."

The name finally registered as she stepped down the sidewalk. She glanced toward the house next door.

Her neighbor, Mrs. Petrovsky, leaned against a porch post. Harry, her Basset hound, wagged his tail and studied his human.

"Hello, Mrs. Petrovsky."

"Rhonda, is that your dog?" Her neighbor pointed at the beagle-shepherd mix.

She paused and her mind raced. How could she explain the sudden appearance of her pet? She didn't want to encourage questions, but Holt's purpose in bringing the animal was to allow her to share her knowledge of animals without arousing suspicions. Here was the first challenge. "I'm dog-sitting. His name is Samson."

Mrs. P. frowned. "Did you check with Bill Parsons before you took that dog in? He has a 'no pet' policy with his renters."

"It's temporary, and the dog's house trained."

"I don't think he'd approve. They chew things." She glared at Samson, glanced at Harry, and then smiled at Rhonda. "You're going on a walk."

"Down to the park and back." Samson pulled her closer to the porch, and Harry.

"Well, my hip's acting up. I barely made it out here from the kitchen. But Harry'd like a walk. Could you take him with you? Leash is here on the glider."

"Sure." When Rhonda released Samson's leash, he raced to the other dog. The animals sniffed each another, tails wagging in unison. Mrs. P grabbed Harry's leash and pitched it to her.

She hooked it to his collar. The dog raised its big head and focused his droopy brown eyes on her.

Together, the two dogs pulled her down the sidewalk. Harry trotted ahead while Samson danced around him, fighting the leash that curtailed his activities.

Two blocks farther, the sidewalk eroded away into a shallow bar ditch of gravel, with clumps of crabgrass and other weeds wilting in the dry soil. Rhonda and the dogs trekked down the bar ditch toward the city park a few blocks away.

They passed an abandoned motor court, set well back from the road. A rusted metal sign by the derelict building creaked as it swung in the wind, the name no longer recognizable. Dried grass covered the narrow strip of land in front of the string of cabins. It obscured the crumbling pavement of a former parking lot.

Harry growled as he and Samson strained toward the old motel. The dogs pushed their noses into the earth and snorted. Samson did a shoulder dive on something. When she tugged firmly on the leash, he yipped and turned a flip. Harry was rooted to the spot, focused on a grass-filled gap between two cabins.

"Come on." Samson bucked and jerked the leash out of her hand. The dog dashed for the cabin complex and Harry charged after him, jerking her forward. Both dogs growled. She smelled what the dogs smelled. Some creature had died, and the sickeningly sweet odor of decay was strong. Whatever lay there had been dead for a while. She fought her gag reflex.

Her first semester in Vet school, when they worked with animal cadavers, the smell of decaying flesh brought up anything that was in her stomach. Gradually, the odor of decomposition lost some of its effect.

Rhonda clamped one hand over her nose and parted her lips to breathe. Late afternoon shadows made it impossible to see into the grass. She moved closer. Harry's long tail wagged slowly back and forth.

No telling what kind of animal the carcass had once been. The air buzzed with flies.

She jerked Harry's leash, tried to pull him back, and stumbled over another animal body, in much the same condition and unidentifiable. The dogs sniffed their way through the grass to another small body, and then another. They darted from one body to the next.

Rhonda grabbed the end of Samson's leash and pulled both dogs toward the street. The scent of decaying flesh threw her gag reflex into full throttle. The dogs came willingly now. Maybe they'd had enough of that smell, too. She was grateful that neither had dived shoulder first into any of the rotting corpses.

She dragged them back to the bar ditch, her stomach roiling.

Traffic had increased on the road. A small school bus passed and then stopped at the next intersection. Three teenage boys tumbled out, punching each other's shoulders. They raced down the street and disappeared into the neighborhood.

At the park, a toddler squealed as a young woman pushed it in the kiddie swing. A stroller sat nearby. Rhonda walked the perimeter of the park with the dogs. They sniffed and peed on trees and grass clumps.

A truck roared past on the road, then backed up and turned onto the asphalt road through the park as she and the dogs completed their loop. The truck pulled off the road to one side and parked. Two figures sat inside.

Rhonda tugged at the dogs' leashes and led them out of the park. She glanced over her shoulder at the red truck and hurried down the bar ditch.

The truck roared past. Rhonda caught the first three numbers, 7-2-4, of the Oklahoma license tag. Mud splatter obliterated the rest. Rhonda checked for traffic then jogged across the side street.

She rushed along the sidewalk, holding her breath, and keeping a firm grip on the dog's leashes as they passed the abandoned motor court. Holt could be at the house, waiting. She'd lost her appetite for pizza. She stopped and bent over, breathing deeply, still trying to clear the awful stench from her nose.

A vehicle roared up the street, then slowed as it came even with her. The tinted side windows of the red truck made it impossible to see inside. As she pulled the dogs down the sidewalk, the truck kept pace beside her.

Were these men strangers, or was it the men from the diner? Neither possibility was good, but a third possibility was too terrifying to contemplate. *No way the drug dealer could have found me so quickly.*

The driver gunned the truck's engine as it kept pace with her. A van pulled up behind the truck and honked. The red truck roared away.

Rhonda jogged the rest of the way to the bungalow.

Holt's truck sat in her driveway; Holt sat on the front step. She hurried up Mrs. P's sidewalk. Her neighbor opened the front door as she climbed the steps.

"Good walk, Harry dear? Is Rhonda a good dog walker? Good boy." She patted the Basset's big head. "Thank you." She took the dog's leash and gestured toward Rhonda's house. "You've got company. We'll talk later."

Rhonda crossed the yard, huffing for air. Holt held up a pizza box and a brown paper bag. "Hope you're hungry," he said.

She unlocked the door and led him inside. After turning on the few lamps, she motioned at the table in the kitchen and unhooked Samson from his leash. She couldn't get the images from the old motel property out of her head. She wasn't hungry.

Holt sat down and pulled two liters of beer from the brown bag. "Hope you like Bud."

Beer had been Daniel's drink of choice. He'd loved a cold beer on a hot night. A spear of grief pierced her heart.

Rhonda grabbed a roll of paper towels from the countertop by the sink, then, joined Holt at the table. Despite the unpleasant find by the old motor court, the smell of the pizza stirred her appetite.

"Have a good day?" Holt bit into a slice.

Rhonda's thoughts raced through her day: the truck, the men at the diner, and the animal carcasses by the old motor court.

"I wouldn't say good." She told him about taking the dogs to the park, seeing the mother and her toddler, the red truck, and then the dead animals. "All those dead animals in one place. They didn't die there naturally."

Holt chewed another bite of his pizza slice before he responded. "I'm more worried about the guys in the red truck. Any chance you got a tag number?"

She repeated the numbers she'd seen when the truck drove away.

"That's a start. I'll find out what vehicles are registered locally with those numbers, and ask that they issue a BOLO, Be on The Lookout. There will be a record of the incident in case anything else happens. And I'll notify Animal Control to pick up those animals at the old motor court."

Chapter 13
Claire

At the Round-up Club, Claire scanned the place for Cade. He wasn't in the bleachers watching the barrel racers practice. She went to the adjacent barn. He wasn't in the barn stalls where she'd found him and Neve yesterday.

After her search, she sat on the aluminum bleachers, watching one rider urge her horse around the barrels, trying to get one more second of speed out of the run. A buzzer rang. Obviously frustrated, the girl whipped her horse out of the arena and toward the stables.

Claire wandered outside. Participants had parked their trucks and empty horse trailers in an organized way. By the weekend, trucks and trailers would fill every space, leaving little room for ordinary vehicles.

A giggling group of girls drew her to an oversized stock trailer where three teenagers leaned against the big truck.

"Hi. Have you seen Neve?"

Two of them shrugged. The third, a brunette wearing a barrel racing t-shirt, said, "She left with a guy about a half hour ago. They took off in her car."

"Thanks." She hoped Neve was with Cade. Where would the two of them go? Maybe someplace private? The backyard patio at the B&B was secluded and empty. The day was warm, they could have gone there to sit in the sun.

"Thanks. If she does come back, would you tell her Cade's mom is looking for her?"

"Sure. She has another practice time later this afternoon, I think."

Claire waved a thanks and headed to her SUV. Seconds later, she turned onto the highway that led back into town. As she sped toward an intersection, a dump truck floated the stop sign and pulled onto the highway in front of her. When she slammed her foot on the brakes, her SUV fishtailed then skidded toward the rear of the dump trunk. Trees lined the sides of the two-lane highway. Any evasive action she took would still result in a crash.

The world around her slowed, and she imagined smashing into the rear gate of the heavy truck. She pumped the brake and shut her eyes.

Her brakes caught and the SUV jerked to a stop. She opened her eyes. The dump truck lumbered down the road, black exhaust pouring from the tail pipe.

Heart pounding, hands shaking, she pulled her SUV off the road. What had that driver been thinking? Didn't he see her? She sat quietly, breathing deeply for several minutes before she drove on into Persimmon.

* * *

When Claire steered the SUV into the parking space in the alley behind the B&B, she was still shaken. She could have died if she'd crashed into the dump truck. The almost-accident was a reality check. No one was guaranteed a tomorrow.

Neve's car wasn't there.

As she got out of the SUV, she lifted her face to the sun. Carrying her satchel, she headed for the back patio. She could use a little Vitamin D.

Claire slid into a lounge chair, pulled out her phone and autodialed Cade's number. After a few rings, voicemail came on. She waited for the beep and said, "Cade, it's Mom. Just wondering what you're doing. I'm back at the B&B. Finished my interview and need to do some research online. Let me know if you need a ride."

The musky scented autumn air triggered a memory of Cade riding Blaze in their yard at home for the first time after Denver had broken the mustang. Her nephew had found his calling with animals after a near-fatal tour of duty in Afghanistan. She was so grateful that he'd come to help her with Blaze. He'd ended up helping Cade, too. Next week, she'd talk with Denver about Cade's recent behavior. It hadn't been that long ago that Denver was 18 himself.

A noisy motorcycle cruised through the alley. She checked her watch. No call from Cade.

"Hello there, Ms. Northcutt. Another beautiful day. Everything tip top for you and your son?" Della Munoz stepped toward her from the house.

"Absolutely. I was enjoying the peace and quiet."

"Humph. Peace and quiet until that motorcycle came down the alley. So disruptive. Day and night. I complained to the City Council but that Mayor of ours just laughed in my face. Any commerce is good commerce as far as he's concerned. But motorcycles and old cars buzzing all over town at all hours of the day and night? Up to no good if you ask me." This owner of the B&B was definitely more cynical than her sister.

Claire studied the older woman. With gray hair and deep wrinkles, she looked many years older than her younger, sweeter sister. Claire recalled what Howard had told her this morning. He'd been complaining too. Was he referring to an influx of motorcycles? He was a vintage car buff. Cars wouldn't bother him.

"This isn't a recent thing then, all the motorcycles?"

"No. For years we've been listening to those loud motors. But it's getting worse, and not just because I'm getting older." She huffed and straightened. "You're doing all right then? My sister sent me out to check. Your son didn't come in for cookies. I can get some for you."

"Thank you, but I'll send Cade in after he gets here. Nice to see you again."

The elderly woman looked at her quizzically before she moved stiffly toward the side door into the house.

Claire picked up her work bag. At the outer door to the suite, she used her key card to enter.

Cade lay on the sofa, his back to the door, sneakers on the floor.

"Cade? Are you okay?" She crossed the room.

"Jeez, Mom. Shut the door. Can't you see I'm asleep?" He shielded his eyes with his arm.

"I see that. Are you sick?" She hoped he wasn't, but it would be a valid excuse for his behavior the past few days. He hadn't been himself.

"No. I'm tired. Shut up so I can go back to sleep." He flipped onto his side, his back toward her.

"Cade, don't talk to me like that. Why are you here?"

"Where else would I be?"

"Maybe the arena? Is Neve practicing?"

He jammed the sofa pillow over his head.

A teenage boy, in bed in the middle of the afternoon. She didn't need an interpreter to know something had happened between the couple. An argument? Had Neve driven him back to the B&B?

Claire sympathized. How many heartaches had she endured during her teenage dating years? More than enough. Sometimes the guy dumped her, sometimes she dumped the guy. Both roles hurt.

"I wish you'd talk to me. What's wrong?"

He tossed the pillow into the air and punched it. It flew across the room. "It's so effed up."

"Language, Cade. You're going to lose privileges."

"You're still threatening me with that? I'm 18. You don't have a right to take away my privileges."

"As long as you live under my roof, I do."

Cade blinked repeatedly. Lip quivering, eyes blinking, he turned away from her. It was what he'd done as a boy. Was he trying not to cry?

"Maybe I won't be under your roof anymore after we get home. Dad said I could live with him the rest of the year."

Claire bit her tongue. She'd thought the nonsense about wanting to live with his father was long over. Two years ago, he could barely tolerate spending a weekend with his dad. But recently ... what had changed? She really needed to talk to Denver about all of this. His perspective could shed some light on what was happening.

"Why are you so upset? Is it Neve?" She took a stab in the dark, although she expected his behavior over the past twelve hours had everything to do with his girlfriend.

Cade glared at the ceiling. "Who says I'm upset?"

"Convince me you're not."

He gulped.

"Cade, please tell me what happened."

His breath exploded. "She won't talk to me. Won't return my calls."

She'd interrupted a fight between the pair Wednesday afternoon. Neve hadn't broken off their relationship, but things were rocky.

"Cade, what happened? Did you lose your temper?"

"No. I was illustrating a point, trying to get her to see what might happen. People could hurt her."

"Who would hurt her? Her grandmother?" Claire didn't understand. Cade's meaning wasn't clear.

"I offered to go with her yesterday, to talk to her grandmother. She told me to stay out of her business."

"Her business? What?"

His frown deepened. "One of her uncles is into drugs. Neve says her Creek grandmother is getting senile, maybe Alzheimer's, she won't do anything about it."

Claire knew this land west of Tulsa had been part of the land given to the Muscogee Creek in Indian Territory. Neve's grandmother could live on her family allotment. She might have a different take on the changes Route 66 had brought. But first, she wanted to know what was going on with Neve.

"Is the uncle living at the grandmother's, where she's staying?" Claire's thoughts churned.

"Neve won't listen to me. She's in danger but she won't let me help." He opened and closed his fists.

Claire sighed. "Sometimes people don't want help. It's hard to stand back and watch bad things happen." She might visit the grandmother tomorrow, without Cade. If he was this worried, he must have good reason.

* * *

After showering, Claire returned to the suite's living room. Cade had relocated to the bedroom. She pulled her laptop out of her bag.

It was frustrating not to have a good lead for the Persimmon portion of her article. She had not yet fully searched the state's newspaper archives. Finding the right keywords to get good results in the database search was crucial.

Newspapers.com was her go-to source for information. Back in the day, every small town had a newspaper. This town was no exception. She'd already done preliminary work using the local news. She pulled up the website and began plugging in keywords.

When she had run through every combination she could think of, she returned to Google. Hopefully, the Oklahoma Department of Commerce had information about business closures by decade. With the addition of business names and owners, she might find an angle for the story.

Claire searched on the internet. She took a few notes, followed names into rabbit holes and out again. But the key item she needed to produce a story eluded her. She found no mention of any new enterprise that would increase car or motorcycle traffic like the B&B owner had mentioned.

The shower came on. Claire checked her watch: 6 p.m. She hadn't heard Cade's phone ring, and Holt hadn't called. Claire was certain Holt knew the waitress at the diner. Attractive and educated, why was she working there? She could be in between bigger or better jobs. She might be earning extra money for something special. Claire had worked a few ludicrous jobs to get extra money for Cade's birthdays and Christmas during her single mother years.

Once again, she thought about the dump truck. The big truck would hardly have sustained a scratch if she'd rammed into it. Had the driver pulled out in front of her on purpose for a thrill or was there another reason?

She'd had no luck so far finding details for her article. It was almost as if the mayor was sending her on a wild goose chase. Was he hiding something?

Chapter 14
Rhonda

Holt bit into another pizza slice. Rhonda put her second piece down after two bites. Despite the wonderful aroma of the baked crust and the cheesy mix of tomato sauce, veggies, and meat, she couldn't eat any more. She leaned back in the chair. "Thanks."

"You're welcome. You deserve a treat." He ducked his head and didn't meet the look she shot at him.

Cut the guy some slack, her inner judge said. And part of her wanted to, but part of her also wanted to reiterate once again the injustices of her recent life. She'd lost Daniel, her children, her parents, her friends, and remaining family. She couldn't imagine her future—never seeing any of them ever again.

She wanted the Feds to catch up with the drug dealers and send them to prison so she could go back to her life. She wanted the world to be as she'd known it. It was unbearable to imagine nothing would ever be the same.

Their life had been so good. Not perfect, but close. It was inconceivable that it was over.

She and Daniel had rolled out of bed at 5 a.m. Thirty minutes later, she cooked scrambled eggs and bacon downstairs in the kitchen. Daniel read the morning paper online while seated on a bar stool at the granite-topped island. Through the wide window behind him, the gray and white trunks of giant sycamores gleamed in the early morning light, and the rolling yellowed rangeland beyond the creek glowed.

His hair, tousled and curly, still wet from his shower, glistened. She had wanted to run her fingers through it, but she flipped the eggs instead.

"Hot today," Daniel said, sipping his coffee. He looked up at her. A smile slipped over her face. Twenty-two years of marriage and two grown children later, his look still caused a tingle throughout her body.

She scooted his plate of eggs, toast, and bacon across the island, then carried her own plate over and climbed onto the stool beside him. "And it's going to be a busy one, too. We're both booked solid."

Daniel ate quickly. Finished, he stretched his arms over his head. His left hand touched her shoulder and then trailed down her back.

"I'll get the operating room ready. Susanna will be here soon." He set his mug down by the sink and crossed the kitchen to the mudroom, where he put on one of the white jackets that hung from the pegs by the back door.

The 7 a.m. operation would be the third one in the past twelve hours that they'd performed on their neighbor's cow. This one was a follow-up repair. Last night, they'd tediously removed embedded barbed wire from the animal's legs and body.

Susanna's blue Mercury chugged up the drive as she rinsed off the cooking utensils. Susanna would help Daniel set things up, then call the house when everything was ready for the surgery. She would walk the fifty yards across the graveled yard to their veterinary hospital to assist in the operation.

The clinic would open as usual after the surgery.

She opened her eyes; terror closed her throat. The memory was too vivid. She was there again, a prisoner of her past.

The surgery went as planned, and they finished the final repair. Mrs. Simpson brought her cat in for a check-up. She gave rabies and parvovirus vaccinations to an entire litter of Brittany Spaniel pups from a local breeder, and a cortisone shot to a ten-year-old German shepherd with an arthritic hip. Jack Dawson brought in his limping blue heeler and she removed slivers of glass from the pad of one foot and wrapped it in gauze.

Meanwhile, Daniel treated two horses, a Shetland pony, and a Billy goat. About 11 a.m., he left the clinic to help a mare foaling at a ranch six miles west.

She was in the lab, checking a fecal sample for round worms, when the phone rang. Susanna buzzed the lab and told her to pick up the extension.

"Daniel not there?" Carson McVeigh asked. "Oh." He paused, then cleared his throat. "Well. Found this dog yesterday. Collar and leash, no tags. Maybe micro-chipped. Can't rightly say. Seems to be in awful pain."

Carson was tender-hearted toward animals but didn't care too much for people in general and women in particular. The man liked Daniel, but barely tolerated her. He wanted to talk to Daniel, but she was the small animal vet, and what he had was a small animal that needed help.

"Dog's not doing good. Can't pass anything, but he sure has tried. Won't eat, won't drink. Miserable, whiny thing. Wish Daniel was there. I need to know what to do with it."

Her mind raced down the list of things that could prevent a dog from eliminating waste. Most of them weren't life-threatening if resolved promptly. "Sounds like a blockage in the intestines, Carson. We may need to operate, but I'd have to see the dog first. Have you tried to find the owner?"

"Got signs posted up and down my block. Gave out my phone number. Sent the info to a couple of radio stations. Got an idiot call, telling me to shoot it. Nothing else."

An animal whined in the background. "Bring the dog out, Carson. Daniel will be back in a little while. I'll look at the dog, and if we need to operate, Daniel and I will do it this afternoon."

"Well." Carson cleared his throat again. "I don't know as how I can pay for this dog to have surgery. He ain't mine. It's just he's in such a state. I feel really sorry for him."

"Bring the dog out, Carson, and don't worry about the cost. Daniel and I will take care of it."

"You ain't gonna put it to sleep, are you, Renee? You're really going to operate?"

"We'll operate to find out what's wrong if we need to. What time do you think you can be here?"

"If I can get him in the car, we'll be there in about ten minutes."

"You want another beer?" Holt reached into the paper sack and pulled out another liter bottle. He twisted the cap off and handed it to her. She took it automatically, and then let the rest of the horrific memory play in her head.

Carson was waiting by the counter, the dog in his arms, when she emerged from the lab. He peered through the doorway to look behind her. "Daniel not back yet?"

"No. Should be anytime. Come in here with the dog, and let's see what's going on."

Carson pushed past and placed the dog on the exam table. The animal, a cross between a lab and shepherd, had eyes full of fear and pain. Every muscle in his body was tense. His legs splayed out in four different directions when Carson placed him on the metal table. The dog cowered, whining.

"Easy boy. Let's have a look at you." She extended her open hand for him to sniff, then carefully slipped a soft canvas muzzle over the animal's nose and secured it at the back of his skull. Slowly she ran her hands over the animal, talking in a soft voice. When she reached the swollen mound of his stomach, he yelped and fought to get away. Probing gently with her fingers, she found a mass.

The dog needed surgery.

"What is it?" Carson twisted his ballcap and shifted his weight from foot to foot.

"He has a blockage. We'll have to operate. And we'll keep him overnight. You can go home if you want. We'll call you after the surgery. If his owner calls you, send them here to get him. We'll hope they see the signs you posted."

"More pizza?"

She'd been sipping her way through the beer and was already feeling light-headed. "I'm not very good company."

"You've got a lot on your mind. I'm a good listener if you'd like to talk about it. Otherwise, I'm fine with sitting here, killing this beer. Want another?"

She lifted her eyebrows. "I'd be tempted if it erased my memory."

"Maybe I should go."

Rhonda didn't want him to go. It felt good to have another person here, as cramped, and crummy as the house was. Samson lay on the floor, his head resting on her right foot. Holt sat on her left, close enough to touch if she had wanted to.

"Stay. It's good to have company." She stretched her arm down to Samson so she could scratch his back.

Holt swigged more beer. "The house deal is done. That's what I want to celebrate. They'll have furniture delivered and stock the kitchen by Sunday."

Rhonda straightened. "Who is 'they?'" She could imagine what the furniture and the interior of the house would look like if a bunch of Feds oversaw turning an empty house into a home. They had not outdone themselves outfitting this place.

"'They' is the crew we use in this region of the country. Decorators. We give them information about you and your previous life, including pictures of the house you lived in before, and they come up with an interior that feels like home to you."

She sucked in a quick breath. The last time she'd seen their clinic, next to the house she'd lived in before— with Daniel—blood spatter covered everything. She couldn't picture it without seeing that blood. As much as she had loved their home, she didn't know if she could go back. Tears welled up and spilled over her cheeks.

Holt reached for her hand. "It'll be great, I promise."

She pushed her chair back and dashed for the bathroom. Inside the tiny room, she splashed water on her face. Her stomach was a tight knot. The beer smell on her breath nauseated her. She sat on the commode. Life sucked.

Holt knocked on the door. "You okay in there?"

Rhonda cleared her throat. "Yeah." She flushed the toilet, although there was no reason to.

"Samson and I are lonely out here. Come out."

Bossy man, she thought. Maybe that was what she needed. It wasn't helpful to sit on toilet lids for minutes at a time. She needed someone to jerk her out of her pity party. She had to deal with life. She had to keep it together. The only person who could help her do that was on the other side of the bathroom door.

A quick glance in the mirror showed puddled eyeliner and mascara streaks down her cheeks. She mopped the mess away with a wet cotton ball, then ran her fingers through her newly colored auburn hair.

"If you're not out here in ten seconds, I'm leaving," Holt said from the other side of the door. "Heck of a way to treat company, even in your rotten situation."

She pulled the door open. "Don't go, Holt. I'm sorry. I just get ... overwhelmed. Let's finish that beer."

Holt moved over to the table. He watched her cross the room, then settled down into his chair. "Okay. Are you going to stay in this room with me?"

"Yes, I am. I'm glad you're here, honestly. I just feel—"

"I know. Overwhelmed." He took a long chug from his bottle, then dug another out of the bag and handed it to her. "Your bottle got warm. I put it in the frig."

She took a long swallow. Samson scooted closer to the chair and rested his head on her foot again.

"By the way, from the looks of your frig, you are overdue for a visit to the grocery store. We'll do that after you move into the new house if it's not stocked with food you like."

"You really think it will be ready this weekend?"

"I'm betting on it."

Rhonda checked out the dismal room. It wouldn't be soon enough. Away from this awful house, she might not feel so miserable. If her surrounding were more homelike, she might be able to deal with the current situation.

She would never accept it, but she could tolerate it if she kept her eye on the resolution. How wonderful it will be to get back to her family, to see the look on her mother's face when she saw her alive. Rhonda could pick up the phone and explain to her children and her family what had been going on.

And she would know that the drug dealers were behind bars, that they could no longer threaten her life or the lives of her family. She would know that the man who had shot Daniel and ordered her death could no longer hurt anyone.

Chapter 15 - FRIDAY
Claire

A beam of light shone in Claire's face from a crack in the drapes. She squinted and rolled over to look at the bedside alarm clock, then bolted upright and glanced at Cade in the other bed. The covers were up to his neck; he snored quietly.

In the bathroom, Claire dressed and layered on her makeup. When she stepped back into the room, Cade was no longer there. She stuck her head out the door that opened to the backyard and the small B&B parking lot off the alleyway and saw him leaning against the back of her SUV, cell phone to his ear.

She gathered her computer and notebook, stuffed them into her work satchel and was about to step back outside when someone knocked on the interior hall door to the room.

"Good morning, Mrs. Northcutt," a cheery voice called.

Claire crossed the room and opened the door. "Mrs. Spoon. How are you?" She smiled at the owner of the Bed and Breakfast. Dressed in a denim dress with a flowered apron over the skirt, the woman stood tall and proud, her brown skin smooth and unwrinkled.

"It's just Betsy, dear. I'm well. Going to be a glorious day, thank the Lord. Good to be alive."

Claire was grateful for the reminder. Sometimes everything going on in her life consumed her, and she forgot to be grateful for each day.

"I thank my lucky stars to be here. Even after Ed died, I wanted to keep going. That's when I joined my sister Della in running this B&B. I was too young to shut down.; I love meeting new people, and my sister … She always needs something to keep her mind busy."

Claire thought about her Route 66 article. "Have you lived here all of your life?"

"Della—I've always called her Dee—never left. She married and lived down the street from our folks. When they passed on, she was divorced and living alone, so she moved into our childhood home and started redecorating. I came back from St. Louis after Ed passed."

The sisters were probably in their seventies, but Betsy could have passed for much younger. Della was the oldest, although her once-black hair had streaked with gray rather than white like Betsy's. When Claire had met them at check-in Wednesday, Della had been grumbling to Betsy about their bakery order. Yesterday she'd been grumbling about noisy cars and motorcycles.

"Are you headed out for the day already? Your son didn't pick up your weekday continental breakfast. Today it's blueberry scones from Tiny's café. Delish. Your son is quite a nice-looking young man," Betsy Spoon said.

Claire scoffed. "He's showing his bad side this morning, I'm afraid. The scones sound wonderful, but we'll have to pass. He's in a hurry. Count on us tomorrow, though. Full breakfast, right?" She stepped back and started to close the door.

"Have a good day. And remember, my house is your house. Come into the living area any time for free coffee and a cookie. This afternoon it's butterscotch, and a few leftover snickerdoodles from yesterday. Still soft, though. Tasty."

Claire smiled as she closed the interior door. She grabbed her work bag and crossed the room to the outside entrance. Cade was no longer leaning against the door of the SUV. She scanned the area. No Cade. Had Neve come by and picked him up? If so, he could have at least taken a minute to let her know. But with the mood he'd been in lately, his bad attitude might have taken over. He had probably jumped in Neve's car and not given his mother a second thought. She shook her head and climbed into the SUV.

Chapter 16
Rhonda

The alarm on Rhonda's cell phone woke her. She turned it off, then lay still. A jackhammer drilled into her brain, and her mouth felt like a sand dune. It had been years since she'd had as many beers as she did last night.

Her last memory was hearing Holt say, "Lock the door behind me. I'll wait on the porch until you do it." She'd struggled up from the table, followed him across the room, and secured the dead bolt after he stepped out.

Now, Samson threw his upper body onto the mattress and whined.

"Okay, okay. I'm up." She stumbled across the room to the tiny bathroom.

After a quick shower, she followed her morning routine and put on the pink tunic that hung from the door hook. Rhonda scratched at a few spots on the uniform. Her evening spot cleanings weren't doing the job. Surely, she wouldn't be a waitress long enough to have to buy a second one, or to learn all the tricks about keeping the pink shift clean.

Samson barked as she pulled on a denim jacket and opened the door. He dashed through the opening and across the porch, then skidded to a stop before tumbling down the steps. What could have been a discarded throw rug lay on the sidewalk at the bottom of the steps. Yesterday, it might have been a cat. This one had lived the last of its nine lives.

Her blood stopped pumping. Rhonda tied the dog's leash around the porch post and moved toward the pile of fur. She made sure the animal was indeed dead, then untied Samson and stumbled back into the house.

Who would leave a dead animal in someone's front yard?

An immediate answer pounded in her head: the drug gang knew she was here. But no, if they knew where she was, they wouldn't warn her with a dead cat. She'd already be dead.

Whoever left this message wanted to scare her. The guys in the red truck, a.k.a. the men from the diner, were the obvious culprits.

Rhonda pulled a trash bag from the box under the sink and went back outside. After carrying the dead animal to the garbage can, she returned to the house where she poured kibble into Samson's bowl and refilled his water. Then, she grabbed her purse and left.

* * *

"Holt," Rhonda said when he answered the phone. "I'm on my way to work. I had a message on the lawn this morning. A dead cat."

"What?"

"If they know I'm here, they wouldn't bother with threats, would they?"

He cleared his throat. "You've irked somebody. Do the words 'lay low' mean anything?"

"They do. And I was. Other than going to work and walking the dog and sitting in my house, I haven't done anything or talked to anyone but you."

"The guys in the red truck saw you at the park, and possibly when you found the animal bodies."

"True. But why do they care?"

"Don't know yet. I'll do a search. Where's that dead cat now? I'm going to get a city crew to clean up the motor court."

"Have someone find out what those animals died of, would you? And the cat at my house. He's in the trash can in a bag. Those deaths couldn't be natural. Why were they placed there?"

* * *

Rhonda opened the café's back door and stepped into the delivery hallway next to the kitchen. The scent of baking scones swirled past. Eduardo was singing; he'd tuned the radio in the kitchen to a Spanish station. Rhonda passed the storage pantry and glanced in as Jean pulled a gallon mayonnaise jar from the shelf.

"Morning. Need help with that?"

"Sure." Jean's gray-blond hair was stiff with hair spray and teased to three inches high on top. A dark blue eyeshadow coated her usually natural eyelids.

Rhonda took the jar from her. "You look nice."

Jean raised her eyebrows and grabbed a jar of pickle relish. "You think so?"

"Anything special going on?"

The older waitress smiled coyly as they walked from the pantry into the kitchen. "You've noticed that repeat customer you got every morning at Table 6."

"Howard?"

"Oh. You already know his name."

"He told me yesterday. What about him?"

"He's a widower. And I think he's in the market."

"He seems nice. You want to cover that table today?"

They set the jars on the worktable, then Jean went to the refrigerators to bring over the table-size containers for refilling.

"Just when Howard's there. Okay?"

"Sure. I'll say hello to him, though. He knows that table's in my section."

Jean nodded. She blushed.

Howard and Jean. She hoped it worked out. Maybe one good thing would happen in Café World while she was working here.

* * *

Howard came through the door at his usual time, went right to Table 6 and sat down. Three other people came in behind him and sat down at Table 5.

"Morning, Howard. Jean will be right with you," Rhonda nodded at him, then moved toward the other new customers and pulled out her order pad. Jean scurried over to wait on Howard.

* * *

Customers came and went all morning. Rhonda was starting to recognize more customers as repeats. She might know most of them by name in another week or so. Nancy came in with a big vat of filleted catfish, ready for frying for today's special, and Rhonda helped her batter them for frying in between customers.

Not all the people at the diner were regulars, but one woman had caught her eye—the one who'd been here Wednesday with Holt. She'd come in again yesterday morning with a young man. The woman had seemed nice, but Rhonda had been too tired to interact. She hadn't seen her yet today. Could be she wouldn't come in again during Rhonda's shift.

Chapter 17
Claire

Claire picked up breakfast at the McDonald's drive-through. Not her usual choice, but it was fast. As she navigated old Route 66 out of town and took the road to the arena, she wished she'd grabbed a scone from the B&B. Her irritation at Cade was building. He should have told her he was leaving. One more thing to talk with him about when she caught up with him.

In the parking lot, she looked for Neve's white Honda, but didn't see it among an assortment of cars and trucks. Claire straightened the shoulder strap of her bag as she got out of the SUV and stepped toward the arena.

She stood at the rail, watching a young woman race her horse around the three barrels. The woman made it look easy, but Claire knew it wasn't. It took skill to get the horse to race to the far end of the arena, stop on a dime, turn close in around not just one but three separate barrels before racing back to the far end where they'd begun. Not a second to waste. Rider and horse must be in perfect sync.

She kept her eye out for Neve and Cade but didn't see either of the teenagers. One of the girls Neve had been eating breakfast with the day before waited with her horse next to a gate.

"Hi. Ready for your practice time?" Claire asked. "It's Brooklyn, right?"

A smile broke across the girl's face. "Oh, hey. You're Cade's mom."

"Yes. I was hoping to watch Neve practice before I go to work. Do you know when her morning practice slot is?"

Brooklyn frowned. "She was first up today, at 7 a.m. Haven't seen her since."

"Just one practice time?" From what Cade had said, his girlfriend's focus was to win the weekend competition in her class. She should be taking every opportunity to speed up her time around the barrels.

The other girl shrugged. "I have two ten-minute slots. Not sure when her second one is. If she doesn't practice, it's her loss, not mine."

"She and Cade must be around here somewhere. Maybe at the stalls?"

Brooklyn shrugged. "Neve left right after her practice. Maybe she went back out to her grandmother's house. She's worried about her."

"Is she sick?"

"She's old, superstitious, and half crazy, Neve says." Brooklyn stroked her horse's long nose. The animal snorted.

Claire didn't like what she was hearing. "Maybe I should go out there and check on them. Do you know where her grandmother lives?"

Brooklyn glanced at the people milling around the arena. "No, but that woman over there with the brown cowboy hat and long braid is one of the organizers. Maybe she knows."

"Thanks. If you see Neve or Cade, would you let them know I'm looking for them?" Claire hurried across the dirt floor. As she approached, the woman flipped through pages secured to a clipboard, and then pulled out her cell phone. Faded jeans, ripped up the seams on the lower part of each leg, flapped over her short boots. Her tan face was sun wrinkled.

The woman squinted at Claire and tucked her phone into her shirt pocket. "Need something?"

"Yes. I'm Claire Northcutt. Neve Bright, and my horse, Blaze, should be practicing, but I don't see her. I'm concerned. Do you have contact info other than her cell number?"

"Let me see." She flipped through the papers on her clipboard and ran her finger down a list on one page. "She's staying at her grandma's, south of Sahoma Lake. I have the house phone number. Let me call. I'm Stella." The woman studied Claire's face before she punched the numbers into her cell phone.

Claire could hear the phone ringing on the other end of Stella's phone. After many rings, Stella punched it off. "No one is answering. I met her Granny last year. She was frail then."

"I can drive out to check on them if you'll give me directions." Claire pulled her note pad from her purse and handed it to Stella. "It could be nothing, but I'd like to make sure."

Stella took the pad and wrote down the directions. She handed it back to Claire. "Better safe than sorry. Could be they need help. Could be they don't. Anyway, you'll meet the old grandmother. She's quite a character. Maybe you can get her to talk to you. She prefers to speak Muscogee Creek, but nobody does much anymore."

When Stella's phone rang, she nodded at Claire and stepped away.

* * *

Fifteen minutes later, in a hilly forested neighborhood, she drove past rundown homes with derelict cars and dilapidated swing sets in the yards. According to her Maps app, she was only one street away from Neve's grandmother's house. She turned the corner, accelerated up a hill and coasted down it toward a curve in the road. She slowed even more, overly cautious after her near collision with the dump truck. Claire studied the mailboxes. When she found the correct name and address, she turned up the driveway.

Fifty yards in, the old white clapboard house sat dwarfed by overgrown bushes. A wide porch across the front of the house would offer shade from the summer heat. The white wicker chairs and settee grouped in front of a window were old, the paint cracked so that the thin brown willow branches beneath shown through.

Claire strode toward the house. Grass was sparse on the mostly-dirt lawn, but the grass had been mowed and the flower beds and sidewalk neatly trimmed. A breeze whipped through, tossing leaves, and bringing with it a putrid smell. Next door, a scrawny black dog stopped to bark by the edge of the driveway.

The screen door creaked open, and a tiny Native American woman with gray hair wound into a braid on the back of her head stepped to the edge of the porch. She wore a brightly colored skirt and a loose blouse of light blue.

Claire headed for the house, smiling. The woman raised her hand, palm flat, toward Claire. Silver bracelets clinked on her arms, and turquoise rings flashed in the sunlight. She cocked her head.

Claire stopped. "Hello. I'm looking for Neve. She's not out at the arena, practicing for the competition. I own Blaze, the horse she's riding. I'm worried about her. Is she here?"

The woman tilted her head back, eyes closed, as if she were sniffing the air.

Claire waited. "I'm Claire," she finally said. "Claire Northcutt."

"Claire Northcutt," the old woman repeated.

"Yes. Is Neve here?"

"I know about you. You write. Sit." She motioned toward the wicker chairs and shuffled over to a rocker with a striped blanket draped over the back. She sat and spread the blanket over her lap. Claire climbed the porch steps and then folded herself into the chair opposite her.

"Neve's not here. Maybe you can find her." Her voice was soft.

"You don't know where she is?"

Neve's grandmother pursed her lips.

Claire focused on the grandmother's heavily creased face.

Once again, the breeze that whipped leaves up to the porch had a putrid scent to it. Claire wrinkled her nose. "Is something around here dead? I keep smelling ..."

"We are all dead or dying."

An old blue truck rattled up the road and turned into the driveway A middle-aged man in blue coveralls climbed out and limped toward them.

"Who's this?" The man asked. Tall, with short straight black hair, he studied Claire. "You with the city? Here about that smell?"

The grandmother waved one hand at him. "No, Cruz. This lady owns the horse Neve's riding. She can't find her."

"Neve was at the arena earlier, practicing," the man said. "But she's not there now. I came to see if something was wrong."

"Plenty wrong," The grandmother said. "You can't help, Cruz. This is about my son Kai."

The old woman gazed out at the sycamore trees.

The man scowled. "Does Neve know about Kai? Did you tell her, Mama?" The old woman remained silent. "Is she with him?" He didn't wait for an answer, but whirled and stumbled to the truck, one leg dragging slightly behind.

Claire watched the old woman. Her reporter senses heightened. There was a story here, and it had to do with the awful smell.

"Let's drink coffee. You listen." The old woman pushed herself out of the chair and moved slowly to the door. Claire followed.

Chapter 18
Rhonda

Early Friday evening, Rhonda delivered a tray piled high with fried chicken and coleslaw to Table 2 next to the front window. Outside, seven Harleys roared up and parked in the designated area beyond the handicapped spaces. Through the front window, Rhonda watched ten riders ease off the bikes, stretch and head for the entrance.

A table for ten meant moving three tables together. The bikers would have to wait until a table opened. Hopefully, that group table wouldn't be designated as hers. Her calves ached and she was overdue for a break. Why had she agreed to work a double shift on a Friday?

Thirty minutes later, Lance helped her carry the food trays out to the grouped tables. Only one of them was technically in her section, but she ended up serving the group of bikers. Before distributing the plates, she checked her order tickets, so she knew which person got which plate of food. Halfway through, as Rhonda placed a plate on the table in front of the customer, the woman grumbled, "That's not what I ordered."

The woman wore a black leather jacket with a purple bandana across her forehead and tied under long thick black hair.

Rhonda pulled out her order pad. "Grilled chicken, no mayo, extra cheese and hickory, sub salad for fries, honey mustard."

The woman's green eyes narrowed. "I said 'breaded,' not 'grilled.'"

Clearly, Rhonda had written 'grilled' on her order pad. But she remembered the old customer service credo— The Customer Is Always Right. "I must have written it down wrong. I'll leave the plate so you can begin your salad, and I'll have the sandwich redone."

The woman's mouth turned up in a slight smile. The man next to her shook his head and studied his hamburger. Chances were when she returned to the table with the new sandwich, the sandwich the woman didn't order would be half-eaten, she'd take the new one and then ask for a 'to go' box for all the sandwich leftovers. That was one way to stretch your food budget.

Rhonda headed back to the kitchen. The bell on the front door tinkled. Tired as she was, she was tempted to ignore it, but she was the only waitress out front. She turned and felt relief to see the woman who'd been frequenting the restaurant the past few days, the one who had come in with Holt on Wednesday.

She strode toward the door, smiling, and motioned the woman toward an open booth by the front window. Each time she'd waited on her she'd been friendly, and as tired as Rhonda was, she needed someone who might not expect her to be the perfect waitress, someone that might even ask her to sit down a minute if she had time.

Rhonda handed her a menu.

"Thanks. I'm not that hungry, but I've got to eat something. Any suggestions?"

Rhonda thought for only a second about what she might eat if she could spare the time and was only mildly hungry. "I think the lentil salad. It has sweet red peppers in it, and purple onion. Just the right amount of flavor. Eduardo does a good job with it."

"Sound perfect, thanks." The woman closed the menu and looked at Rhonda before glancing around the dining room at the tables cluttered with dirty dishes, and the busboy who was busily trying to clean them up.

"We've had a crazy afternoon. And now, a group of bikers." Rhonda tipped her head toward the large group at the back of the room. "I'll get your order out as soon as I can. I should be able to dish it up while the cook is working on food for that bunch." Rhonda started for the kitchen.

One of the men had pushed his chair back from the table and was staring at her and the woman she'd just seated at the booth. An electric current raced through Rhonda. Her heart thudded beneath her ribs. She held her breath, expecting to hear her name—her real name—any second as she hurried past his table and toward the kitchen.

Was it happening? Surely not already? Who was that man? But as Rhonda glanced over her shoulder just before she passed through the swinging door between the kitchen and the dining room, the man, who wore a leather jacket and jeans with a red bandana around his neck, was making his way across the dining room toward Claire.

"Rhonda? You alright? You look a little sick." Jean squeezed past, carrying a tray of food.

Rhonda shook her head. "Feeling the long day."

"Hang in there, honey."

She lurched over to the pickup window. "Eduardo? Got a re-order. Breaded on that last chicken sandwich, not grilled."

Eduardo put down his metal spatula, rubbed his hands on his apron, and stepped over to the window. "*Que pasa?*"

"Customer says she ordered 'breaded' chicken. I wrote down 'grilled.'" Rhonda shrugged.

"She is lying. You been here *cinco dias*. Five. No mistakes. *Nunca*."

Rhonda forced a small smile. "And I need a lentil salad. Can you pull that together while those burgers are cooking?"

Rhonda staggered to the employee's bathroom next to the storage pantry. The unisex bathroom was small, but the ladies kept extra makeup and hair spray there for touchups. She peered into the mirror.

When she'd entered the witness protection program, she'd changed her hair color to auburn. The hair color made her eyes greener, and her new hairstyle was curly and short. Heavy eyeliner on both her upper and lower lids was not her usual look. She wouldn't be easy to recognize.

Someone knocked on the door. "Don't take all day." It sounded like Wilson, the dishwasher.

She flushed the toilet and turned on the faucet.

When she left the bathroom and returned to the kitchen, Sylvie, a part-time waitress, was leaning against the serving table. She winked at her. "Guy out there thinks you're cute. He asked your name."

"Which guy?"

"Biker. End of that big table we pulled together."

"Not my type. You want to finish that table for me? I'm going to serve up this salad and then I need a break, or I'll never get through the next two hours."

Sylvie shrugged and tucked the side of her long, brown hair behind her ears. "You've done the hard part. Taking and delivering orders. Guess I could. He's kind of cute, really. More my type than yours, although he's a little old. I'll check their drinks and give 'em their tickets. First, let me grab a quick smoke." She headed toward the back hallway.

"Thanks," Rhonda called after the other waitress.

"Reorder up, Rhonda," Eduardo said.

Sylvie was already outside. Rhonda took the plate into the dining room, holding her breath to suppress the anxiety that had taken over her body. Most of the people at the big table were eating. Her 'redo' customer was munching on her salad. She set the new sandwich next to her. "There you go. Sorry again for the mistake. Enjoy."

She was a few steps away from the table when a voice called, "Hey sweetness?"

Something about the voice, the tone of his words, sent chills through her body, amping up the anxiety level once again. She kept walking.

"Come on. Give a guy a break?"

Rhonda pushed into the kitchen and sped toward the back hallway. What was wrong with her? The man didn't know her name. He didn't recognize her.

Rhonda prepared the plate for the lentil salad with shaking fingers. She placed it in the freezer as she gathered her belongings, ready to dash out the door when Eduardo had her own take-out order ready. She planned to take it home to eat, and then come back for the final hours of her shift.

Sylvie hollered across the room to her, "I'll check your table now, Rhonda. Any message for the biker?"

"No message. I think he's trying to pick me up." She shook her head. "Not interested. And I'm headed home to eat a bite as soon as I drop off this salad. Long day."

"I'll tell him." Sylvie pushed through the swinging door and into the dining room.

Rhonda crossed her fingers that the bikers would be gone by the time she finished her dinner and returned to the dining room for the last 90 minutes of her shift. Then, she retrieved the chilled salad from the freezer and carried it out to the woman at the booth by the window. The biker with the red kerchief was now sitting across from her.

Chapter 19
Claire

A man approached Claire's table. Grinning from ear to ear, he wore black jeans and black leather motorcycle chaps, a black leather jacket with a red t-shirt underneath. His black hair was long, and a scruffy beard covered his jawline. His eyes flashed as he grinned a lopsided, wide grin.

Claire recognized that grin. She'd last seen Vince Matheson at her 25-year high school reunion two years ago. The two of them hadn't spoken until after they'd had a group picture taken with others who'd attended the same grade school. They'd talked about how goofy they'd appeared in sixth grade, with crooked teeth and pre-pubescent bodies.

Vince Matheson wasn't the biggest kid in her sixth-grade class, but he'd been the cutest. Half the girls had crushes on him. She would say that he only had eyes for her, but in hindsight, he didn't care about girls yet. He talked to her, wrote her a few notes, but back then nothing much happened in the sixth grade, and no one had date parties. Boys and girls didn't go out alone together after school, and when they played together at recess, it was always girl versus boy games. In class, they sat in rows, alphabetically. Matheson sat behind her in home room.

"It's Claire, isn't it? Claire Martin? It IS you." He slid into the other side of the booth and extended one hand across the table toward her.

"Yes, it is. Vince. What a surprise to see you." She touched his fingers with hers but didn't shake his hand.

"You got that right. What are you doing here in small town Okieland? Thought you'd be working for some big shot news outfit. You were headed that direction when we talked at the reunion. Weren't you working on something for the Associated Press? Something about a do-good horse rancher?"

Claire nodded. "Good memory." She wished he'd forgotten. She didn't want to explain what a fiasco that had turned into. The rancher, J.B. Floren, had been far from the wonderful animal lover her article had made him out to be. She'd been lucky that AP hadn't asked for a retraction. Instead, as the real story behind Floren revealed itself a few weeks after his murder, they'd let the sun set on the article, and no one had pursued it.

"So, you got the accolades you wanted, but no job offer?" He leaned across the table toward her.

"Didn't really want a job offer. My son wouldn't have wanted us to move. Timing wasn't right."

"Oh. Guess I got the wrong impression. But if that's what you want, that's good."

She nodded and lifted her iced tea glass to her lips, studying the man who sat across from her. She hadn't recognized him or anyone else at the 25-year reunion. She'd missed the 10-year. When they posed for a grade school pic, they'd all been checking each other out, trying to decide who was who. Afterward, Vince had most likely told her where he lived and what he did for a living, but she'd forgotten. And she didn't remember him saying anything about motorcycles. They'd hardly talked long enough for each to recognize the other years later in different circumstances. She searched her memory for details about him but came up empty. He was handsome, but bells weren't ringing.

"What are you doing here? Working on another article?" He eased back in the booth and kept grinning.

"I'm writing something about Route 66. Big anniversary coming up."

"Ah, I guess that's true. This town went boom, and then bust. That your angle?"

She took a long drink of tea. "Sort of." She wasn't ready to talk about it yet. The story was still coming together in her head. "What about you? What are you doing here?"

"Riding with my buddies on the Mother Road. I make time to do that most weekends. And I'm stopping in to see an uncle who lives here."

"Longtime resident? I'm interviewing some of those for my article. Think he'd be willing to talk to me?"

"Probably. I can give you his phone number. Got a pen?"

Claire dug a ballpoint out of her purse and tore a blank page from her notebook. She slid both across the table.

When he'd returned the page, she glanced down at the name *Howard Noble*.

She pushed back in the booth. "He's your uncle? That's a coincidence. I've already talked to him. This morning."

"Hope he gave you something you could use."

"I'm still looking for the right angle." Claire sighed.

Vince crossed his arms, studying her with an appraising look that made her squirm.

The waitress, Rhonda, stepped up to the table and set a lentil salad plate in front of her. She eyed Vince. "Are you moving over here? Want me to bring your plate over here? It's coming out in a minute."

Vince glanced at Rhonda, and Claire picked up her fork and dug into her salad. She didn't need Vince Matheson to distract her from her focus on the article.

"No. I'm joining my buddies," Vince said. "I'll be back over there by the time you bring my steak out." Vince gave Rhonda a long look. A muscle in his cheek jumped.

"Great. Coming right up." The waitress crossed the room to the swinging kitchen door.

His look followed Rhonda. "I'll get back to my friends, then. Nice to see you, Claire." He scooted out of the booth and leaned toward her. "Say, will you be here all weekend? Like to meet up for dinner tomorrow?"

Claire swallowed. "Thanks for the offer, Vince, but I'll be busy the next few days with this article, and then I've got to get Cade back to Stillwater for school on Monday. It was nice to see you again."

She hoped her smile covered her discomfort. Vince would be a good distraction if she were willing. But she wasn't. And it was clear he had a roaming eye. He would probably ask Rhonda out to dinner before he left the café.

Besides, if she couldn't find time to spend with Holt, why would she make time for anyone else?

Chapter 20
Rhonda

Rhonda trudged across the pavement to her car. A fourteen-hour day, her feet and lower back ached. She hadn't heard from Holt all day. Hopefully, the adage was correct, no news was good news.

The streetlights glowed; dark was settling on the little town. Rhonda cruised down the main street past storefronts, most of them dark, many of them empty. The buildings were constructed of yellow and white limestone, quarried from the nearby hills. Most older structures had been built around the turn of the century, others shortly after Oklahoma became a state in 1907.

It had been a long time since she'd studied the history of her home state but snatches of it popped into her head with little prompting. She remembered that the eastern half of the state featured forests, abundant water in wide rivers and lakes, and mountains. Designated Indian Territory, the region became home to many relocated Native American Indian tribes from the southeastern US. In contrast, the western, drier half of the state had been taken from the Plains Indian tribes who used it as a hunting ground. As Oklahoma Territory, it had been opened to white settlement in a series of free land runs.

She'd studied that history in the ninth grade and found it boring. Now she knew that what she'd studied was only half of the real history. They'd not learned about the emotional, moral, and economic toll paid by the Native Americans so European settlers could come to the U.S.

After high school, her parents moved the family to southcentral Texas, where she'd done her undergraduate work as well as attended veterinary college. She'd met Daniel.

The Witness Protection program staff had thought it risky for her to come back to Oklahoma, but they had also agreed that most times the 'Hide in Plain Sight' philosophy worked. She was 600 miles from her former home in Austin, and she'd never picked up a heavy Texas drawl.

So far, so good. She hadn't run into anyone who had identified her. At least that she knew of. But two of the disagreeable men who'd been talking about the dead woman had returned. Was there any possibility that they were connected to the drug dealers? Did the drug dealers know where she was?

Her cell phone rang. "Holt?"

"Long day?"

"Yeah, just headed home."

"I'm in town. I'll meet you there. And I've got ice cream."

"Hmmm. What kind?" Not that she was picky—she loved ice cream. But if, by chance, he'd brought her favorite, the government agent was going to move up a few notches in her book.

"Chocolate chip?"

A man's usual favorite—and one of hers, although not in the number one position. "That would be great. I'll be there in five minutes."

The homes in the neighborhood she drove through were decorated for Halloween; fiber spiderwebs had been stretched across many front windows, and lighted jack-o-lanterns glowed from front porches. Scarecrows posed on poles in many front yards, and others featured hay bales, pumpkins, and sheaves of grain.

She remembered her own Halloween experiences, back before people worried about razor blades in apples and candy bars, or poison sprinkled into home-baked treats. It had been her favorite holiday. And as her kids grew up, she tried to make it just as special. Yet, with national news focusing on real boogie men and popular films featuring zombies and the Michael Myers of the world, it had become difficult to enjoy a creepy, but still safe, night on the streets.

How would the celebration go here? Would she have any trick-or-treaters at her bungalow after she got home from work? Most likely, tomorrow night, instead of going door to door, these kids would be at the Community Center, trick or treating in a safe setting of booths rather than neighborhood houses. According to the local news, one room at the Center would be a shop of horrors, and another had been turned into a crawl-through maze. She'd heard it all from Nancy, Lloyd's wife, at the café.

Rhonda drove past a local wedding chapel. Lights illuminated the sign out front, but the windows of the small church-like building were dark. She doubted it saw much use this last week in October. The focus was on tricksters, and free candy. But she did recall one wedding she'd attended on Halloween, held in a community theater.

She stopped for the stoplight at an intersection. A rumble moved up on her left, and she glanced at the noisy vehicle. The red truck's engine roared.

Rhonda couldn't tell if it was the same red truck without seeing the license plate, but it didn't matter. She couldn't see through the truck's dark windows, and she was grateful that they couldn't see through her own tinted windows. She doubted the occupants of the truck would realize who was in the car.

The light changed, but the truck didn't rev its engine and zoom off; instead, it waited until she accelerated into the intersection before it pulled out. In another two blocks, the street narrowed from four lanes to two. The truck got behind her.

Rhonda turned left, and the truck continued straight. She zoomed to the next corner and turned left again into an alleyway, where she pulled over close to the garages on one side and waited. The truck didn't appear.

Was it the same truck? Was it those men? Maybe they hadn't recognized her. Maybe it wasn't the same truck. She was overthinking everything.

Her cell phone rang.

"Everything okay? I'm at your house." Holt spoke quickly, in a quiet voice.

"Be there in a few. I'm not far away." Rhonda dreaded telling Holt about another encounter with the red truck. Would he have anything new to tell her? Was it too much to hope that he might have good news, that they'd captured the rest of the Mendosa gang, and the trial was on the docket? She navigated down a few more streets and pulled into the crumbling driveway. Holt's truck was parked in the street.

Holt climbed out of the truck and headed toward the house with a sack in his arms.

She unlocked the front door. Samson yipped and jumped as they entered the house.

"I'll run him outside," Holt offered. "You change your clothes, relax a minute. We'll be back." Holt grabbed the leash from where it hung on the back of the ladder-back chair and hooked it to Samson's collar. Then they were out the door.

Rhonda moved around the house, closing gaps between the curtains after checking the window locks. Then, she pulled a sweatshirt and pants from her suitcase and went into the tiny bathroom to wash away the grime of the day.

When she came out a few minutes later, Samson and Holt had come in from outside. Holt sat at the table with two bowls, two spoons, and a half-gallon of chocolate chip ice cream.

"Yum, thanks!" Rhonda sank into one of the chairs.

Holt grinned, and a little dimple popped up on one of his cheeks. His five o'clock shadow was gone, and the faint scent of cologne lifted as she slipped into the chair across from him.

"One scoop or two?" He dug into the creamy contents of the carton with a big spoon.

"I think, because of the really long day I've had, I've earned two scoops tonight."

He spooned the ice cream into her bowl and pushed it across the table. Likewise, he spooned two scoops into his own bowl, closed the carton, and got up to put it in the freezer section of the refrigerator. His smile was gone when he sat back down.

"About those animals …" he began.

She laid down her spoon.

"Or maybe it should wait until after you've eaten?" He cleared his throat, reached down, and scratched Samson's back. The dog sat at his feet, shivering with energy.

"Yeah, let's leave it until then." She didn't like discussing medical matters while eating. And it was bad manners to discuss what had happened to those animals over ice cream. She wasn't naïve. In the world of veterinary medicine, she was witness to most of the worst that humans could do to other living beings. She picked up her spoon again.

They ate in silence. Her head filled with memories, all leading to the reason she was here in this town with a fake identity. Someone had murdered her husband, and if they found her, they would murder her, too.

Holt's spoon clattered in his bowl as she scooped up the last bit of melting ice cream. He grabbed the bowls and took them to the sink, rinsed them, then set them in the dish rack before returning to the table.

"Okay, about the animals. One of the local vets, Chuck Baxter, did autopsies on three of them and found the COD in all three to be suffocation. And he found elevated levels of carbon monoxide in their blood."

"Suffocation? Outside a building? Did the animals die at the site or were they dumped there?"

"I went to the old motor court with them and did a little CSI work. Lots of tire tracks running in between the cottages, back to a ravine, and down to the road. No way to tell when vehicles made the tracks, but our last rain was a week ago. According to Baxter, the animals had been dead between three and five days."

"So, they were brought to the site and dumped."

"Looks like it. Weird. Why not drop each carcass in a different location? No one would connect them. Individually, the deaths would be attributed to natural causes."

"Somebody wanted those animals found." Rhonda frowned. "Why?" If the person who dumped the animals was not the person who killed them, what was the message? Was there a connection between the dead woman and all the dead animals?

She wished she could investigate, but it was none of her business. And if she wanted to stay alive and remain hidden, she had to be sure that no one thought she was making it her business.

"The locals interviewed the owner of the old motor court. Elderly, longtime resident. Seems he doesn't stop in to check the place often. Probably infested with rats and bats. The city will hit him with a fine for nuisance property. Oh, and another thing. Two of the cats had microchips. The tabby belonged to a Della Munoz, and the gray was registered to Sheila Biggs, the murdered teacher."

Chapter 21
Claire

Claire closed her laptop and pulled the drapes over her room's only window. She flexed her fingers and stretched her back. Too many hours at the computer, researching, since stopping at the café for a bite of supper after returning from Neve's grandmother's. At least Cade was communicating with her by text. *With friends. Back after supper*. Was Neve with him? She guessed so. He didn't have friends in town, but Neve knew other riders from the barrel racing competition.

The seed of worry that Claire had been sheltering all day after hearing what the elderly woman had to say, took root, and grew.

She'd been researching and writing, investigating the grandmother's allegations, chasing rabbits into holes that led nowhere. All the letters to the editors, news articles, and county records that mentioned complaints, lawsuits and protests about the old landfill resulted in no final judgments against anyone. They dissolved into thin air. Payoffs?

The grandmother didn't believe her granddaughter was in danger, but Claire wasn't so sure. The son, Kai, didn't come to the house while Claire was there. The old woman seemed to believe he could solve her problems, and that Neve was in no danger from her uncle.

For a woman who had seen the best and the worst of what life could dish out, she was amazingly unafraid. If she felt fear, Neve's grandmother had buried it deep below a layer of stoic acceptance.

Claire pulled out her cell phone and scrutinized it. She checked missed calls, texts, and voice mail. Two days since she had heard from Holt. She wanted to ask his advice, to use him as a sounding board as she so often did. But he was working. Wouldn't it be okay for her to call him?

When she punched in his number, the call went straight to voice mail.

"Holt, can you talk? I've run into something interesting, not usable for my Route 66 article, but another story. I'd like to talk to you about it. Can you call me? Over the phone, I can tell you that it has to do with the Muscogee Creeks, their land here in Creek and Tulsa Counties, and possible pollution. Could be this issue falls under federal rather than local or state jurisdiction since it's tribal. Need your advice. Call me."

Claire hung up. The sky outside had darkened as she worked, and the nearly full moon had risen. Moonbeams outlined shadows from the old elms and oaks bordering the parking lot.

Two other cars occupied the allotted spaces for B&B guests. Slow for a Friday night. With the barrel racing competition going on this weekend, shouldn't the place be full? Not everyone at the competition could afford a Tulsa hotel. Perhaps, she reasoned, the other B&B occupants were at supper or out for a round of drinks before returning for sleep.

Her phone rang. She punched it on. "Hello."

"Claire. You called? I just have a minute. Sounds like it could be a federal issue to me. If you really want to get involved, call the Tribal offices down in Okmulgee. They could answer your questions better than I can." Holt's voice sounded harried. "Look, sorry, I can't talk now. I hope I can catch up with you sometime tomorrow, out at the Round-up Club. You'll be there for the qualifying competition, right?"

"I hope to be. But that's the other thing. Neve and Cade went AWOL today after her first practice. And her grandmother is right in the middle of this issue I mentioned. It could have something to do with the reason Neve was gone most of today. I'm a little worried."

"Is the grandmother worried?"

"Neve hasn't been gone a full 24 hours. And I think Cade's with her. He should be back here before long. Maybe he'll have some information."

"Let me know what's happening."

"Talk to you later, Holt. Thanks for calling me back."

"Miss you."

The phone clicked off. She was on her own. Was Neve really in danger? She glanced at her watch again. Where were they? Cade did not like Neve's uncle. She hoped he was staying away from him, and that the allegations about her uncle dealing drugs weren't true.

Her mind went places she didn't want it to go. Dark images of hands, groping her in the dark, a naked man lying dead on her living room floor. The gun in her hand. Another man, bleeding from a severe leg wound. And the pitchfork responsible for the injury, in her hand.

Stop. She shouldn't go borrowing trouble, as her own grandmother used to say. Right now, there was no sign anything bad had happened. She needed to talk to Cade.

Where r u? her text to him read.

She waited for a response. And waited. And waited. Finally, the message dots appeared. His text flashed. *TTYL*.

"Talk to You Later?" What kind of message was that? It told her nothing about where he was or who he was with. Her mother-blood started to boil. But he was 18. He would be on his own at the university for the spring semester, in only another two months. It was too late to expect him to be her obedient little boy again, wasn't it?

Chapter 22
Rhonda

"Someone wanted those animals found." Rhonda's words hung in the air.

Holt agreed. "I think so, too."

"Why? Animal abuse? Did someone want them discovered? Did they pick up all the animals and bring them to one place?" Rhonda leaned forward, her elbows on her knees. Animal abuse always got her stirred up, and someone was abusing animals here. "Animals don't suffocate accidentally."

"I checked with the local police about cases of carbon monoxide poisoning. Know what I found?"

"More animal cases? People cases?"

"The woman found dead earlier this week had been stabbed postmortem. The ME found high concentrations of carbon monoxide in her blood, and that's what killed her."

Rhonda crumpled her paper napkin and wiped the table. If she correctly remembered what Lynnie had said, her friend had been found in her own backyard. "Did they find evidence of carbon monoxide inside her house, or indications of a faulty heating system?"

"Not in her house. Or in her car in the garage. Interesting case and no leads on the killer, yet." Holt pushed back in the chair and downed half his glass of water. "And now you've found her cat."

"Did you tell the police about the men at the restaurant?" All three men were clear in her memory. Why had two of them returned to the restaurant?

"Yes, but I left you out of it. We can't jeopardize your cover by pulling you into this investigation. And even if the detectives connect the men to this dead woman, overhearing the words, 'She was dead' would not convince a judge to make an arrest. He could have been talking about anyone or anything."

"You mean like a dog or a cat? This woman's death and those of the animals could be related, couldn't they?"

"They could be. But it's not my case. And you shouldn't be involved."

Rhonda chewed her lip.

"What?" He watched her. "Is there something else?"

She got up from the table and went to the sink to fill her drinking glass. "There was a guy at the diner today. He wanted to talk to me. Just flirting. But it threw me for a minute."

Holt sat forward in his chair. "You didn't know him?"

"No. Nothing familiar at all about him. Like I said, he was just flirting. I didn't speak to him personally, except to take his order after the group came in. Another waitress bussed their drinks and took out their tickets." She stretched, feeling the tension in her back muscles. "While I was taking my dinner break, they left."

"What did the man look like? Any clue where the bikers were from?"

"I didn't talk to any of them, Holt. I don't know where they were from. Another waitress took care of them when I went to dinner. Maybe she learned something. Oh, one of them talked to the woman you were with the other day. She came in for a salad tonight, alone." Rhonda rubbed her lower back.

A crease deepened between Holt's eyebrows. He smoothed his dark hair. "Oh? That was Claire, a friend from home." He cleared his throat. "I'm concerned about you, Rhonda. If someone flirts with you, my undercover agent at the café should have reported it to me."

"Report a flirting customer?" Rhonda tore off a paper towel and wiped out the sink. "Holt, that's overkill. And there's always a chance I'll see people I know. Neither of those things mean they know who I really am, or about the incident in Texas. I'm just another waitress, right? That was the plan." She bit into her lip. 'The incident in Texas.' Had she really said that? How about, 'the horrific murders at my vet clinic that turned my life into a living hell'!

Holt leaned back in the chair, frowning. "We can't be too cautious. These are bad men."

She didn't need a reminder.

Rhonda suspected he was upset with the agent who was supposed to be watching her at work. She had no idea who it was. Mentally, she ran through the people who worked at the café. None of the men or women there seemed remotely capable of being a trained undercover DEA agent.

She trusted Holt. Not that she had a choice. His job was to get her established and to keep her safe for however long it took the authorities to arrest and try the remaining members of the drug gang. Then, she'd show up for court. Once her testimony was on record and the gang was in jail, she would go back to her real life—as a veterinarian.

"Okay. We'll play it day by day." He ran his fingers through his hair. "Lloyd is giving you Sunday off."

"I work a long shift tomorrow. Seems only fair. Not sure what I'll do with time off."

"It will be moving day! Your new place should be ready."

Rhonda glanced around the shabby little house. "Good." When she stepped toward Holt to give him a High Five, every muscle in her back screamed. "Ooh. My back hurts." She stretched. "How long will it take me to adjust to this routine?"

Samson got up, too, stretched, and then stiffened. He ran toward the front door, barking.

Holt hurried to the door and peered through the peep hole. "Nobody out there."

She grabbed the edge of the table as she stood. Had someone dumped another animal in her yard? "What did you find out about that dead cat?"

Holt stepped away from the door. "Nothing yet. Animal control picked it up. Waiting to hear the autopsy results. It could have died in a fight with another animal in your yard, or some jerk could have left it there as a sick joke. If the animal died from carbon monoxide poisoning, that's something else entirely." He leaned against the door. "I should leave. You've got another long day tomorrow. Need anything before I go?"

She didn't want him to leave. After he left, she could either read or go to sleep. She wasn't much good at either of those things lately. "Evenings are boring around here. I worry and pace the floor."

"Got any cards, or dice?"

She and Daniel had often played card games like Go Fish or Crazy Eights when the kids were small. Card games became Poker and Canasta as they grew older. Cards could be fun, but not so much with only two people. The only games she could think of for two players were War and

Strip Poker. She shook her head. "No cards. Maybe the decorator will throw in a deck or two when she outfits my new house."

"If you had cards in your former home—puzzles, games, whatever—there will be similar things in your new place. I promise."

"Then I can't wait to get into my new house."

He went through the door, and she locked it behind him. Then Rhonda eased back into the chair at the table and laid her head on her arms. Samson sat on the floor beside her, his head on her knee. She stroked his ears and scratched his muzzle. "I'm glad you're here, boy."

The dog whined and looked at the door.

"Need to go out? Let's try the back yard."

She led Samson to the back porch and into the yard. One section of the screened-in porch was torn, leaving a hole big enough for Samson to get through. She hated leaving him locked in the house when she went to work, but she had no choice.

The dog pulled her across the grass toward the back fence. Beyond it, an alleyway wound through the neighborhood. Rhonda dropped the leash to let Samson roam. He sniffed along the fence.

Wisps of mist hung in the air and stars of the Milky Way twinkled between the clouds. Rhonda picked out the Big and the Little Dipper, the North Star and Cassiopeia. The same constellations had hung in the night sky above her home a week ago. She could almost believe that the events of last weekend were a nightmare rather than a memory.

"Yoo-hoo, Rhonda? What are you doing out there?" Mrs. P called from her back porch.

Startled, Rhonda turned toward her neighbor's house. "Letting Samson out before bed. Are you okay?"

"Got the heebie-jeebies tonight. Someone's walking on my grave, I think." Her voice sounded shaky and weak. "Come on out, Harry."

Rhonda's grandmother had used that phrase. Mrs. P must believe Death was near. Renee hadn't believed it, but maybe her new persona Rhonda did. She jumped at every shadow. Harry's dog tags jingled in the darkness as he trotted down the porch steps and into her neighbor's yard.

"Need a cup of herbal tea? I can bring some over," Rhonda offered.

"Won't help—demons in my past. My life's full of regrets, things I did when I shouldn't, or didn't do when I should've. It's all catching up with me, now." Her voice quivered.

Rhonda peered through the shadows toward her neighbor's porch, but Mrs. P stood in the dark. "Do you want to talk about it?"

"If you catch me in this mood tomorrow, in the daylight, maybe I'll talk about it then. This time of the year brings too many memories. Come on, Harry. Let's go in. Good night, Rhonda."

The dog tags jingled again, and then a door closed. Rhonda turned back to the night sky. Behind her, in the east, clouds had scuttled away and uncovered the full moon in the sky. Just in time for Halloween.

"Wooo-ooo."

The sudden mournful sound rumbled up from Samson's throat. It lifted the short, fine hairs on the back of her neck and sent shivers throughout her body. Was the dog reacting to the sudden revelation of the moon, or was something lurking in the brushy alley that snaked through the neighborhood? She didn't wait to find out.

Rhonda grabbed Samson, snatched up his leash, and carried him back into the house. She slammed and locked the door to the porch. Gently, she put the dog on the floor. He strained on the leash, pulling toward the front of the house, toenails scratching the floor. She unsnapped his leash and he bounded across the room to the table. A paper sack, folded and closed, lay on the surface.

Hadn't they cleaned up the table and thrown all the trash away after eating ice cream?

The dog jumped onto a chair and put one foot on the table as he nosed at the sack. Had Holt come back inside the house after she and Samson went out to the backyard? Maybe brought a donut for tomorrow morning?

"Samson, get down." Rhonda grabbed the bag, unfolded the end, and peeked in.

When it fell to the floor, Samson jumped for the paper sack. A mouse fell out.

Rhonda's heartbeat thumped in her throat. The dog nudged the animal with his nose, but the mouse didn't move.

She scanned the empty room, then checked the front door. Locked. The bedroom and bathroom were empty.

Whoever had come into the house had opened the door with a key. As far as she knew, only she and Holt had keys.

Holt answered his phone on the first ring, "Missing me already?"

"Samson and I came in from the back yard just now. A paper sack was on the table with a dead mouse inside it. On the table, Holt, where we had ice cream." She swallowed the glob of spit in her mouth.

"Someone brought in a dead mouse and left it on your table? After you locked the door behind me?" She could imagine his handsome face as he talked, eyes wide, mouth slightly open, frowning.

"Someone got in. I'm not safe."

"I'll be right there."

Rhonda dragged the table to the front door and piled both chairs on it. She flicked off the lights and sat on the floor against the table. Samson crawled into her lap and snuggled close. She clutched the dog. Who had gotten in? And why would they leave the mouse? She didn't want to be here alone.

Surely Holt had made sure the locks were changed before she moved in. And where was the agent Holt had assigned to watch her house?

Her keys were always either with her in her purse or in her locker at the cafe. The lockers weren't locked. Any of the workers had access. Someone could have gotten into her purse, taken the key, had a copy made and returned it a short time later. The hardware store was only a block down the street from the café.

The other waitresses were as busy as she was. Most of them took their dinner breaks at the café, but sometimes they had errands to run. No one knew where she lived. Had someone followed her home?

Another minute passed. Headlights pulled into the drive. After Rhonda heard the key in the lock, she flicked on the porch light. "Holt?'

"Yes." He tried to open the door, but the table stopped its movement. She pulled the chairs off and shifted the table so that the door opened a crack.

"You barricaded the door. And you're hanging out in the dark?" He shoved the table open a few more inches and squeezed inside. Then he put his arms around her. Her body wouldn't stop shivering.

Holt reached back through the doorway to the porch, then pitched a backpack into the front corner of the living room. "I'm spending the night, and I'm changing your locks. I called your guard, asked him where he was. It seems he was up the street grabbing a sandwich and was only gone for five minutes. Someone had to have been waiting for me to leave. Maybe, those men who saw you at the motor court when you found the animals are trying to scare you away from investigating."

"Killing animals is a crime. Isn't it the usual first step toward becoming a serial killer?" Rhonda wrapped her arms across her chest and backed farther into the room.

"The vet will report his findings to the mayor and the police chief. There will be an investigation." Holt closed and locked the door.

"What if there isn't? What if they just let it go?"

Holt shrugged. "Is it worth risking news coverage that would reveal your whereabouts to the drug dealers? Your call."

"Couldn't I stay anonymous?"

"Whistleblowers are rarely able to maintain their anonymity. And in a small town …"

"But nobody knows me."

"Doesn't take long. Especially if you make the news."

She clenched her fists. She'd always prided herself on speaking up when injustice was done. Someone had murdered a woman and senselessly killed helpless animals. What else was going on behind the scenes? How could she stay silent?

"How could you help and maintain your cover as a waitress?"

"I could–"

"What?" Holt glared. "Reality check. You think Mendosa's gang would hesitate to kill you if they knew where you were? You saw those henchmen, and you tricked one of them to his death in the lake. You think these beasts are going to let that go? Whatever it takes to get your mind off these animal deaths, you need to do it. Jigsaw puzzles, crossword books, a flower garden, piano lessons … Whatever it takes. Let it go, Rhonda."

"Someone has a key to this place. Who?"

"I'm changing the locks. And I'm sleeping here, on the floor. You only have to spend one more night in this place alone. Meanwhile, try to think about something besides those animals, or what brought you here in the first place."

She knew he was right. She wanted a distraction from what had happened to her and Daniel, but she had to let the dead animal mystery go.

"I'm going to bed." She stomped into the bathroom, locked the door, and sat on the toilet, shaking, until she gathered enough strength to wash her face, pull off her clothes, and put on her night shirt. She stayed in the little bathroom until the hammering and the sound of an electric drill had stopped.

When she left the bathroom, the room was dark except for a tiny camp light on the floor in the living room, and the lamp on the table beside her bed. She couldn't imagine Holt was already asleep, but she had nothing more to say to him. She was glad he was there.

Rhonda tried unsuccessfully to go to sleep.

Chapter 23
Claire

Claire settled into the B&B suite and continued her internet investigation. She learned about the Muscogee Creeks, one of the so-called Five Civilized Tribes, their relocation to Oklahoma in the 1830s as part of the Trail of Tears, and the government's promise of land for the Tribe. She learned about the Dawes Rolls, and the federal government's attempt to sublimate the cultures of the Native Americans.

It was disheartening. The government made no reparations of substance. Recently, the tribal governments had asserted themselves as Sovereign Nations. Their casinos were flourishing, bringing money used for education and healthcare to the tribes. Of course, there was corruption. Someone always wanted to cheat another to get more money in nefarious ways.

Could what be happening to Neve's family land be another effort to steal from those who still lived on the allotments, more than a century later?

She glanced at her watch. 11 p.m. Cade should have been back by now. He'd sent his last text, *TTUL*, more than three hours ago. She'd been patient; she had sent no more texts. But now she did. *Cade, you need to come back to the B&B. I'm worried.*

No response.

Her brain considered her response when Cade returned to the B&B. She'd keep her voice smooth and soft as she learned to do during her marriage to Tom. It usually accomplished what she needed. She hoped it would work with Cade.

She'd tell him what she'd found out about the pollution on Neve's grandmother's land. Claire had been researching the issue herself and would help if she could. The grandmother didn't want to involve the police. She thought her son, Kai, could take care of it.

She'd ask Holt to do a background check on Kai.

Claire glanced at her phone again. Where was Cade? Why didn't he check in?

Chapter 24
Rhonda

"He has a blockage. We'll have to operate. And we'll keep him overnight. You can go home if you want. We'll call after the surgery. If his owners contact you, send them out to get him. Surely they'll see the signs you posted."

Daniel's words repeated in her head. The signs 'you' posted. Carson McVeigh had led the dealers to them. It was Carson's fault that Daniel was dead.

She lay there in her bed hating Carson. He disliked her because she was a woman. Why? An unrequited or rejected love? A mother who was a little too hard, or a little too clingy, or a drunk? Not everyone celebrated Valentine's Day or Mother's Day or Father's Day. She hated Carson because he'd led the drug devils to her clinic.

Her mind revisited that day, not quite a week ago.

They prepped the operating room for surgery. She weighed the dog and checked her charts for the correct amounts of anesthetic to administer to keep the animal sedated during the surgery. They didn't expect any problems. Although not exactly a routine surgery, like spaying or neutering, if the mass was localized, they should be able to remove it and make repairs quickly. The animal would be out for an hour or two, and then on the road to recovery.

Susanna stuck her head into the operating area. "Someone's driving up. I'll tell them you're tied up for an hour, at least. Or are you closing up after this?"

It had already been a long day between regular appointments and emergency appointments, not to mention the foal Daniel delivered this morning. "I think we'll close for the day," she'd said. "It's nearly 4 p.m. Make them an appointment, unless it's life-or-death."

Daniel grunted his approval. They gloved up, he administered the anesthetic, and she prepared to make the incision. They'd pinpointed the location of the blockage and didn't think it was a tumor or something inedible the dog had swallowed. She made the cut, reached in with the forceps, and pulled something out. A round packet covered in tough plastic. She set it in the nearby tray.

Daniel pulled off his surgical gloves and ran his fingertips down her arm. She knew what he was thinking. "Who could ever do something like this? The animal was nothing more than a sacrifice to them. The dog had been as good as dead after he crossed the border." Anger lines deepened around his eyes and mouth.

She felt the same misery and anger as Daniel. Ever since they'd met in vet school, they'd been kindred spirits, soul mates and lovers. Her lower lip trembled.

Daniel stitched up the incision. She carried the animal to the adjacent room used for recovery and laid him in a nest of clean, soft towels in one of the crates. When she returned to the operating room, Daniel was bent over the sink, running water over the packet, which was stapled shut. Not much doubt about what was inside.

"I'll call the sheriff." She crossed to the recovery room, where the nearest phone hung on the wall.

From that area in the back of their building, she heard the front door bang open and felt the walls of the sturdy building shake.

"Help you?" Susanna's startled voice carried down the hallway. Heavy footsteps stomped across the floor of the reception area. "You can't go back there!"

A gun blast shook the clinic walls. Footsteps pounded down the hallway fast.

"Where's the dog?" A gruff voice shouted in the adjacent operating room. "El perro. Donde?"

She peeked around the corner into the room. The two men in the doorway were both tall and muscular, each with dark hair and eyes. One wore his chin-length hair tucked behind his ears. A rim of dark hair circled the second man's bald head.

"The dog. You operated? Where is it?"

Daniel turned his back and sprayed cleanser on the operating table. "Who are you?" He glanced over his shoulder at them.

The gun blasted and Daniel crumpled, screaming, clutching his left leg.

"Where is the dog?" The gunman scowled, a grim smile on his face, dark eyes wide-set and deep, a black beard rimming his jawbone.

She took a step deeper into the recovery room and jammed her fist into her mouth.

"Tell me!"

Another shot blasted. Daniel screamed. She grabbed the phone and punched in 911, then laid it on the counter beside the bank of recovery crates.

"I have many bullets. You have many limbs. I shoot each one, many times, until you tell me. I know the dog is here. I want what you removed from the dog. Now."

"We sent the dog to animal control in town," Daniel groaned.

"I don't believe you."

The gun blasted again.

She pressed her fist harder against her teeth. Faintly, she could hear the 911 operator responding to her call.

"Tell me!" Once more, the gun fired.

She darted across the opening, catching a glimpse of Daniel on the floor, curled into a ball next to the operating table. Blood splatter covered walls, table, and floor.

"I don't know," Daniel said, his voice barely audible.

She jerked the exterior door open and ran for the garage, digging the car keys from the pocket of her shorts and stuffing the small plastic bag deep inside.

A black Chevy Blazer had been parked haphazardly near the front door; both front doors stood open. It registered in her brain that there could be a third man. Inside, with Susanna. She had to get help.

She raced to the garage, jumped into their SUV, turned the key, and floored the accelerator. The tires bit the cement pad, and the car fishtailed out of the garage and down the drive. Her tears blurred the figure who dashed from the clinic and ran toward her. Bullets splintered the windshield.

Shots pinged against the sides and top of the vehicle. The back window shattered, so did the passenger window behind her. She punched the accelerator, willing the vehicle to go faster. It blasted out onto the road.

What had the man done to Daniel? Was he dead? She couldn't go back. If she went back, they'd shoot her. Or kill her. Susanna might be dead as well.

Behind her, an engine roared. In the rearview mirror, she watched the Chevy Blazer drive over the yard and bump onto the road.

Rhonda sat up in bed, heart pounding. Samson whined; his body tucked against hers. His tail wagged as she stroked his warm body. "It's okay, Samson, it's okay."

But it wasn't. The memory was so clear. Daniel pleading. The angry man yelling. The gunshots. And the Chevy Blazer behind her. She floored the accelerator and closed her eyes.

Her SUV squealed around the corner. Trees flashed past, she took the next corner on her two right wheels and came dangerously close to losing control. The tires squealed around another corner, and then another. One more short stretch and the road would curve around the lake.

Through the broken window, the black Chevy Blazer was catching up fast. The vehicle slammed into her rear fender.

She jerked the wheel and pulled away from the Blazer. Frantically, she searched for side roads, someplace to get away. Another window exploded as a barrage of shots rang out.

An access road was just ahead. She knew where it went. She and Daniel had been there many times. Beautiful sunrises and sunsets over the lake below the overlook.

She was nearly to the road, the Blazer close behind. She pulled the wheel to the left, cutting over the curb and up onto the access road—less than a half-mile to the lake.

A motor roared; the Blazer had made the turn. She glanced at both side of the road. Vegetation, rocks, stubby trees. No place to go. She accelerated.

The lake was deepest near the overlook. If she were lucky, she would survive. If the man caught her, she wouldn't. She fastened her seat belt and pushed the automatic switch to roll down all the side windows.

The barricade at the edge of the cliff was ahead. The Blazer was nearly on her bumper again.

She had no choice. If he caught her, she would die. If she drove into the lake, perhaps she wouldn't. The thug behind her believed she would chicken out, that is, if he knew what lay ahead.

At the curve in the parking area, she punched the accelerator. Her SUV skidded and then smashed through the dilapidated guard rail at the edge. Solid ground fell away. For brief seconds, bright blue autumn sky, cloud smears, and the puffy line of a jet contrail appeared through the front windshield, next to the bullet hole and the spider-webbed cracks around it. Her SUV arched and plunged toward the shimmering surface of the lake.

She forced her look away from what lay ahead. A dried-up French fry lay on the floor in front of the passenger seat.

Would Erin and Sean lose both parents in a single day?

The surface of the lake rose to meet her. She pulled as much air into her lungs as she could. The airbag and the front windshield exploded, shoving her back against the seat, covering her in chunks of glass. Then, blackness.

She clutched Samson. Shivers shook her body. She had lived through it, and here she was, alive, but not really. Tears streamed down her face. Why had she survived? Why hadn't she let the water fill her lungs? Why hadn't she let the lake take her? *Oh, Daniel.*

Cold water crept up to her armpits as she touched the ceiling of the SUV. Water gushed in through the ragged hole of the windshield.

Arms shaking, her fingers fumbled with the latch of the seat belt. Icy water inched toward her chin. She jabbed repeatedly at the latch as the car settled deeper into the lake. Water crawled up her neck and nose. The latch released. She fought to shove the inflated air bag away so she could move.

She thrust her body through the gap of the open window and out into the lake, then kicked, up, up through the black water. She reached the surface, gasping for air, flailed, then began to swim. Across the surface, the lake swallowed the Blazer only twenty yards away. She kicked away from the two rapidly sinking cars. She swam, not looking back, not wanting to see that the other man was swimming too, or treading water, looking for her.

The muddy bottom of the lake suddenly solidified beneath her shoes. Rocks tore at her legs as she crawled out of the water. Pain throbbed in her left arm and leg, as well as her head.

The sound of sirens screamed through the air, grew loud, softened, then wailed again. She wasn't sure if her brain was screeching or if emergency vehicles were coming to help.

She stumbled over a boulder and sprawled on the rocky shore. The sky tumbled above, beams of red and white light splashed into the blue.

Voices shouted. Her legs wouldn't move. She squinted and tried to focus.

Shivering, she pushed to her hands and knees, tried to stand, but fell. She crab-walked toward a thicket of sumac bushes. Voices shouted. She kept her head down and pushed on.

She stumbled and lost her balance as she reached the bushes and shoved into them. Rivulets of blood—her blood—ran down her legs onto her feet. Pain hammered her body. Her breath came in gasps, her heart pounded. She had no reason to get up, no reason to move, ever again. Where was she going to go, anyway, and how was she going to get there?

Then, voices, shouting. Her legs wouldn't move.

"Renee? Are you okay?" Holt's voice floated to her. She opened her eyes to the dark, dingy room, to the faint light seeping through the flimsy curtains. And a huddled figure across the room, on the floor near the front door.

"No. Just my regular nightmare," she snipped. Did he expect her to be having happy dreams about running through a flower field?

"I should have died." She believed it. Her husband was dead, her kids were grown, living their own lives. Her parents were old, at the end of their lives. She couldn't be a veterinarian anymore or let anyone know she was one. She had no future. And no past that she could share.

"You're a survivor, and you're going to get through this." Holt's voice, strong and steady, charged across the room. She didn't want to hear it.

"You don't know anything about me. You have no clue how hard this is. I hate every minute of every day. I hate who I must pretend to be. I hate living here. I hate not knowing when—or if—that devil will go to hell."

She rocked on the mattress, holding Samson close and stroking him so hard that he squirmed to get away.

The silence grew and made her angry. Was Holt falling asleep again? So much for caring any little bit about what she was going through. Some "handler" he was. She vaulted up and crossed the room to the little bathroom, slamming the door as she went in.

The needle-like blasts of hot water pounded her back. Could she shower away her despair? No. But she could get comfort from the hot water pounding on her back.

Chapter 25 - SATURDAY
Claire

Claire lay still in her bed in the B&B suite in the wee hours of Saturday morning, awake. Cade had not come back.

Last night, for hours, she'd watched her iPhone, expecting it to light up any minute with a message from her son. Nothing.

She kept expecting to hear his key in the door lock. He'd come in with a sheepish look on his face. He'd apologize. He'd explain. After all, he was 18. He probably believed he didn't owe her an explanation if he spent the night out.

But he did. This was unacceptable.

She needed to talk to Holt. He had a way of settling her down so she could see a clear direction. Sometimes, he offered advice about Cade that helped solidify how she should manage a situation as a parent. He didn't tell her what to do. He'd backed away from that after their initial rocky six months. And she was glad. Not that things weren't still rocky. Part of her knew that if they didn't smooth out soon, she might lose Holt to someone else.

She couldn't be the only woman in the world Holt was interested in.

Her memory flashed back to the café. How distracted he'd been when he'd taken her there for a burger. Her second time at the cafe, she'd noticed an attractive redhead waitress. Could he have been watching for her on their first visit?

She pinched her eyes shut and flipped to her other side. Why was she spending time thinking about Holt and whoever it was that might be distracting him?

Where was Cade? Where was Neve? Her stomach tightened. Did it have something to do with the grandmother and that stinking property on the edge of town?

Her research had uncovered nothing about a landfill that might be oozing toxic substances. Neve's grandmother insisted there was such a landfill and that the materials in it had been illegally dumped for years. She had said the poisonous materials were travelling through the earth, seeping into cracks and underground water flows before eventually oozing to the surface.

She'd gone to the city's website to search the departments to determine who to contact. From her experience as a journalist, the Public Works Department would be the usual overseer. She'd found the names of those directing waste disposal.

But it was Saturday, these employees wouldn't be in their offices again until Monday.

Where was Cade? Where was Neve? Would the girl miss today's preliminaries? Should she contact the police now, before she did anything else?

Claire flicked her phone on and navigated to her text messages. The last one she'd received had been at 8 p.m. *TTUL.* Not something Cade had ever texted to her before. What if Cade hadn't sent that message? Somebody else could have his phone.

She punched in Holt's number.

"Hey, there. I was just thinking about you." He answered after the first ring.

"Holt—" she interrupted. "Cade didn't come back to the B&B last night. I don't know where he is."

"Okay." He spoke in his calmest voice. "When did you last see him? What happened yesterday?"

As Claire told Holt about Friday, she realized that she'd last seen Cade early that morning, standing outside, waiting for her next to her Jeep Cherokee. The rest of the day, they had not communicated. Then in the evening, the short texts were all she had received.

Her throat tightened. "I was giving him some space. He'd been so upset about Neve. He hadn't been acting like himself. Holt, this is not like him." The words caught in her throat.

"No, it's not like him. So actually, he's been missing 24 hours. Could the texts you received have been sent by someone else?"

"Oh my God, Holt. Where is he? What's happened?"

"I'm on my way. I'll make some calls while I drive."

Claire showered and dressed on autopilot. Every few seconds, she stuck her head out of the shower to glance at her phone, afraid she might have missed the tone that signaled she had a text message or a call.

The room seemed foggy. Her concentration was off.

When someone knocked on the interior door, she jerked it open, heart hammering.

The gray-haired owner of the B&B peered in at her. "Reminding you that our full breakfast will be served at 8 a.m. Looks like you're already dressed. Come down for a cup of coffee if you'd like."

Claire blinked.

The woman leaned toward her. "I'm Dee Munoz. We met at check in. My sister and I are the owners.

Remember? You have reservations for two for a full breakfast this morning."

Claire blinked again.

"Are you all right, honey?"

"Um. I don't know. My son didn't come in last night. I'm too worried to eat."

"Can I box it up and bring it to you, or put it in the frig for later? You paid for it, might as well eat it. Homemade biscuits, scrambled eggs, sausage, sliced tomatoes, potatoes, peppers and onions ... Mighty good."

"Thank you, but I'm not hungry. A friend's coming by and we're going to go look for him."

"How upsetting. Is there anything I can do for you?"

"Let me think. Watch for my son. And call me if he comes in." Claire wrote her cell number on the desk notepad, tore off the sheet and handed it to the woman.

"My sister and I will keep our eyes and ears open. Hoping for the best. He's probably fine. Teenagers don't realize how mothers worry, do they?"

Chapter 26
Rhonda

When the alarm on her iPhone went off at 6 a.m. Rhonda touched the SNOOZE button and kept her eyes closed. This would be a long Saturday, working a double shift from 7-7. She was weary to the bone after a night fraught with nightmarish memories. Had her imagination made them worse than they were, or were they more horrific than she allowed herself to remember? A series of memories flashed.

Daniel's expression had frozen as he slumped to the ground after the first bullet hit his knee. Red-faced, the shooter had repeatedly growled, '*Donde? Donde es el perro?* Where is the dog?'

She struck the icy water and forced her legs to kick away from the pull of the sinking SUV. She'd crawled across the rocky shore to lay under the sumac bushes, too weak to move another inch.

Then, voices. Immobilized by fear, she waited for someone to jerk her from her hiding place, hold a gun to her head and fire it. She cowered, praying they couldn't see her, wouldn't find her. Closing her eyes, she prayed she was invisible, just as an ostrich did when it buried its head in the sand.

But she wasn't invisible.

A nearby footfall shifted the sand beneath her cheek. She opened her eyes, and not six inches away was a brown hiking boot and the cuffs of dark green khakis.

"Here," a voice said. She braced for the action to come, being jerked from her hiding place, thrown about, battered, and then killed. Goodbye, Daniel. Goodbye Erin. Goodbye, Sean.

Instead, a gentle hand touched her shoulder. Another wrapped her in a blanket. Sirens screamed, loud, louder, up on the road. Red lights brightened the darkening sky, then disappeared.

"You're okay," a man said. "You're safe, now. Lean on me. We're with the DEA. Drug Enforcement Agency, and the US Marshals' Office. Can you hear me?"

An arm circled her shoulders. A hand gripped her elbow. The man helped her walk down the beach; she was unable to do more than put one foot in front of the other.

He squinted at her. "Other than bruises, you seem all right. How do you feel?"

"I don't feel anything." She ran her tongue over her dry lips. Even her heart felt only numbness.

"Drink some water. It's a tough walk through this thick sumac. Let's get you out of the open." He unscrewed the top of a water bottle and handed it to her. She took a long swig.

"Drink a little more."

She did.

"Ready? Follow me. Grant will be right behind you. Stay low."

They moved through sumac bushes as tall as she was. The branches snagged her arms and clothes. She wanted to be safe. She had no choice but to believe that if she endured the trek through the shrubs, she would find safety.

The agent led her through bushes and then trees. Straight ahead, three black vehicles were parked on the dirt track road that circled the lake.

He helped her into the back seat of a large black Expedition with tinted windows. She huddled under a thick blanket, shivering. Water dripped from her hair and down into her face.

She peered at the man who had helped her off the beach. A camo shirt, pants, smears on his face below a beige cap; a strand of dark hair stuck out from the hat, above his ear.

The SUVs zoomed up a boat ramp, backward. While braking, the driver turned the squealing tires so that the Expedition twisted sideways, then righted itself. The powerful motor raced as they blasted down the road through shadows cast by the setting sun.

"Are you Dr. Renee Trammel?" The driver asked.

She tried to swallow and choked on her dry throat. "Yes," she finally croaked.

"You drove through the guard rail into the lake."

"Someone ... was chasing me." She turned her body toward the window and glanced back at the darkening landscape.

"Yes. We're searching for his body now. He wasn't as lucky as you were, but you planned ahead to survive, didn't you?"

She drained the rest of the water from the bottle.

"I'm going to tell you what I think happened, and you correct me if I get something wrong. Okay?"

"Okay." Her hammering heart had slowed, but a fog had dropped over her. Was she dreaming? Was she dead?

"Someone brought a dog into the clinic, and it was in a lot of pain." His voice was low, quiet, almost hypnotic. "You operated, removed a blockage from the animal's

stomach, and were cleaning up when someone burst in with a gun. He shot up the place, and you ran for help. Someone followed you, shot at you. You tried to lose him but couldn't, so you drove into the lake as a last resort, with your seatbelt on and your windows down so you could escape the sinking car. Am I right?"

She opened her mouth to speak, but instead of her voice, a croak came out. She cleared her throat. "He killed them, my husband and Susanna, our assistant. I wanted to get help. But it's too late. They're dead, aren't they?"

"I'm sorry for your loss."

Silence filled the car. Her head swam with swirling memories.

Renee gasped. "Who were they?"

"Ernesto Mendosa. We've been tracking him for weeks. Drug dealer. Ruthless."

"How did you know he was at my clinic?"

"We had word that he'd lost part of a shipment and was searching. We located his vehicles. Drones followed them, and we followed the drones. We saw what happened outside as he burst into your clinic. Your security cameras caught what happened inside, I hope."

"He got away." The words eased out in a whisper.

"No. We caught Mendosa trying to escape out the back way as our team swarmed the area. With your testimony at the trial, he'll stay locked up for a long time. But we want to get all of his guys, the entire network, across the southcentral U.S."

Rhonda's alarm buzzed again, and this time, she switched it off and rolled out of bed. She glanced across the dimly lit room. Holt's sleeping bag had been rolled up and tied and stood by the door. The rest of the room was empty.

She put on makeup and did her hair, returned to the living room, and switched on the lights—still no Holt. Samson sniffed at the front door and darted out when she opened it, letting in the subdued light of a misty dawn. She grabbed his leash and quickly followed, but the dog hadn't gone far.

Holt sat on the step, drinking a cup of coffee. A take-away holder on the cement porch floor held a second cup. "Brought you some joe. Figured you could use a cup after the night you had."

"Didn't sleep much. Did you?"

"I slept enough. Are all of your nights like that?"

"Yes." She doubted they'd get better any time soon. Maybe when she could hold her children again, and her mom and dad. She dropped down beside Holt on the step and gazed out at the foggy morning.

"I'm sorry," he said. "I wish I could make this easier. At least you're moving into a better place tomorrow. It's a nice house. You should drive by today, check it out. They'll be moving furniture in, and decorating, but you could get a quick glimpse."

He handed her a business card with an address scribbled on the back of it.

"Thanks. I'll do that. Where is it?"

"The addition is on the other side of town, about fifteen minutes from here. Closer to the Creek Turnpike on the way to Tulsa. Not far from a nice little lake that serves as the city's water supply."

"In the country? Large lots?"

"Quarter to half-acre. Used to be in the country. Developers built a nice neighborhood; most of the houses back up to pastureland that drops into a ravine, so nothing will be built there."

"I won't be here long enough to care. At least, I hope not."

Holt nodded. "Yeah. Nothing for you to worry about."

"I need to get on to work. Long day. Double shift. And it's Halloween."

"Are you wearing a costume?" He grinned.

"I wear one every day, remember?" She smoothed the front of her pink tunic.

Holt's phone rang. He glanced at the screen. "Got to take this. Excuse me." He turned away and Rhonda said goodbye to Samson and locked the front door.

Only one more night in this dump. She was counting the hours. With new locks, surely that last night would be peaceful.

Chapter 27
Claire

Still hopeful, Claire wrote Cade a quick note:

Missed seeing you. PLEASE call or text me. I need to hear from you.

She hurried to her Jeep Cherokee, not wanting to encounter either of the B&B owners. She slipped inside and closed the door. Unshed tears stung. After she talked to Holt, she'd be calmer. He'd help her figure out what to do.

She wondered if Cade might go to the cafe for breakfast with Neve after they'd spent the night … wherever. She was betting the auburn-haired waitress would be at the cafe this morning. She and Holt would swing by there.

She hoped Vince wouldn't return to the café for breakfast. She didn't want to talk to him, or even see him when she was with Holt.

Holt's truck roared down the alley and parked next to her SUV.

Claire hopped out of her vehicle as Holt came around his truck to meet her. His arms enfolded her, and she let him hold her. She held back her tears. He kissed her forehead.

"Any word from Cade?" He asked, his mouth against her hair.

She pulled away slightly and looked up at those eyes. Worry creased his brow. "No. I left a note inside the room in case he comes back."

"Good. I'm hoping the two of them made up and stayed together last night. You have the grandmother's phone number? We should start looking there."

"Yes, and the barns out at the Round-up Club."

"You've tried texting and calling today?"

Claire frowned at him. "Only a thousand times."

"Have you had anything to eat?"

She shook her head. Who could think about food?

"First things first. Chances are, Cade's fine. He could be trying to show you he's an adult—or thinks he is. When he comes back, he'll act like nothing has happened."

"But what if he doesn't come back? Aren't we wasting valuable time by pretending he's being an inconsiderate teenager?"

"Believe me, I've thought about that, honey. I've contacted the local police. They'll meet us at the café. Do you have a picture of Cade on your phone you can share?"

"Yes."

"Ride with me?"

"I'll follow you there. I don't want to be stuck without my Jeep when you have to go to work." Not only that, but the two of them could cover more territory separately. She didn't intend to spend all day letting Holt lead her around town.

* * *

The bell above the doorway tinkled as they entered the diner. Customers occupied a few tables, but many were empty.

The auburn-haired waitress—the stitching on her uniform said *Rhonda*—pushed into the dining room from the kitchen, carrying a pile of rolled-up silverware in her arms. She went to the cash register, deposited them into a half-empty bin, and smiled at Holt and Claire. "Morning. Table for two, or is the young man joining you?"

Claire scanned the room, searching for Cade or Neve. "Have you seen him?"

The waitress tilted her head. "He hasn't been in. Is something wrong?"

Claire pulled in a breath, then let it out, slowly. "Not sure. I hope not."

The waitress led them to a booth by the front window. "In case he comes in, there's plenty of room for him to join you. Can I get you some coffee?"

Claire nodded and picked up the menu. Holt and the waitress exchanged glances. She didn't care. Rhonda crossed the room to the coffee station, and then returned with cups and a hot pot of coffee. Claire studied the waitress as she filled their cups.

Waitresses in small town cafés were usually of two kinds, an older woman who'd been waitressing a long time, or a young woman who was working her way through college or just working, a bit desperate for money. In today's world, most of the younger girls would have piercings (ears, nose, lip, eyebrow) and tattoos that peaked out from their necklines. This waitress had neither of those. Plus, she was middle aged.

Where was Cade? The ever-present thought circled in her mind.

Claire tried to focus on Rhonda. The waitress had pulled out her order pad, and Holt was telling her what he wanted. She had dark circles under her eyes and a stain on her uniform. Her voice had a slight southern lilt much like Claire's and she was obviously well-educated.

A wedding ring set flashed as the waitress wrote down Holt's order.

Then she looked at Claire. "And what can I get you? I'm betting you don't want another lentil salad, although it was good last night, wasn't it?"

Claire nodded. The salad had been good, but life had changed overnight. Nothing sounded good to eat at the moment.

The bell over the front door tinkled, and she leaned sideways around the waitress to see who had come in the front door. It wasn't Cade. Another waitress led the couple to a table.

"Your order?" Rhonda asked again.

"Just wheat toast. And the coffee. Thank you."

Rhonda set the coffee pot on the table and stepped away as the bell over the doorway tinkled again. Rhonda led the three men to a table.

Claire stared toward the café's front door, wishing Cade would come in. He'd never stayed out all night before. Doing it at home was one thing, but doing it in a strange town, where they were visiting for a long weekend, was something else completely.

"I'm sure this is difficult. It's normal to think the worst, but that may not be what's happened. He's 18." Holt peered into her face.

"A mother worries." And couldn't stop. She didn't think she would ever completely stop wondering where Cade was or what he was doing, even when he had a family and career of his own in some other city in another state. But he had to come back this time. He had to.

A policewoman entered the restaurant and walked into the dining room without stopping, her look searching the room. Holt motioned to the officer, and she crossed to their booth, where she stood beside Holt.

"I'm officer Payne. Agent Braden called me this morning about your son. Would you like to file a missing person's report?" The petite officer peered at Claire with deep set brown eyes, her dark hair gathered in a bun at the nape of her neck.

Claire glanced at Holt. "Agent Braden asked you to come, and I don't want to waste your time. I don't know where my son is, and frankly, I'm not sure the texts I got last night were from him. I haven't actually seen him since yesterday morning." She'd ask Holt about the 'Agent' bit later. Right now, all she could think about was Cade.

"Could you fill out this report for me?" The officer pulled a file folder from her backpack and handed it to Claire. "A current picture of your son would also help. When you've finished with this, I have some questions. Take your time, please."

Claire picked up the pen and filled in the blank spaces. The form made it real. Cade was missing.

* * *

Thirty minutes later, the officer placed the file folder and the completed paperwork in her briefcase. "This information will be useful. A team will be out at the Round-up Club within the hour. We'll also be looking for Neve Bright and will interview her grandmother. One final question: other than the arena and the B&B where you're staying, has Cade been anywhere else during the three days you've been here? Any other activities he's mentioned?"

"No. As far as I know, he's either been with Neve at the Round-up Club, or with me."

Claire glanced at the plate of toast Rhonda had set in front of her some time ago. It was cold, and unappetizing. As if she could think about eating, anyway.

"I have your phone number, as well as Agent Braden's. I'll keep you informed about what we're doing, and what we've found. Meanwhile, try not to worry. Keep your mind busy. Likely, your son and his girlfriend will turn up unharmed and embarrassed."

"Thank you." Claire knew there was nothing to be gained from worrying but it was impossible not to do it anyway.

As the policewoman walked away, Rhonda approached the table and refilled their coffee cups. "Can I bring you some fresh toast? I noticed you didn't have time to eat this while the policewoman was here. Something's happened, hasn't it? Your son?"

Claire saw Holt toss Rhonda a warning glance, but the waitress didn't drop her eyes. Claire nodded. "I haven't seen him since yesterday morning."

"I'm so sorry." Rhonda glanced at Holt. "I've lived through teenagers. I know what a worry they can be."

Claire folded her hands and stared at them.

"I'll get some fresh toast, and some jam. Eat a bite if you can. You need it to stay strong and focused." Rhonda removed the plate of cold toast.

"Right." Holt cleared his throat. "You talked to Neve's grandmother yesterday, didn't you Claire? What did she say? Anything that might give us a clue as to where Cade and Neve might be? I'm sure the old woman won't be as up front with the police as she was with you."

"Probably not. She thinks someone's trying to get her off her land, which was part of the allotments to the Muscogee Creeks in the early 1900s." Claire rubbed her forehead. It seemed ridiculous to be talking about this when she didn't know where Cade was. How could she even think about the article she'd been researching?

"I know this part of Oklahoma was Indian Territory in the 1800s. Tribes from all over the U.S. were forced to relocate here so colonists could move into the eastern and midwestern states." Holt's look never left her face.

"The Muscogee Creeks were one branch of the resettled Creeks. Their allotments were in this area. I think Neve's grandmother must be the daughter of an allottee."

"Who wants her land?"

"She didn't tell me, but they're not offering to pay a fair price for it. Pollution is seeping up from the ground. Maybe from an old landfill. It stinks out there, and who knows if the fumes are poisonous. Neve was upset about it, and she's been asking questions. The grandmother thinks that's why she hasn't seen her. And one of Neve's uncles is supposed to be 'taking care of it,' but Neve has a history with him. According to Cade, that uncle has physically abused her."

Holt straightened. "That's bad. A possibility of pollution. Any dead animals around?"

Rhonda stepped up to the table with a plate of fresh toast and several small containers of jelly. She set it in front of Claire. "Dead animals? Are there more of them, Agent Braden?"

Holt's face went blank.

"Where?" Rhonda's wide-eyed glance darted between Holt and Claire.

Holt opened and closed his mouth.

Claire had never seen him this uncomfortable before. What did the waitress know about dead animals? And why did she know Holt as 'Agent' Braden?

Chapter 28
Rhonda

The bell over the doorway tinkled again, and at the same time, a voice called from the kitchen. "Order up."

Rhonda glared at Holt and whirled toward the kitchen. "Be right with you. Sit anywhere," she called toward the door. An elderly couple scanned the room and headed for an empty table in the center of the dining room.

Her temper steamed. Holt was more open with the woman he was eating with than he was with her. He knew something about more dead animals, and he hadn't told her. Never mind that he really hadn't had a chance to.

Claire had mentioned she was working on an article about Route 66. Someone in the café had mentioned a reporter recently. Who was it? As she added garnishes to the plates Eduardo had dished up, she thought back. She overheard so many things every day, snatches of conversations, jokes, comments. Most people stopped talking when she approached their table, but others continued their conversation as if she were invisible.

Her memory clicked. The mayor had said something about a reporter in town. Had he meant Claire?

Rhonda pushed out of the kitchen again, holding two platters. She delivered them to the correct table, and then walked up to Holt's booth. "We've got to talk, Holt. I have a break in 15. Wait for me."

Claire gave her a questioning look. Rhonda didn't respond.

Whatever Claire was to Holt, she didn't know anything about Rhonda. Not yet anyway.

A loud group of men entered the café, ignored the 'Please wait to be seated' sign and bustled into the dining room.

Rhonda paused at the coffee station, watching the group. Chair legs screeched against the linoleum floor as they pulled out the chairs at a table in Vivian's section and sat. She picked up a coffee pot and headed for their table, intending to pour their coffee as they considered the menu, but as she approached the table, Vivian flew out of the kitchen, smoothing her hair with one hand. She'd applied fresh red lipstick.

"Hi, fellas. What can I help you with this morning?" Vivian asked.

"Hey, Vi. Coffee all around, and pancakes."

Vivian glared at Rhonda and reached for her coffee pot. "I'll take care of these gentlemen, thank you."

"No problem." Rhonda returned to the coffee station and filled another pot, then made a round of the café, refilling coffee when needed. Vivian's loud voice and the men's laughter dominated the typically low volume banter of eating customers.

She glanced at the other waitress as she continued to work her group of tables, grabbing more butter for some, syrup for others, and placing empty dishes in the dish bin for Lance.

Vivian was unusually buoyant today. She obviously knew the men. Dressed in jeans and wearing flannel shirts over t-shirts, they must be regular Saturday customers.

Vivian left their table, order pad in hand, and one of the men turned in his chair to stare at Rhonda. His piercing look rose the hackles on the back of her neck.

Avoiding Vivian's section of tables, she ducked into the kitchen.

Chapter 29
Claire

Claire swallowed the last bite of toast and watched Rhonda cross the room and enter the kitchen. "What did she mean about dead animals?"

Holt leaned toward her across the table. "I'm undercover here," he said in a low voice.

Claire's eyes widened. "'Agent' Braden. She's part of the assignment?" She'd long suspected his involvement in law enforcement. He was finally admitting it.

"She *is* the assignment. I can't say anything more. I'll explain what I can later."

"I think I'll call Neve's grandmother." Claire pulled out her phone, found the number in her list of contacts, and called, turning down the volume and putting the phone on speaker.

"Hello," an old voice muttered.

"This is Claire Northcutt, Cade's mom. We met yesterday. Have you seen Neve or Cade recently? I haven't, and I'm worried. I've filled out a missing person's report on my son."

"They're not here. My son Kai is taking care of things. No need for the police."

"Do you know for sure where she is? She could be in trouble. If she's missing, you should file a report."

"We take care of our own."

Claire pulled in her breath. She couldn't believe what she was hearing. Holt shrugged and lifted his hands.

"Is your son also going to take care of that awful smell on your property? That smell could indicate something toxic and harmful to you and your family. You should report that, too. It's not your fault."

"No. It's Mother Earth's fault. For having all those cracks running below the land white people say they own. You own nothing. You are caretakers. Bad caretakers."

"Can I talk to someone about the pollution for you?" Claire asked.

"Who would that be? Talk to the Great Father. Talk to the Great Rainmaker. Tell Coyote to see if he can get Mr. Skunk to stop stinking up my land. Nothing will happen, Claire Northcutt." The connection went dead.

A blond woman pushed past as Claire dropped her phone into her purse. The woman slid into the booth behind Claire and pulled out her cell phone. When Rhonda approached, she said, "You're going to get slammed in about an hour. I'm here to cover the meeting. Does Lloyd know about it?"

"What meeting?" Rhonda asked as she filled the woman's coffee cup.

"Local environmental group. Protesting the leakage from the old landfill."

Claire turned sideways in the booth to glance at the woman.

"I haven't heard anything about any meeting," Rhonda said.

"You're going to hear all about it before long. Things could get heated." The woman glanced around the diner and took notice of the already-seated customers.

Claire turned back to Holt. "Are you hearing this?" she whispered.

He nodded and sipped his coffee.

"What do you mean by 'heated?'" Rhonda asked the woman.

"Liable to be a shouting match, and a few people could get fired up."

"An old landfill. Where?"

"No one knows exactly how far it extends. But gas fumes are coming up into yards and homes. Methane, and other toxic stuff. This meeting is to discuss who's responsible for the cleanup. I'm betting those people will shift blame. My cameraman should be here in fifteen. Bring him a cup of coffee when he comes in, okay?"

An environmental issue related to the landfill. Sounded like what Neve's grandmother had told her.

"Claire, excuse me for a minute, I need to make some calls. I'll step outside." Holt slid out of the booth and crossed the room toward the hallway leading to the restrooms.

Was he leaving so he could talk to Rhonda? Something about dead animals? If Rhonda was his assignment, was he protecting her, watching her, or collaborating with her?

Someone stepped up beside her.

"Morning, Claire. Mind if I join you?" Vince Matheson flashed her his brightest smile as he slid into Holt's side of the booth. "Saw you sitting here. Thought I'd say hello." He settled in. "Still working on that article? Have time for a drink tonight? It's Halloween. We might as well have an adult celebration. I can pick you up about 8. Which B&B are you at?" His eyes sparkled.

Claire looked into his handsome face. She could see the little boy around his eyes. He still had that innocent look about him, but she also recognized a cunning gleam she'd not noticed before. Who was he, really? "Thanks for the invitation, Vince. I can't tonight. Sorry."

"We could find a lot of interesting things to talk about." Vince grinned and leaned toward her across the table.

"Thanks, but no. And my friend is coming back. That seat is taken."

Matheson frowned as he scooted out of the booth to stand beside the table. He tapped his fingernails on the slick surface. "I guess I won't see you until the next reunion, unless you give me your phone number." His frown changed into an enticing smile, but she wasn't enticed.

"I'm not dating right now, Vince. I'll see you at the reunion."

He glanced around the dining room, and then back at her. "Until then, I guess. Oh, and I hope you can get some sleep soon. You look like you definitely need it." He lifted a hand and stepped away from the table, his face now an emotionless mask.

Chapter 30
Rhonda

"What were you saying about dead animals?" Rhonda grabbed Holt's arm and tugged him farther from the café's back door and into the employee parking area. "Have more been found? And this meeting about the landfill? That could be where the pollutants that killed those animals are coming from. Could they have killed Lynnie's friend, too?"

Claire burst through the back entrance. Rhonda lowered her voice. "Are there more dead animals? You can stay to listen, can't you? It could have something to do with that woman's murder."

Holt glanced at Claire and pulled his arm out of Rhonda's grasp. "I didn't introduce you, but I think you know my friend, Claire, from Stillwater."

"Does she know about me? Isn't that bad?" Rhonda spoke in a whisper, her forehead wrinkled in concern.

"Claire knows you're involved in my current assignment, but that's all she knows."

"You didn't tell her about …?" Rhonda glanced at Claire. Were they a couple? She didn't care if they were. She had no interest in Holt, personally. But he had to stay on task, to protect her, and to keep her informed. Could he do that if this lovely lady from Stillwater distracted him?

Her son was missing. How could Holt be focused on protecting her if he were helping his friend find her missing son?

Claire stepped closer. "Was someone you know murdered?"

Holt ran his fingers through his hair as he turned to Claire. "A young woman was murdered earlier this week. The medical examiner released the cause of death as carbon monoxide poisoning. And Rhonda found several dead cats at an old motor court on the edge of town. They died of carbon monoxide poisoning, too."

Claire glared at Holt. "And you were going to tell me about this when?"

"This is an active case. I can't discuss it."

Rhonda watched the pair face off. *Interesting.*

Holt's glance moved from Claire to Rhonda as he spoke. "Claire, I think you should stay for the meeting. I need to check on a few things. I'll be back soon. Okay, Rhonda?" The line between his eyebrows deepened.

"I'll watch out for her, Holt. Don't be too long." Rhonda crossed her arms. Claire's face fell. She wasn't happy about being left here, about being unable to help in the search for her son.

"You'll be okay here, Claire. It'll give you something else to think about. Could be good info for that article you're writing, right?" Rhonda mustered an encouraging smile and walked with Claire to the café's back entrance.

Chapter 31
Claire

The local group gathered at one end of the dining room; the audience filled all available seats. Claire left the booth to sit at the back of the group, sipping her coffee and avoiding attention. She pulled out her note pad and stared at the blank page.

Why had Holt left her here? How could he think she could concentrate on this meeting when Cade was missing?

The woman reporter took an empty chair front and center near the podium someone had pulled into the room. Claire watched the reporter speak to several people. Slowly, the seats around Claire filled.

A middle-aged couple took the chairs to her right. A woman entered with a young boy in a Spiderman costume, reminding Claire that it was Halloween. Claire's focus had been on Cade today. She'd forgotten all about trick-or-treating and the community's Fall Festival, not to mention her article and the barrel racing competition.

"Hello again, Mrs. Northcutt." Howard Noble nudged her elbow. "Here for the meeting? Hope this won't be part of your article. Minor hubbub, really. May I join you?"

Claire glanced up at the man, then indicated the empty chair to her left. "Sure. How are you, Mr. Noble?"

"Better, now that I'm sitting next to a lovely lady. All the men will be envious."

Claire's eyebrows rose. "I doubt anyone is taking any notice."

"Beautiful day. Going to be a perfect afternoon. I'd rake leaves if the wind would stop."

"Mr. Noble–'

"Howard, please."

"Howard. About this leaking landfill issue. What do you know about it?"

He studied his hands. "The topic comes to the surface—literally—every now and then. Everyone used to dump trash in some corner of their yards. Buried it if they couldn't burn it, or just left it there to rust or rot. We didn't have trash service. Everyone poured God-knows-what into the earth without a second thought. Never dreamed it might stay down there, travel around, and come back up as a poisonous fume."

"Do you think a lot of small landfills are contributing to the pollution, not one big one?"

His eyes narrowed. "Don't know. Somebody could be using their property outside city limits as a dump. Guess we'll find out."

More people sauntered into the restaurant, filling up the tables. Another middle-aged couple sat down in front of Claire.

Jean, the waitress, came by and refilled Claire's coffee cup.

When the meeting began, Claire noticed Rhonda removing breakfast dishes and helping to clean tables. Their eyes met several times as she moved around the room.

Holt had said the waitress was part of his current assignment. They were friendly, so he wasn't watching her for criminal activity. Why was he keeping tabs on her? Or she could be undercover, too. Were they keeping an eye on someone at the café?

A man got up from one of the tables and moved to the far wall. He turned and spoke to the crowd, "Good morning. Could I have your attention? Good morning." The crowd quieted.

A man introduced himself as the president of the Tulsa Chapter of the Sierra Club and said there was only one item on the agenda, the seepage of toxic landfill waste in the community. "It was first brought to our attention several years ago, then, six months ago, several residents came to me and asked for help. We enlisted the help of local environmental scientists, who have been sampling soil in several locations and testing for heavy metals and other contaminants. I'll let that scientist introduce herself and explain what her research revealed."

The environmental researcher reported the findings of her research to the crowd. In six of the seven research areas, toxic materials were found in surface water and soils. Claire took notes, recording what the woman was telling the crowd. Her mind filled with questions she hoped someone asked before the meeting ended.

But none of them would provide an answer to the question that burned in her mind. Where was Cade?

Chapter 32
Rhonda

Rhonda circulated around the room, filling coffee cups and offering water to the crowd. Normally, this was a quiet period in the café, somewhere between breakfast, brunch, and lunch. She was sure that was the only reason Lloyd had been willing to let them meet here. If the meeting went on much longer, it would cut into the lunch crowd and the usual Route 66 travelers that passed through on Saturdays.

"What are we going to do about it?" Someone shouted at the speaker.

"We tackle this in a reasonable way, and we'll get results. If we act like a bunch of hot heads, they'll put up brick walls faster than you can imagine. We have retained an attorney, a specialist in environmental law, who is preparing our case. Your case."

"And who's going to pay for this attorney? I don't have money for this, and this toxic stuff is oozing up on my land."

"It will be a class action lawsuit. Sierra Club will cover the expenses, and each of you who has faced hardship because of the toxic waste will receive reparations. Document the effects of the toxic materials, illnesses you've experienced, respiratory problems, cancer, mental illness, insomnia. Send those to me. Here's the address."

He repeated the address twice, and Rhonda committed it to memory. Holt would want to know this, and if the carbon dioxide deaths he'd told her about were a result of materials oozing up from the landfill, the lawsuit could include an indictment for cruelty to animals. The SPCA would get involved.

The meeting adjourned. People left the café, but others stayed behind to speak to the leaders. Claire Northcutt remained seated after her table companions left; Howard Noble sauntered away after winking at Jean.

Rhonda cleared coffee cups off tables and put the dishes on the cart that Lance, the busboy, filled as he cleaned tables. When she reached Claire, she paused. She could see Holt in a relationship with this woman, but she didn't think it was in full bloom, yet. There was uncertainty in his eyes and wariness in Claire's.

"Think you'll include anything about this in your article? Is this town another Love Canal?" Rhonda remembered one of the most notorious cases of landfill misuse in the history books.

Claire added more sugar to her coffee and stirred with a spoon. "That was a long time ago. There've been lots of incidents since. And lots of companies who have been fined for similar negligence all over the country."

"Something like that could be happening here." Rhonda set the coffee pot on the table. "A person doesn't have to look far before they find incidents of pollution. Oklahoma has several Superfund sites where hazardous waste was dumped by mining companies, or oil and gas. The Pitcher Zinc mines for one, and around Tulsa early to mid-Twentieth Century manufacturers buried hazardous waste at several sites."

"You know a lot about it," Claire said.

Rhonda chewed her lip. She was talking too much, giving too much away. "I read a lot. Always have. You need more coffee? I'm scheduled for a lunch break, so Jean will be taking over my tables." She tore a sheet off her small order tablet and handed it to Claire. "You can pay either of us."

"How about I pay you, and then you and I go somewhere nearby to get a bite to eat. I need a change of scenery, and it would help me to be able to talk to someone. Otherwise, I'll go crazy with worry about Cade."

Rhonda's eyes widened. She shouldn't have lunch with Holt's friend. She wasn't supposed to open up to anyone. But then, she *was* Holt's friend, too. If he'd approve of her getting to know anyone, wouldn't it be Claire Northcutt?

As she grabbed her jacket and purse from her locker, her mind buzzed a warning. She shouldn't do this. She'd hear about it from Holt later.

"Low down dirty idiot," Jean cursed as she came in from the dining room. "The jerk stiffed me."

"Who?" Lynnie asked as she added parsley and condiments to the tray she was preparing.

"That damned Roger Benson."

"He's a snake," Lynnie said under her breath. "I know he had something to do with Tatia leaving. He was always hitting on her, trying to get her to go out with him. I never trusted him."

"Well, she didn't go out with him, did she? I was the one who spilled the beans about Benson," Jean ranted. She glanced at Rhonda. "He's a meth dealer. Has his own little meth plant set up somewhere. Wish we could get Lloyd to ban him from the café."

Rhonda stood by the back hallway, her jacket and purse in hand. "Not sure I know who you're talking about. Hope he doesn't sit at one of my tables."

"Oh, he will one of these days, but not if he figures out which tables Lynnie is working first."

Lynnie rolled her eyes. "You've seen him, Rhonda. Spooky-looking guy. Big gut, brown hair, always sweating. Gross."

She was describing the man who'd been talking about the dead woman earlier in the week. Rhonda hadn't noticed him in the dining room today, but she'd been busy with her tables, the meeting, Holt and Claire Northcutt.

"He's gone now, and I may give him a piece of my mind next time he comes in," Jean said. "Joker left me a ten spot for a $16 tab. Does he think I'll make up the difference?"

"I can chip in, Jean, if it'll make it easier for you. You shouldn't have to pay for that." Rhonda dug in her purse for her wallet.

"You're a sweetheart. Wouldn't be the first time, though. And no tip, either."

"Maybe he thought he was leaving you a Twenty. Simple mistake." She handed the older woman a ten-dollar bill.

"You don't know Benson like I do. Stay away from him. And you, too, Lynnie. He's no good. Thank you, Rhonda. That's real sweet of you. Going to lunch?"

"Yeah. I'll see you all in about an hour."

***

Claire Northcutt was leaning against a red SUV in the parking lot when Rhonda came out of the café. Her phone to her ear, she didn't look pleased with the conversation she was having.

Rhonda took her time crossing the lot. She lifted her face to the sun and felt the warm rays. A slight breeze stirred the leaves, and already fallen brown ones skipped across the parking lot. A crow flew over, cawing.

"What can I do? I'm going crazy sitting here." Claire's voice boomed.

Claire was probably talking to Holt. She wondered if Claire would tell Holt they were going to lunch together. He was not going to be happy.

"Okay, then. I don't want to argue. I'm going to grab a quick lunch with Rhonda. Then we'll be back here to the café. Call me. Soon. Whether you find out anything or not." Claire dropped the phone into her purse.

Rhonda skirted the front of the vehicle and opened the SUV's passenger door.

"Any news about your son?" She slipped into the Jeep's passenger seat.

"They haven't found anything yet. And his girlfriend has disappeared, too. The police are pursuing the runaway theory. They say there's no evidence that they were coerced into leaving. And the grandmother didn't seem to know anything. Totally convinced them she was senile." Claire sat behind the steering wheel but didn't start the car. She shook her head and chewed at her lip. "Those kids didn't run away. She was scheduled to compete. I know Neve, and I know Cade. They're teenagers, and they've been having a tough time. They didn't just suddenly run away together."

"Doesn't sound like it. I can't tell you how many girlfriends came and went while my son was in high school. Constant parade. Those girls were so dramatic. And college girls don't seem to be much better." She spoke the words before she could stop them. It had felt so natural, sharing thoughts and experiences with another woman, not having to pretend she was not who she was.

"You've got kids? Tell me about them."

Rhonda closed her eyes. What was she going to say now? She'd blown it. Claire had only asked to be polite, but she was sure the woman needed to be distracted from her worry.

"Rhonda? Are you alright?"

Rhonda took a deep breath. "I miss them. Haven't seen them in a while. But someday ..." She straightened her back. She needed a distraction too. Surely Holt wouldn't hold it against her to use Claire as a distraction. It felt good to have another woman to talk to. "I'm so sorry about Cade. I can imagine how worried you are." She felt a little guilty turning the conversation back onto Claire's son, but she couldn't let Claire return to the topic of her children.

"I don't know what to think. They're qualifying in time trials today. But if Neve's not there ... I need to run out and check on Blaze. Who knows if he's even been fed. That was Cade's job."

"We can grab a quick lunch and drive out to check on your horse. We can get everything done in an hour."

"Thanks."

The restaurant wasn't busy. They were seated and placed their ordered in less than a minute. Rhonda studied Claire but flicked her look to the window when Claire turned to her.

"Is Holt a regular customer when he's working in the area?" Claire asked.

Rhonda's thoughts spun. She wasn't sure how to answer that question. Claire was fishing for an explanation as to how they knew each other. It wasn't Rhonda's job to tell her. She shrugged. "I hardly know him. Just started working there on Monday."

"Really? He's my neighbor in Stillwater. Told me he was working in the Tulsa area this week, and we happened to cross paths when Cade and I came for the competition. And for my article. You two are extremely comfortable with one another."

Comfortable? Rhonda knew it was more than that. She was trusting him with her life. She sipped from her water glass.

"He likes the food at the diner. But he did tell me you two were working together. How exactly?" Claire asked.

Rhonda opened her mouth to speak and then closed it again. She blinked. "Really, I can't say. But I hardly know Holt. We met a few days ago."

Claire studied her.

Rhonda shrugged and looked around the restaurant, hoping her face didn't reveal her inner feelings. Why had Holt told her they were working together? Granted, it wasn't exactly a lie.

"He's a good guy, Rhonda, but it's hard to be sure who is and who isn't these days. Cade used to hate him, but I think he's okay with him now." Claire's voice faltered.

Rhonda wanted to keep the ball in Claire Northcutt's court, but the topic of Cade was too painful, too uncertain for his mother. It wasn't fair for her to press it. She had to take a different tack. "Are you two dating?" She hoped her voice sounded flippant. She didn't care if they were. She wasn't interested in Holt.

"We spend time together when he's home. We have dinner, watch movies, hang out. I don't really think of it as dating." Claire fumbled over her words. "I could go out with someone else if I wanted. So could he."

Rhonda lifted her eyebrows. "I think you'd like to be dating. You care about him."

"Um," Claire blinked.

"It's okay. You don't have to confess anything. I just sense that the two of you aren't being honest about your feelings. But how would I know? I hardly know either of you. I'm just making conversation."

The waitress delivered their salads and left the tab on the table.

"I've been trying to figure my feelings out," Claire said as she stabbed some lettuce with her fork. "Do I want something more from him? I'm divorced. Cade's dad and I split up when he was five. Haven't remarried. And I'm not sure I want to go through that again."

Rhonda worked the wedding ring on her finger. She wasn't ready to take it off yet. She wasn't sure if she would ever be. She picked up her fork and stirred the barbecue ranch dressing into the greens. How could she respond to that? She'd been married to the same man for over twenty years. She'd married a good one the first time. Would there be a second time? She doubted it.

Claire's cell phone rang, and she pulled it from her purse.

Rhonda could hear an agitated voice on the other end of the phone. Claire ran her fingers through her hair and listened. "Thanks for calling me. I'll be there soon to take care of it."

Claire dropped the phone back into her purse. "I need to go out to the Round-up Club. Blaze is kicking the walls of his stall. Do you mind? I'll take you back to the café as soon as I've gotten things under control." She frowned as she rubbed at her scalp.

Rhonda glanced at her watch. "Let's have these salads boxed up. I'll finish mine later."

"Good idea." Claire scooted out of the booth. Both of them left money on the table.

Rhonda glanced at Claire as they hurried toward the SUV. Claire was close to tears. She had to keep Claire talking. Claire wouldn't lose control on her watch. "I'd like to know more about this newspaper story you're working on. Route 66? Who have you interviewed so far?"

***

Five minutes later, they pulled into the parking area at the Round-up Club arena. Unlike the day before, the parking lot was overflowing with trucks and SUVs. Horse trailers were parked all along the sides of the asphalt lot. Horses, some already saddled, waited in the paddocks.

As they walked toward the arena. Rhonda saw more red trucks than she could count. What was the likelihood that one of them belonged to the men who'd followed her?

Inside the arena, the timed qualification rounds were underway. Rhonda stopped to watch.

A horse raced down the arena and circled the triangle of barrels, its body leaning at an almost 45-degree angle as the rider urged it along.

"Stables are this way," Claire said, walking on.

Rhonda scanned the viewing stands and saw a group of teenagers on the top row. Claire should talk to them, ask if they'd seen Cade or Neve.

She followed Claire into the adjacent barn and down the long alley between rows of horse stalls. Horses neighed as they walked by. Riders dressed in colorful shirts and jeans led horses out of stalls and into the wide alley. Others were using combs or brushes to curry their horses before saddling them. Above all the noise, Rhonda heard pounding, as if someone were slamming a hammer into a board.

"Hey, Blaze. What's wrong, boy?" Claire called into one of the stalls. A horse whinnied. Hooves slammed into the side of the stall. "Hey, stop it. I'm here. Let's get you something to eat. And your water's empty. No wonder you're upset." Claire opened the gate to the stall and stepped inside. Rhonda lingered in the alley, watching Claire stroke the horse.

"The kids haven't been here for a few hours. Blaze needs water. Can you walk him for a minute while I take care of that?"

Claire hooked a lead onto the horse's halter.

"Sure. Where?" Rhonda stepped up to the horse, running one hand down his neck and then stroking his nose.

"Paddocks are down that way. And the exercise yard. Just walk him around a bit. He'll throw his head and roll his eyes because he doesn't know you. You're not scared of horses, are you?"

"No. I'm an animal person," Rhonda said. Claire handed her the rope, and Rhonda led the horse out into the alley. "Come on, Blaze. Let's stretch those legs a bit."

Her husband had been the large animal vet, but she'd worked on plenty of horses, too, during her years as a vet. She scratched Blaze's white nose and patted his withers. "That's a good boy. Tired of being cooped up in that stall, aren't you?"

The horse tossed his head and knickered, letting her lead him away from the stall and down the long alleyway to the wide gate at the far end, away from the arena. They stepped out into the sunshine and Blaze picked up his pace, eager to be moving. Rhonda walked faster, matching his stride as they walked the open space beside the paddock.

The scent of animals, as well as all of the familiar barn smells, transported her back to home and the clinic outside Austin. Just a week ago. How could that be? She closed her eyes, walking blind with the horse, letting the sounds and scents engulf her. Her throat thickened. She kept walking with Blaze, keeping her eyes open only a slit to be sure her steps didn't take her into a rut, or a fresh pile of manure.

Blaze's steps finally slowed, and the horse nuzzled her arm. She turned toward the barns. "You're hungry, aren't you? I bet Claire has your lunch ready. Let's go see."

When Rhonda reached the stall, Claire was gone. A full water bucket sat on the floor, and the feed bucket had been filled with oats. Fresh hay had replaced the soiled. Blaze nuzzled the grain. Rhonda unhooked the lead and hung it back on the wall peg. She closed the gate behind her as she left the stall and headed up the alley to the arena.

Shouting and cheers lifted into the air. Another racer must have successfully qualified for tomorrow's competition. Rhonda stepped through the crowd that had gathered along the arena's fence and looked up into the stands. The group of young people stood in a huddle on the top row, and Claire was making her way toward them, hopping up the levels as if they were steps.

A middle-aged man in a black ball cap joined the group of young people. He turned his back to the arena, and the kids looked at something he held in his hands. As Claire hurried toward the teenagers, Rhonda kept her eyes on the group, assessing the height of the back row of the bleachers. Her stomach churned.

Claire stomped up to the older man and touched his shoulder. As they talked, Claire stiffened. He laughed. Claire stepped to one side, gesturing toward the arena. The teenagers pulled back as the conversation escalated into an argument.

Panic hammered into Rhonda's brain. "Claire," she shouted, even though there was no way the woman could hear her over the shouting crowd as another racer made the final dash toward the finish line. She pushed through the crowd surrounding the fence around the arena.

The man stepped closer to Claire, and then shoved her shoulder. Claire took a step back. He shoved her again. She tottered, lost her balance, and disappeared off the back of the bleacher.

Rhonda ran toward the bottom of the bleachers, pushing her way through to a huddle of young people. Claire lay on her back, eyes open, clenching her stomach and gasping for breath.

Quickly, Rhonda squatted next to her. "Claire? You're okay. You fell, but you're okay. I'm right here." Rhonda checked her pupils for dilation and felt her pulse before she ran her hands quickly over each of her arms and legs. "Can you move your feet? Your fingers?" Once she had stopped gasping for breath, Claire moved each hand and foot in turn.

"Good. Nothing seems to be broken. Can someone bring me a blanket?" Mentally, Rhonda assessed outward signs of trauma. There was a danger of internal bleeding, and the possibility that Claire had suffered a spinal injury. She could also be going into shock.

"Get back, please stay back. Give her some air. Someone call 9-1-1. Claire, does anything hurt?" Rhonda smoothed Claire's hair, pushing a wayward strand out of her eyes. When someone handed her a folded horse blanket, she spread it over Claire's body.

"My shoulder. I tried to tuck it and roll." Claire's voice cracked.

"Good job. That was totally the right thing to do."

Claire struggled to get up.

"No. Don't get up yet. Breathe in and out slowly. There's no rush."

Claire focused on Rhonda's face, and gradually her breathing normalized.

Rhonda looked up at the metal structure next to them. "That was a good twelve-foot fall, Claire You should go to the hospital, to be safe." She continued to study Claire's pale face.

A man in a black ball cap shouldered his way to the front of the small crowd that had gathered around Claire. Rhonda stood, recognizing him as the man Claire had been arguing with.

"Sorry you lost your balance. I tried to grab you, but you slipped away. You seem to be all right. I'm glad of that." He leered at Rhonda, grinning as he groomed his thick black mustache.

"Stay away from her. I'm having you arrested for assault."

"Hmmm. Like that would ever happen." The man turned and stalked through the lingering crowd.

"Who was he?" Rhonda asked the nearest teenager. The boy shrugged and exchanged looks with two friends standing close by.

"He was here the other day with that Stillwater girl. She said he was her uncle or something. Said he might try to sell us drugs. And he was, just now. This lady interrupted him."

"Thanks for telling me. I'll pass that on to the police." Rhonda knelt beside Claire once again to recheck her pulse. "Is there a medic on duty, or a body board here?" Rhonda shouted.

"Coming. We're coming." A woman with a gray braid pushed through the crowd, followed by two women in white EMT jackets pulling a collapsed gurney behind them.

"Let's get you to the hospital, Claire." Rhonda's throat was dry. Her head was spinning. "I need your keys."

"In my purse. Where I fell." Claire closed her eyes.

Rhonda let the EMTs take over. She retrieved Claire's purse from the trampled ground behind the arena grandstand.

Carefully, the pair of EMTs lifted Claire onto the stretcher, keeping her neck and back immobile. They strapped her down, and then extended the collapsed legs of the gurney.

"Who are you, really?" Claire whispered to Rhonda as she walked to the ambulance beside the gurney with the EMTs.

Fireworks exploded inside Rhonda's head. She patted Claire's arm. After they'd placed the gurney in the ambulance, she rushed to Claire's SUV. Then, she followed closely behind the ambulance as it zoomed toward the hospital.

Chapter 33
Holt

Rhonda was waiting on the bench outside of the emergency exam rooms, hunched over, her auburn hair hanging lose. Holt took a deep breath and moved through the white hall toward her, trying to ignore the antiseptic air and the bad memories it evoked.

"How bad is it? Is she going to be all right?" He looked deep into Rhonda's eyes, searching for the truth. His heart had hardly been able to beat since her call.

Rhonda had called him from Claire's SUV, as she followed the ambulance to the Persimmon Hospital. He was sure that Rhonda had taken charge of the situation at the arena. As a medical professional, she wouldn't do anything less. But he knew that once things had slowed down, and she'd had a chance to think, she had been terrified. Her medical knowledge compromised her identity as a waitress at the café. Who else had seen her take charge? Who else thought it out of place for a waitress to have medical knowledge? Were there any reporters there? Would the local newshounds get wind of what had happened?

He had a lot of questions, and only time would reveal the answers.

But meanwhile, Claire was here, in the hospital after a fall. She could be severely injured.

"They've taken her to Xray. She'll have a CT scan. No indications of a back injury. Or internal bleeding. I didn't let her get up. I think she'll be fine, Holt."

"Thank God." Holt sank into one of chairs that lined the hallway, leaned over, clasped his hands, and watched Rhonda's face. His heart had begun to pump normally. Soon, if the news continued to be good, he should be able to breathe. "Can you tell me exactly what happened?"

"Only the part I know. Claire got a call while we were having lunch. Someone from the arena said that her horse was trying to kick his way out of the stall at the Round-up Club. We drove out to check on him. I walked the horse while she replenished his food and water. When I got back to the stall, she wasn't there, so I put up the horse and went to find her." Rhonda paused and took a breath. Her face tightened. "Claire was climbing up the stands toward a group of teenagers. I assumed she wanted to ask them if they'd seen Cade or Neve. But by the time she got to the top, a man had approached the kids. He was showing them something. I couldn't tell what. When Claire arrived, the two of them argued. He shoved her, she stepped back and when he shoved her again, she lost her balance and fell off the back of the bleachers."

Holt winced. It wouldn't have happened if he'd been there. It wouldn't have happened if he hadn't insisted that Claire stay at the café while he went looking for Cade. "Who was this guy?"

"One of the kids told me he'd been trying to sell them drugs when Claire interrupted."

"Can you describe this man?" Holt pulled his phone from his pocket and opened Notepad. He wanted every last detail. He'd see the man in jail before the day was done.

"Dark hair. Dark jeans and a windbreaker over a red shirt. Cowboy boots and a black baseball cap. Squinty eyes, brown complexion. Acne scars on his cheeks."

Holt typed into his phone. "Great details. I'll get this out to the locals. Any idea who he might have been?"

"The kids said the man had been there previously with the girl from Stillwater. I think they meant Neve. Later, she had told them he was her uncle, and that he might try to sell them drugs."

Holt typed more into his phone. "Thanks." Neve. Her suspicions had been correct. And now the possible problems between Neve and Cade were becoming clearer in his mind.

"Any news about Cade? Or Neve?" Rhonda scooted to the edge of the chair and faced him.

"No. The local detectives are out asking questions. No leads yet." Holt frowned at her. He wasn't used to feeling so helpless. He knew his focus had to be on Rhonda, but, when it came right down to it, his life had become Claire and Cade. How could he sit back and let someone else be in charge of finding and protecting them? He shook his head.

Rhonda exhaled a long breath. "Now that you're here, Holt, I've got to get back to work. The café is probably getting slammed. I've been gone nearly two hours." She stood. "I can call an Uber. Claire's SUV is outside, I'll leave it with you."

"No. Take it. Claire won't need to drive it. They'll probably keep her overnight, and we'll worry about getting her vehicle back to the B&B tomorrow. You go. We'll talk later. Thanks for taking care of Claire." He stood up when Rhonda did, and gave her a quick hug.

Rhonda stepped back to look at him. "She means a lot to you, doesn't she?"

"More than she knows." Holt watched Rhonda hurry out of the hospital. He'd finally admitted it himself, and to someone else. He hoped he had the chance to admit it to Claire.

A doctor in a white coat, carrying a clipboard, stepped up to Holt. "I was looking for the woman who came in with Mrs. Northcutt. Her friend."

"She had to get back to work. I'm the closest she's got to family here. I'll be taking care of her. How is she?"

The doctor eyed him. "We need some identification. This is irregular."

"You can ask the patient. Tell her Holt Braden wants to take care of her. I'll wait while you do it." He pulled out his wallet and handed the doctor his driver's license and his DEA identification badge.

The doctor headed down the hallway, motioning to a nurse as he went through a door into the Emergency area.

Holt's hands sweated. He needed to know how Claire was. Had she broken her back? Did she have internal injuries? He swiped his forehead with one hand, perched on the edge of a chair and waited.

Minutes later, that same nurse came through the doors and walked up to him.

"Mr. Braden? Ms. Northcutt has identified you. She's going to be fine. No signs of internal bleeding, x-rays show no broken bones, C-Scan was clear." She handed over his license and ID.

"So, what's the diagnosis?" His body felt lighter.

"Her shoulder is bruised, but not broken. She was relatively uninjured in the fall, but we need to be vigilant. Sometimes internal injuries don't show up right away."

"What does that mean? How do I know if—"

"Watch for unusual bruising, unusual behavior, headaches, fainting. No strenuous activities for the next week. No heavy lifting, moving furniture, no workouts, no risk of falling."

"You're releasing her?" He had conflicting feelings about that. He couldn't be with Claire 24/7. Not that he didn't want to be, but he had to work. He had responsibility for Rhonda. And besides that, Claire wouldn't agree to a 24/7 monitor. And Cade was missing.

"No need for her to stay. Not as long as someone will be with her." The nurse looked at Claire's chart. "Stillwater is home, right? Any family members there?"

"Her nephew. And she has a son. Unfortunately, we don't know where he is." Holt scratched his head. How was he going to manage this?

The nurse jotted a note on the clipboard. "Okay. So, she'll be going with you? I'll leave the paperwork with the discharge desk, and we'll bring her out to you in a few minutes."

Holt signed the necessary forms at the discharge desk, and then paced around the emergency waiting room. He clicked through the texts and emails he'd received that afternoon, hoping for good news to share with Claire.

His police contact reported that Neve Bright had competed early Saturday and did well enough in the timed trials to make it into the finals on Sunday. No one could confirm if Cade had been at the arena with her. The grandmother refused to talk to the police. Her neighbors were also unhelpful. Not even the two elderly sisters at the B&B could offer any new information about either of the teenagers. Cade had vanished.

A wheelchair rolled toward Holt, pushed by an orderly.

He turned toward it. His heart lifted. She was pale, but it was Claire, smiling up at him. "How do you feel, sweetheart?" He bent to kiss her cheek.

"I fell, Holt, but I'm okay. Nothing broken, just a little bruised. Tell me what they've found out about Cade, and Neve."

"Sir, if you'll pull your vehicle up to the pick-up area, I'll have her waiting for you there," the orderly said.

"Soon, Claire. Let me go get the truck." He sprinted out of the building and over to where he'd parked the F-150. He started the truck and drove it around to the hospital entrance. Together, he and the orderly helped Claire up into the passenger seat.

"Thanks, I'll take it from here," Holt told the orderly. He circled the truck and climbed in behind the steering wheel. He reached across the seat and took Claire's hand.

"Tell me now, Holt," Claire insisted.

Gently, Holt told her what he knew and didn't know. "I'm sorry, Claire. Surely, we'll hear something about Cade soon. When we find Neve … she probably knows where he is."

"But what if she doesn't? What if Cade has vanished? What if he's never found?" Her breath was jagged, her words low and faint.

"We won't stop looking." He felt a pain in his gut. He couldn't bear to see Claire so miserable.

Her eyes closed. Holt started the truck and pulled away from the hospital.

"I have a couple of questions for you," she said quietly.

"I'll answer if I can, but I've told you all I know about the investigation." He navigated the truck out of the parking lot and onto the busy street. A vintage Hudson Hornet turned in as he waited on traffic.

"I want to know about Rhonda. Who is she?"

That was the last question he'd expected her to ask. Why was she thinking about Rhonda? "We're working on a case together. That's it." He sensed she was watching him and gauging her words.

"Your friend knew exactly what to do after I fell. Very efficient. Very thorough. Made sure I didn't move in case I'd injured my neck or my back. She's not really a waitress, is she, Holt?"

"Of course, she's a waitress. You've seen her at work. And I told you I'm collaborating with her on this case."

"But she's really a doctor, or a nurse. Tell me the truth. Why is she working at Tiny's Route 66 Diner? With her training, why is she undercover?"

Holt Braden glanced across the front seat of his truck at Claire. Rhonda couldn't stop being a doctor any more than he could stop being an investigator. Her professionalism had made it obvious to Claire that Rhonda was not who she pretended to be.

Holt didn't want to lie to Claire. Any possibility of having a deeper relationship would fly out the window if he did. Over the past four years, he'd been so careful to make sure that their two worlds didn't collide, that he'd never have to explain who someone was or what he was doing.

But this time was different. The first time he'd taken Claire to the café for a burger, he'd known he shouldn't go there with her. He'd been nervous from the minute they walked in the door, although he'd been sure that Rhonda would treat him like a stranger. How was he going to manage this?

"Holt?"

"Yes, I know, and I'm going to explain. It's complicated. And it's also secret. An entire operation could be jeopardized."

He glanced at her. Her green eyes shone with curiosity. She was not going to let him off the hook.

"The three of us should talk about it. I'll ask her to come by the B&B after her shift." He hoped that would give him time to decide what he should and should not tell Claire.

He was going to recommend that she return to Stillwater. She wouldn't want to, especially with Cade missing. What mother wouldn't want to stay? He would contact Denver. Maybe her nephew could come here to get her. He couldn't leave town while he was assigned to Rhonda's case.

He should never have told Claire he was working in the Tulsa area, shouldn't have suggested they get together while she was here for the barrel racing event. He hadn't considered that Claire would be so curious about Rhonda.

Although it didn't seem obvious right now how this might endanger Renee, it was a possibility. Nothing was ever as it seemed. People were not as they appeared. Someone in that crowd had seen Rhonda act and had realized she was wearing a waitress uniform. What was a medical professional doing in a waitress uniform? One mention of that unusual fact to the wrong people and Rhonda suddenly became Renee, and the hit squad was camping on her doorstep.

He had to move her. Her cover was blown whether Claire stayed in town or not. Renee needed a new town and a new job. She had too much exposure at the diner.

"Holt, are you and Rhonda both undercover?"

Sweat beaded on his forehead. "Ye-e-es. You could say that. And that's all I can say until Rhonda joins us."

"You are going to tell me, aren't you?"

"Yes. Absolutely. With Rhonda. Later."

He focused his look on the street, hoping Claire would sense he did not want to discuss this further right now. His truck passed yard after yard where autumn decorations—scarecrows, ghosts, and witches—swayed in the wind. He had hoped this Halloween season would be calm for a change. Not going to happen. His life was never calm when he was on a case.

Chapter 34
Rhonda

Rhonda's hands would not stop shaking. She'd blown it. Claire was smart. She knew it was unlikely that Rhonda, as a waitress, would know so much about first aid and injuries. Claire believed her to be a nurse or a doctor. Never entered her mind that she might be a veterinarian. That was a good thing, wasn't it?

What worried her more was that the man who'd attacked Claire might have recognized her. She'd seen his eyes widen, and a grin spread over his face. He wouldn't hesitate to tell his buddies that the waitress at Tiny's Diner knew an awful lot about medical issues.

Jean glared at her as she hurried across the kitchen. She entered the dining room with her order pad and headed toward her tables. "I'll take it from here, Vivian. Sorry I'm late."

Vivian pursed her lips and tore the top order off her pad. "I have the lady's order. You get the gentleman's order. Thanks for nothin'."

The harried waitress moved to a table where the glaring customers were tapping their menus.

The dining room had only one empty table.

"My name is Rhonda, and I'll be serving you today. I have your order, ma'am. What would you like, sir?"

She jotted down the man's order and then quickly surveyed the tables as she headed for the kitchen. Customers at three more tables appeared irritated. She turned in the order and turned back to the dining room. Through the front window, she saw that two parked tour buses filled one side of the parking lot. That explained the mid-afternoon rush of customers.

* * *

Two hours later, Lynnie showed up for her shift as the second bus pulled back onto Route 66. Vivian bustled out of the kitchen to take a break, but not without one more sarcastic remark to Rhonda. "Screw me around again, girl, and I'll have your hide. You need to split tips with me if you want me to cover for you again."

Rhonda reached into the pocket of her uniform and came up with a wad of bills. She handed them to Vivian. No reason to explain why she'd been late. Vivian didn't trust her. Maybe she never would, after today. And Rhonda didn't really need the cash. "Again, I'm sorry. Shouldn't happen again."

"Hmmm," Vivian muttered as she stomped out the back door.

The jitters started again when the crowd thinned. As soon as Rhonda had time to think about what had happened, and how she had reacted, she'd be all over Holt with questions. Holt would defer to Rhonda. It was her story. It was her tragedy. She could refuse to answer her questions, but from what she already knew about Claire, the woman wouldn't take no for an answer. If Holt had any hope of a serious relationship with Claire, he'd want to tell her the truth.

She helped Lance bus a table and was replenishing the silverware bin when the bell tinkled on the front door. She took one quick glance and ducked through the door into the kitchen, her heart in her throat. The man wore a black ball cap and had a thick mustache. Neve's uncle, the drug dealer. He had two friends in tow, and a smug look on his face.

She wanted to run. She wanted to go back to the house, pick up Samson, load her car, and drive until she was too tired to see the road. But what good would that do? She'd be alone, without a destination, and when she was needed in court for the trial, they wouldn't know where to contact her. She would be more lost than she was right now.

"Rhonda? *Tu es enferma?* Are you unwell?" Eduardo touched her arm.

"No. I'm fine. *Solo cansada.* Only tired. Thank you." Rhonda forced a smile onto her face and squared her shoulders. She had to manage this.

She charged back into the dining room, order pad in hand, and marched up to the table where the three men sat. "What can I get for you? My name's Rhonda, and I'll be your server."

She didn't make eye contact with any of them.

"You can get me a chicken-fried steak with mashed potatoes and gravy. And a bandage. Maybe a tourniquet. Or a splint." The man with the black ball cap laughed.

She rolled her eyes. "Why? Somebody beat you up? You were the one who pushed my friend over the railing. You should be arrested for assault, and attempted murder."

His beady eyes drilled into her. All three men straightened. "Now wait a minute. That's not what happened. She came at me. And you're no waitress. What's a doctor, or an EMT, doing working at a diner—Rhonda?" He eyed the embroidered name on her uniform.

She held his look. "I was in nursing school. Got divorced. Ran out of money. And it's none of your business. What can I get you two gentlemen?"

Rhonda glanced at the other men. The blood drained from her face. One of them—skinny with a goatee—studied her. The third man had gray hair on his temples and a white scar above one eyebrow.

Her fingers tried to write down their order, but the room buzzed, and she didn't register their words. "Excuse me a minute." She moved from their table across the room to the kitchen.

Jean stood near the set-up station, talking to Eduardo. Rhonda headed her way.

"Jean. Do me a favor. Can you confirm their orders at Table 11? I'm not feeling well. I need to—" The room whirled.

Eduardo grabbed her arm and guided her over to a chair. *"Te sientas, mi amiga, por favor."*

Chapter 35
Claire

"Holt, I can't just lie here and take it easy. I've got to look for Cade." Claire threw off the quilt that Holt had pulled up over her and rolled toward the edge of the bed. The room spun. She blinked to get it back in focus and tried again.

"Claire, stop. They gave you a mild painkiller, and it's my job to keep you quiet. You aren't making that job easy."

A series of sharp knocks sounded on the interior exit door. "Ms. Northcutt. Answer, please," an insistent voice commanded.

Holt left the bedroom and went to the door while Claire lay still, trying to steady the room around her. She blinked, peering toward the door, certain that one of the two B&B owners was checking on her.

"And who are you, sir? I was expecting Ms. Northcutt. I rented this room to Ms. Northcutt and her son. Let me pass." The gray-haired sister shoved past Holt and into the sitting area. She stood in the center of the room, staring into the bedroom at Claire on the bed.

"Ms. Northcutt. This is not that kind of establishment. Your visitor will have to go."

"You misinterpret this situation, Mrs., er, um. Who are you?" Holt stammered, then recovered. "Ms. Northcutt was in a serious fall today. I brought her here from the hospital. She needs to lie still and rest. Doctor's orders." Holt held the older woman's glare.

She looked from Claire on the bed to Holt.

"He's telling the truth, Della," Claire said. "I fell this afternoon. And I'm stuck here, recuperating when I need to be looking for my son. Have you seen him today? He didn't come back last night, and I'm frantic with worry." She picked at the bedspread with her fingers. She wanted to get up, to charge out the door to her Jeep and look for her son.

Della Munoz stalked into the bedroom and hovered over the bed. "Oh, my dear Lord. That's bad news. When was the boy last here? Yesterday morning? Did I …?" She pinched her eyes shut and held one finger to her forehead. "I saw someone. Betsy was in the kitchen, and I went out back with the garbage. There was a car in the alley. I didn't know that car. No reason for it to be around here. I went back in and asked Betsy about it. She didn't know it either. One of those fixed up cars from the 50s, like they have out at the Route 66 museum. An old Chevy." Mrs. Munoz nodded at Claire.

Holt stepped into the bedroom. "That's important information. Thank you. I'm Holt Braden, Claire's friend from Stillwater. I'm in Tulsa on business. Glad I was able to help today."

"Me, too, Mr. Braden. Sorry for the confusion at the door. You wouldn't believe what people pull sometimes. I knew Miss Claire wasn't like that. Would you like me to sit with her for a while? I sure can if you've got something else you need to do. I'll turn on the television. But don't you go to sleep, Miss Claire." Della pulled the room's one extra chair up to Claire's bed.

Hands tucked in his pockets; Holt turned and peeked out of the curtained window of the suite.

"I'm not a baby. I can stay awake. You don't have to sit with me, Della. I don't have a concussion," Claire insisted.

"Could be a slow bleed. I've heard about slow bleeds. Might not show up for a while. I'll be right here." Della sat on the edge of the chair seat and studied Claire's face. "It's no problem. Betsy can get on without me for a little while. When she misses me, she'll come lookin.' And then I'll let her take a shift until Mr. Braden gets back. We got you."

"But I need to—"

"You need to stay here and be still, Claire," Holt said in a quiet voice.

"I'll stay with her. Me and Betsy will take turns. We've made the afternoon cookies—lemon drop today— and iced tea is in the frig. You go out there and do what you have to do. Find that boy." Della settled back in her chair, hands folded in her lap. "Go on now, Mr. Braden. We girls will be fine."

Holt stood far enough back from the window that his face was in shadow, the bright and glorious fall afternoon outside the window. Claire wished she could see his eyes. What was he thinking? Did he know something he wasn't telling her? And why couldn't he tell her the truth about Rhonda? Who was she?

"I'm going out to the grandmother's house. And back to the Round-up Club. We'll find him, and the two of you will go back to Stillwater tomorrow. You'll check in with your doctor in Stillwater first thing Monday. To make sure everything is okay."

"Everything is okay. Nothing's wrong. I should be going with you." She clenched her hand and hammered the bed with it.

"Call me if you need anything. I'll be back soon." Holt planted a kiss on her forehead and then crossed the room to the outside door. "Thank you, Miss Della. Oh, I didn't catch your last name."

"Munoz. Della Munoz."

Holt paused on the doorstep. He looked at Claire and then opened the door.

"See you soon."

"Be careful."

Claire wasn't sure why she said it. He hoped he wasn't going into a dangerous situation. She hoped Cade's absence was just teenage forgetfulness, that Holt would come back to her room with Cade in tow, and that Cade would be apologetic and contrite.

Her head hurt. Her back hurt. And her shoulder really hurt. She sighed.

"You need anything, Miss Northcutt. Sip of water? Something for the pain? I'm sure you feel like you been stomped on."

"I do. But I'm okay for now, Della. Next pain pill at 4. I'll rest now. Does Betsy need you? Maybe you should check in with her, tell her you're here. I'll be fine alone for a few minutes."

"You sure of that? I guess I should let her know where I am. She's probably wondering."

"Sure. Do that. Just leave the door unlocked."

* * *

Her cell phone rang from the nightstand. Claire didn't recognize the number, but there was the possibility that Cade was calling her from someone else's phone if his was dead. She answered.

"Claire! So glad I caught you. Can we meet for a drink? I just can't let you get away without seeing you again. I'd really like to see you."

Her mind analyzed the voice, sorted through the possible identities of the caller, and quickly settled on the most likely one. "Vince? How'd you get my number?"

"Nothing nefarious. So how about that drink? I'd like to get your thoughts on the meeting today. I'm wondering how it's going to play into your article."

"The meeting about the toxic waste? Were you there?" She's seen him before the meeting, but not during. There had been so many people there, she could easily have missed him if he slipped in and stood at the back of the room.

"I'm not convinced anyone did anything intentionally. Just a culmination of bad practices over decades. Anyway, let's have a drink. What do you say?"

"Thanks for the invitation, Vince, but I had an accident today. I'm resting. And waiting for my son to come in. We'll be driving home tomorrow."

"An accident? Hope it wasn't serious. And you're headed home tomorrow. But you didn't get much information for your Route 66 article."

"I didn't. Maybe it wasn't a good idea in the first place."

"You would have made it an interesting piece, I'm sure. Sorry I couldn't have been more help."

His voice was friendly and familiar, almost comforting. Claire almost wished they could have gotten together. But it was out of the question. She had to rest and wait for Holt. *Holt.*

"Vince, I can't see you. My life is busy right now. I'm not interested in dating." She swallowed and her heart pounded. *She would wait for Holt however long it took.*

Vince sighed into the phone. "I recognize a brush off when I hear one. Guess I'll see you at the next reunion. Take care, Claire."

He disconnected before she had a chance to say goodbye.

Chapter 36
Rhonda

Exhaustion fogged the edge of her world. Her legs felt heavy, as if she'd attached 100-pound weights to her ankles. Her heart hammered. *Danger.*

Two of the men she'd overheard had come back to the café. With Cade's attacker. Were they still watching her, trying to decide if she'd told anyone about the dead body discussion? Vivian was at their table. Flirting? Rhonda grimaced. Not much to flirt with there.

When she'd talked to the attacker, she had played it as cool as she knew how. Calm, smiling, and glancing at customers throughout the cafe. Her trembling body had wanted to run. Anywhere but here.

She thought of the missing boy, Claire, and the man who'd brutally shoved her over the railing of the bleachers. The short fall was unlikely to kill someone. But if she'd landed on her head and broken her neck, the outcome could have been disastrous. Claire could have died.

Now he'd come to the café, and his companions were the same two customers she'd seen earlier in the week with the man who'd said, "she was dead, I'm sure."

All of them peered at her with narrowed eyes. Wondering if she had told anyone?

Rhonda sat in the employee area behind the kitchen, breathing deeply and trying to get a grip on herself. She had to get back to work. Otherwise, she'd confirm their suspicions. They'd know she knew something, and they'd come after her.

Wasn't it bad enough to have the drug dealers looking for her? Did those long fingers of evil reach all the way up into northeastern Oklahoma?

Jean brought her a cup of strong tea and a chocolate chip cookie. She munched it slowly, savoring the brown sugar and the chocolate, feeling energy return to her body. She could do this. Just as she'd pulled herself out of the lake a week ago and crawled under the sumac bushes on the shore.

* * *

Three hours later, when it was time for dinner break, she left the café. Jean, Vivian, and Lynnie had picked up the slack as she moved slowly through the tables, taking orders, and delivering food.

"I'm worried about you," Lynnie had said. "You don't look like yourself. You haven't picked up a 'bug' have you?" She'd asked before hurrying into the back office. Moments later, Lloyd was in his doorway, watching her.

Good, she thought. He'll let me leave work. The three men were long gone, but it was excruciating to be there. She didn't feel safe. Her false identity was at risk. She needed to talk to Holt.

"Take the rest of the day, Rhonda." Lloyd pulled her into his office and sat her in an office chair. "You're pale, you don't feel well. I think you need to go home. So, go home. The customers don't need to wonder if their waitress is passing a virus on to them. Get your coat. You're off tomorrow anyway. See you, Monday."

Rhonda stumbled on the way out to her Camry. A blustery wind kicked up the fallen leaves and more of them swirled down from the trees. The musky scent of sycamore fell in a cloud around her as she slid into the driver's seat.

She wondered about the boy. She wondered about Claire. They had to talk to her. She would drive Claire's SUV back to the B&B. For now, the vehicle still sat in the corner of the parking lot. Were Claire and Holt still at the hospital? What if Claire were more seriously injured than she'd thought?

Rhonda rolled down her window and sat in the car, letting the fresh autumn air clear her head. The last place she wanted to be was in the dismal bungalow. When she finally started the car, she left the lot and turned in the opposite direction on Route 66, away from the bungalow and toward her new home. If the movers were still there, she could get inside. Maybe she'd stay there overnight. Call Holt and ask him to pick up Samson and bring him over. Start her new life in the house one night early.

Little kids in costume, racing ahead of their parents, were already making their way from house to house. When her children had been young, she hadn't had a lot of money, so many of their costumes were home-made. Old shirts became ball gowns and worn-out jeans morphed into chaps and a vest. A couple of times, she'd bought them pre-made kiddie costumes of flimsy material worn over regular clothing. A plastic head mask secured with elastic, with holes for eyes, nostrils, and mouth, fit snugly over their faces.

The kids had faithfully pulled on the masks while waiting on porches for the homeowners to bring them candy. In between houses, they pushed the masks back onto the top of their heads.

Her heart ached. Although those days were gone, she'd hoped to recreate them with the grandkids—if there were grandkids. She pulled the car over to a side street and sobbed. Once the tears had dried on her cheeks, she drove off again, following the directions Holt had given her through town to her new home.

* * *

The houses in Dunaway Acres were brick ranch-style homes, built in the late 80s or early 90s. A nice step up from her 40s bungalow. Most front yards boasted a mature tree, sometimes two, each soaring 30-50 feet into the air. The immaculate lawns and trimmed bushes indicated that these homeowners had money to spend on lawn care or cared enough to do a good job themselves.

Halloween decorations festooned the trees and front porches. Cobwebs, jack-o-lanterns, ghosts, and scarecrows hung from trees and gutters. A witch clung to a telephone pole, her face smashed into the side, her broom protruding. It was a homey neighborhood, like so many in Austin.

Would she ever see Austin again? Maybe, if other members of the drug gang were captured. Otherwise, she'd make a visit to the city on the sly, a quick drive-by, a look through the car window with tears blurring the scene.

She braked to a stop at a corner stop sign. Two kids and their parents crossed the street in front of her. She glanced at the street numbers. Her new place was ahead on the right. A furniture delivery truck sat in the driveway.

A truck horn blared behind her. She glanced in the rear-view mirror. The driver of the red truck wore a black ball cap and had a thick black mustache. He grinned. She accelerated through the intersection, passed the house that would soon be her home, and drove on.

Rhonda fumbled for her phone, keeping her eyes alert for children and parents. The street was crawling with them.

She punched Holt's number on autodial and waited.

His voice mail came on.

"Holt, please pick up. Holt." She waited an instant. The message clicked off. She punched autodial again.

"Holt, it's me. The red truck is following me. I'm near my new place. I don't know where to go. I don't want to lead them back to the bungalow. Where do I go? A convenience store? There's a Quik Trip on the corner. Meet me there?"

She clicked off the phone and pulled in, parking her car in a handicapped space by the front door. She locked the doors and searched the front seat for something to use as a weapon. Candy wrapper on the floor. Instruction manual in the glove box. Tissue box beneath the passenger seat, next to a small, collapsed umbrella. She squeezed her upper body between the front seats to look at the rear bench seat. Empty. An ice scraper lay on the floorboard.

Rhonda grabbed the ice scraper and the small umbrella and waited for something to happen.

Chapter 37
Claire

Claire tried to relax. The television program was annoying, a talk show that seemed to condone bad behavior in teenagers while they 'found' themselves. She didn't want to hear it. She was living her own bad behavior nightmare. Would she ever see Cade again? Had he run away? Or had something happened to him? Had Neve's uncle done something to him?

There was nothing abnormal about teenagers getting in verbal fights with their significant others. Cade had told her a little, but she wanted more information. Had it really been about the uncle, about Cade wanting to protect her? The uncle was certainly a threat.

Why was it that these days, her son only responded to questions when she'd made him angry. She didn't relish provoking him to that point.

Their arguments reminded her too much of those she and Tom had had during their five-year marriage. Their relationship had always been tumultuous, but she'd thought, as so many young women did, that things would get better once they were married. Instead, he'd demanded more of her and cut her off from friends and family at every opportunity. Finally, after a girlfriend pointed out that Tom had control issues, she decided it had to stop. She'd found an apartment and enlisted a friend to help move Cade and her on a Saturday morning when Tom would be fishing.

Early that Saturday morning, her husband had risen early, and, as soon as he had backed out of the driveway, she got up. She filled the boxes she'd had in the back of her old SUV with plates, silverware, and cookware, a few bed linens, and towels. Two hours later, she and Cade pulled out of the driveway of their home and headed to their new place. Behind them, in a Ford F150, came her friend with Cade's twin bed, her grandmother's sewing machine, two folding chairs, and tv trays.

She'd never felt so frightened or so exhilarated. Later, her lawyers told her that she hadn't quite done it the right way. She should have asked Tom to move out, talked about division of property, talked about how a separation would affect their son, and gotten his responses in writing. Sounded easy enough. But getting a man with a hair trigger temper to do it was another story. She had been more frightened of those talks, and the way he would react—violently—than she was about the act of leaving her husband without a word. In the end it had worked out for the best.

Claire wished she could see more through the curtained window. Although she'd drawn the drapes to one side, the sheers prevented any view of the sky. She lowered the volume on the television. Outside, she heard laughter and children squealing.

She remembered seeing a sign the day they arrived that said the B&B's lawn would host a celebration late this afternoon for the church next door. She imagined that booths would be set up like a country fair, with bobbing for apples at one, a dart game for prizes at another, a beanbag toss, a dunk tank, and maybe even a scary 'ghost' tent.

Volunteers would hand out candy somewhere, and caramel apples. It had probably already started, the noise level outside had increased. Soon, the yard would be a frenzy of activity.

Someone knocked on the door. "Who is it?" she called. She didn't want to get up and wished that Della or Betsy would come back to the room so that one of them could answer the door.

"Trick or treat!" Little voices yelled.

"Sorry, I don't have any candy," she called. She did have some coins in her purse. She inched to the edge of the bed and slowly sat upright. If anyone else came trick or treating, she could give them a quarter.

She dug all the quarters out from the bottom of her purse and lined them up on the bedside table. Quivering, she moved to the edge of the bed, and then carefully, step by step, she crossed the bedroom, the coins clutched in one fist. She laid them out on the end table by the outside door and sat in the armchair, ready. She could take care of six kids, and then she'd have to do what she did at home when she ran out of candy: stop answering the door.

Another knock came. She called, "Who is it?"

"Trick or treat!!" high voices responded. She used the arms of the chair to push herself to her feet, took a step to one side and opened the door, smiling, quarters in hand.

The men shoved into the room. Claire tumbled backwards toward the chair. As they reached for her, she kicked out, swung her fists. One man grabbed her hands, the other her feet. She bucked and twisted, screamed. But a third man shoved something into her mouth and slammed his fist into her face.

Chapter 38
Holt

Holt hunched over his desk and glared at the computer. He didn't like what he was seeing. He was gathering the pieces, trying to tie them together. It was like working a jigsaw puzzle and not being able to connect two areas of the puzzle. Where was the missing piece?

He'd used the whiteboard in his office to sketch out the two women in his life, the two mysteries that had developed. One might not be a mystery, but the second most certainly was, and a dangerous one.

He studied the wall beside him.

Rhonda – he'd titled the board. And below that, pictures:

- Renee Trammel, disheveled, as they'd found her at the lake.
- The small vet clinic operating room, blood spattered.
- The animal recovery area, only one crate occupied, frightened brown eyes staring.
- A man, bloody, gunshot wounds to the arms and knees.
- A woman, in the reception area, lying on her side, a bullet through her heart.

- A man, medium build, pale, brown hair. Cuts on his face, neck, torso. Drowned.
- Another man. At booking, in the police station. 70 inches tall. Deep set dark eyes. Scar above right temple. Scar on left jaw line. Ornate cross tattoo on his neck.
- Suspect sketches of three people. A 'Wanted' poster for one. BOLOs for two.

And below the board, a narrow table with files. Emails, reports, notices, memos. Folders dating back two years. Inside the files were more pictures, suspect sketches, memos, notations.

But there was more. He'd added a column and listed more items:

- Murdered woman, stabbed, cod=carbon monoxide poisoning.
- Dead cats at old motor court, cod= carbon monoxide. Two microchips. Owners Sheila Biggs, Della Munoz.
- Dead mouse at Rhonda's house. Break-in or keyed entry?
- Dead cat in Rhonda's yard.
- Environmental meeting
- Red truck
- Diner customers: Three men. One overheard saying, "she was dead, I'm sure."

And then to the right, at the end of the board, what he'd written there a few hours ago. Because he had a feeling. Just a feeling.

Claire: the headline. And beneath it, he'd written in All Caps:

- Route 66 news feature.
- Barrel racing event at the Round-up Club arena.
- Cade
- Neve
- Neve's grandma. Creek Indian. Toxic landfill ooze?
- Environmental meeting
- Claire injured in fall.
- A sketch of the man Claire had fought with, and a brief description. Late 20s to early 30s, black mustache, black ball cap. Red truck. Name=Kai? (Neve's uncle)

He saw two connections between the two cases: the environmental meeting, and the red truck. Every muscle in his body screamed with tension.

He closed his eyes and peered into the blackness. He needed time to think. Claire was safe at the B&B, and Rhonda was at work. Another hour, then he'd check in with both, and the three of them would have their heart-to-heart at the cafe.

He dreaded it. But it was necessary. He wasn't worried about how Claire would react. He trusted her with his every confidence. He was a fool for having kept things from her for so long. He'd been burned once when his confidence in someone had been betrayed. Someone he had been protecting had been compromised, and as a result, killed. Once was enough. He couldn't risk it again. But things were different with Claire. She kept things to herself, just like he did. He had no doubts he could trust her with his life.

He focused on the whiteboards, sifted through everything he knew and sorted through the possibilities. He made a few phone calls, ordered some directives.

Then he went into the bathroom and turned on the shower.

His phone, lying on the table where he'd dropped his keys, lit up as he closed the shower door and let the needles of water pound his tense shoulders.

Chapter 39
Rhonda

Rhonda huddled in the driver's seat of her Camry. Cars pulled up to the pumps, owners pumped gas, got back in their cars and drove away. SUVs parked beside her, kids in costumes piled out and tramped into the store while a parent pumped gas. The little ones rushed from the store with soft drinks or bottled water. Young men driving trucks parked a few spaces away. They went inside the store, laughing, and appeared minutes later with 6-packs of beer.

She kept an eye on the rearview mirror. Where was Holt?

Had he gotten her message? Maybe he was still at the hospital. Claire could have taken a turn for the worse.

She punched his number into her phone and listened as it rang and then went to voice mail again. "Holt. Where are you? I'm at the Quik Trip. They were following me, but they haven't come here. Should I go home? Call me. Please."

She dropped the phone into her lap. She took deep breaths.

Since when did she get so dependent on someone else to tell her what to do? She'd always been independent. Insisted on going to vet school despite her father's obvious scorn for her chosen profession. *An animal doctor? Why not a people doctor? That's where a doctor makes a difference.*

His opinion hadn't changed her desire. It hurt that he didn't trust her heart. Vet school had been just as hard. She'd spent long hours studying, conducting difficult experiments on living animals. She and her fellow students had done cadaver work, learned each muscle, organ, bone, and soft tissue in mammals, reptiles, amphibians, and fish. During her small animal rotation, she learned even more about the cats, dogs, pot-bellied pigs, rabbits, and guinea pigs she might be caring for in the future.

So why couldn't she decide what to do and where to go at this moment?

Her mind jumped backward.

Daniel read the morning paper, sitting on a barstool at the black granite-topped island in their kitchen. The bacon sizzled, and she cooked the eggs until they were no longer runny. Through the wide window behind Daniel, the gray and white trunks of giant sycamores gleamed in the early morning light. The rolling yellow rangeland behind them glowed.

"Hot today," Daniel had said. He sipped from his coffee mug. His warm blue eyes looked at her; a smile slipped over her face. Twenty-two years of marriage and two grown children later, his look still made her tingle. She scooted his plate of eggs, toast, and bacon across the island, then carried her own plate over and climbed up on the stool beside him. "And it's going to be a busy one, too. The morning is booked."

Daniel ate quickly. Finished, he sat back on the stool and stretched his arms over his head. His left hand touched her shoulder and then trailed down her back. Her entire body warmed.

At that moment, she had believed that life—her life— couldn't be more perfect.

Someone banged on the car window. Rhonda startled. A white mask with drooping black ovals for eyes stared in. The saliva in her mouth dried up.

The mask lifted. A teenager laughed and pointed at her. His companions guffawed and elbowed each other. They rushed to a car parked several yards away, two of them stopped to gawk and point at a Vintage Cadillac Eldorado with its trademark giant red fins that had just pulled into a parking spot.

Her heart slowed. She couldn't sit here forever, she had to go somewhere. The red truck and its occupants might still be out on the street, watching for her, waiting to follow her.

Rhonda backed out of the parking space and drove away. Tiny's Diner was a few blocks away. People would be there. She'd go inside and wait. The men in the red truck wouldn't dare do anything to her if she were in the diner, would they?

A half dozen cars had parked near the diner's front door. She pulled in next to them so she could see her car through the front windows, from inside the building. She sent Holt a text—*At Tiny's now*—dropped her phone into her purse and ran into the diner, locking the car doors using her key fob.

Once inside, she slid into a corner booth where she had a clear view of her car and anyone approaching the restaurant.

Vivian was taking an order a few tables away. When she finished, she sauntered over. "You're not supposed to be here. You're not working. And you've still got on your uniform. Why're you here?" She tapped her long, pink fingernails on the Formica tabletop.

"I'm waiting for someone." Rhonda tried to compose herself, letting her fluttering heart slow to a steadier rhythm.

"Jillion other places to meet up, you know? Like a bar?" Vivian frowned at her. "Something wrong?"

"Lots of trick-or-treaters out there. Streets are busy. You had any in here?" Her voice quivered. *Why is my heart still pounding?*

"Why would we? No candy here. Except maybe you. Eye candy." Vivian snorted.

"I don't need anything. If you want this booth, I'll move somewhere else." But if she moved to another open table, could she still watch her car, still see the men if they approached the café?

"You're not in my way. Jean's got this section tonight. And as you noticed, no one is sitting here. I'll bring you a glass of water." Vivian eyed her, head tilted.

"You don't have to do that."

"But I want to," the waitress said. "I'll bring coffee. One cream, one sugar. That right?" Vivian's voice had lost its snarky tone.

"Yes. Thank you." She eyed the soda fountain counter, where two teenagers sat drinking malts. She frowned. She'd worked that counter so many times, something had changed. Then she knew. Someone had taken down the photos on either end of the mirror. In their places were photographs of palm trees, a pier, and a beach. A hand-printed sign beside the pier picture read, 'The End of the Road, - Santa Monica Pier, Pacific Ocean.' Why had Lloyd changed the display? Could be he often did, she'd only been here a week. How could she know what he did, or why he did it?

Vivian sauntered to the coffee service, filled a cup, and brought it to her. "Here you go, Rhonda. How 'bout a piece of pie while you wait? Got one coconut crème left. Or a slice of cherry."

"No pie, thanks." She wasn't hungry, but lunch with Claire had been hours ago. Her stomach roiled at the smell of the coffee. *How is Claire? Where is Holt? And why is Vivian being nice?* "Lloyd changed the photos behind the soda fountain."

Vivian looked over her shoulder at the photos and shrugged. "Hmmph. I hadn't even noticed. He's been grumpy today. I think that meeting this morning set him off. Maybe he's decided to go see the Pacific. Long as someone signs my paycheck, who cares?"

Rhonda glanced out the window. No red truck. She hoped that Claire's Jeep was still in the employee's lot where they'd left it hours ago. She couldn't see it from here.

She punched autodial on her phone again. The call clicked over to voice mail. "Holt? I'm at Tiny's. Can you come, please?"

A car drove up outside and a young couple got out in Halloween costumes, she, dressed as a tempting princess and he, wearing a clown suit. They entered the diner and glanced around the dining room. Their looks rested on her. She wasn't on duty but was still wearing her uniform. She buttoned her cardigan sweater, covering up the pocket and the stitching that read, *Rhonda.*

She took a tiny sip of coffee and glanced out the window. Night was falling. Leaves were swirling. The streetlights came on. Why didn't Holt call?

Three policemen entered, laughing. They took a table not far from the front door. Rhonda felt the muscles in her back relax. She was safe here with the police on guard. The diner dimmed.

A policeman stood outside her hospital room, and another uniformed man stood inside the doorway. Her body ached because of the deep, empty hole in the cavity where her heart had been. The scratches all over her legs and arms didn't bother her like the hole did.

She'd been crying when a man dressed in khakis and a light blue golf shirt entered the hospital room. He signaled the guard, and the guard stepped out.

"Is my husband alive?" Her voice emerged soft and cracked.

Sorry lines bracketed the man's blue-gray eyes. "There was a man named Carson McVeigh, and your employee, Susanna. Did McVeigh bring the dog in?"

Cold settled like a damp fog around her. She nodded. "It was a stray. He wanted to help it."

Carson McVeigh had loved animals, but not people. Susanna had loved animals and people, like her and Daniel. Their life had been so complete. They'd been doing what they could to make life easier for animals and the people who loved them.

And it had gotten them all killed.

The man held out the pouch she had tucked into the pocket of her shorts earlier at the clinic. "We've been after this drug dealer for a long time. And now we're the closest we've ever been. We just apprehended one of his top men at your clinic. And the local police are dragging the lake for you."

The shivering started in her head and moved down each limb of her body.

"We need your help. You saw the killers. They think you're dead. Will you testify, once we've got all the evidence gathered?"

"They'll kill me if they find out I'm alive, won't they?"

"Not if we can help it."

"But what about my family? My children. My parents. You've got to protect them, too."

"We will. But everyone must think you're dead, that there are no witnesses. Maybe they'll drop their guard enough that we can pick up the rest of the gang. Will you agree?"

Jean slipped into the bench seat on the other side of the booth. "Rhonda? You're white as a lily on a fresh-turned grave. What's going on?"

Rhonda let out the sigh she'd unwillingly been holding. "I'm meeting someone. That's all. I'm not having a good day."

"No, you're not. You haven't been home to change your clothes. And that Jeep you left here at lunchtime is still out there. Lloyd asked about it. Think you can move it? He might have it towed."

"He wouldn't do that without talking to me first, would he?"

Jean shrugged. "Don't know. Maybe."

Rhonda reached into her purse for Claire's keys. "I'll move it. Could you walk out with me? It's dark in that corner."

"Think the boogeyman will get you? Sheesh. Guess it is Halloween. Michael Myers might show up early around here, though." She glanced at the few customers and then scooted out of the booth. "Let's go now, before somebody new comes in."

Together, they passed through the dining room and the kitchen and out the back door. Claire's SUV sat in the far corner. Their footsteps crunched on the gravel as they crossed the lot and came up to the car.

"Hey," Jean muttered. "Looks like someone's taking a nap in the front seat. Is that your friend?"

Rhonda squinted through the side window. Then she jerked the SUV door open and reached in to feel the man's neck. There was no pulse. She stared into the dead man's face.

"I'll call 911," Jean said, moving back a few feet. "Sheesh."

Rhonda took another look at the man and reached for Jean's arm. "Don't call yet." She touched his icy gray hand.

"Why the hell not? There's a dead man in this car."

Rhonda shook her head. "Give me a minute. I need to call someone."

"A minute is all you get. Something's getting riper by the second." Jean covered her mouth and stepped back, farther away from the SUV and the corpse. The smell of overripe vegetation rose from the car.

The remains of their salad lunches had been in the heating car all afternoon.

Rhonda grabbed her phone from her purse and called Holt again, praying 'please pick up' each second that passed.

The phone clicked as he answered. "Rhonda? Got your messages. I've just left the office. I'm on the way to the café." Holt sounded harried.

"Holt. Thank God."

"You sound panicked. What's happened?"

"Get here fast. There's a dead body in your friend's SUV, here at the diner."

Chapter 40
Claire

Slowly, Claire became aware of her surroundings. The room was warm, the air close, with the scent of decay, rotting wood and … something else. Another odor, something unpleasant she'd recently smelled. Where? The B&B? The arena? Her pounding brain couldn't name it.

Her arms ached, and she couldn't move them, they were secured together at the wrist, behind her back.

Claire tried to swallow but her mouth was dry. Something stretched across her mouth, she could neither open nor close it.

Claire strained to peer through the blackness around her. Where was she? A vague memory crept in. She'd pulled the B&B door open, and someone rushed in. The sound she made wasn't any word she knew. She moved her jaw trying to shift the gag. It cut into her lips.

She squirmed and tried to move her tingling legs. They were tied together, knees bent; she was unable to straighten them.

The floor beneath her had a little padding, enough so that when she shifted, her legs started tingling. She tried to sit up but couldn't. Claire searched the darkness. Across from her, one area was not as black as the rest. A window? A doorway?

Faint voices spoke outside the room, but she couldn't make out any words. Were they both men? She wasn't certain. One voice sounded vaguely familiar, but his words came out in an angry snarl. What were they talking about? Their voices came louder, faster. Arguing.

Her head pounded, and she hurt everywhere. They'd tied her in an uncomfortable position. She tried to shift her body. Pain shot through her every nerve, stabbing her back and every limb. She gulped in a breath and let it out slowly, trying to ease the pain. She wouldn't move again.

Claire concentrated on breathing deeply and slowly. What had happened? She'd heard children's voices, but when she opened her outside door to pass out the quarters she'd salvaged from her purse, it had not been children wanting a treat.

She closed her eyes in the darkness, hoping to catch a glimpse of memory, but the men had moved quickly. She had no recollection of their faces. How did she know they were men? The smell of their bodies. Sweat, adrenaline? And the faint scent of spices. Cumin.

She smelled it in the room now. As well as the scent of … gasoline.

What did they want with her? She'd argued with the man at the Round-up Club. Was he behind this? Why would Neve's uncle carry it so far? Kidnapping? Murder? Why would a simple meth dealer take such a drastic action?

He'd been trying to sell drugs to the teenagers.

Claire brooded about Neve's grandmother. Did she know her son was selling kids drugs? Did she know that he'd hit Neve? Why was she protecting him?

Something rustled several feet from her. Her heart stopped. She lay very still. The rustling came again.

Her heart hammered. Was there a rodent in the room with her? Another animal? Another captive?

She reached with her fingers as far as she could with her wrists bound. Her fingertips touched wire. A cage. The rustling was close. In the cage?

Claire poked a finger into the wire cage. Whatever it was inside the cage moved, rustled closer. What would be in a cage? Her mind raced through the possibilities. A rabbit? A guinea pig? A mouse? A snake?

She jerked her finger out of the cage. Whatever animal was in the cage could stay in the cage. She didn't need to know what it was. Didn't want to know what it was.

Her heart pounded, and she hurt everywhere. Her mind was still foggy with the medicine the nurses had given her at the hospital. She closed her eyes and imagined she was somewhere else. Stretched out, on the sand, with ocean waves crashing nearby and an ocean wind caressing her skin.

Chapter 41
Holt

Holt turned into the parking lot of the diner and navigated around police cars and an ambulance to the employee's lot behind the building. He scanned the crowded lot and found Claire's Jeep in the corner, surrounded by uniforms, a trio of EMTs, and a man in white coveralls whom he suspected was the coroner. Off to one side, Rhonda, still in her waitress uniform, stood with her arms crossed next to another waitress. Nearby, Lloyd gestured as he spoke to the police.

"Crap," Holt muttered. He had to nip this in the bud. Rhonda's cover would be blown to smithereens. "Who's in charge?" he blared into the crowd as he displayed his US Marshals' badge and credentials. "I need to speak to the officer in charge."

A man in a suit who'd been talking with Lloyd stepped back from the older man and glared. "That's me, Detective Stanton. And you are ..." He reached for Holt's credentials and studied them. "What's your interest here? This is a crime scene. We have a body."

"I need to speak to you privately."

"Well, I'm a little busy."

"You can use my office," Lloyd said. "I'll show you." Lloyd started toward the back door of the diner. The police detective shrugged and motioned for Holt to follow. "I've got about one minute."

"I won't take much of your time." He hoped the detective would grasp the situation quickly so he could get Rhonda out of here.

Lloyd led them in and then closed the office door once the two men were inside.

Holt cleared his throat. "You've got a crime scene. But one of the women who found the body is in the Witness Protection Program. I need for you to release her at once. She's a crucial witness in a drug investigation. Lloyd, the diner's owner, has employed her. He's former CIA."

The detective pulled back. "Oh? Witness Protection. Lloyd, CIA?"

Holt explained the situation succinctly as Stanton listened.

"Okay," the detective agreed. "I'll get a few details from the ladies, then they can go. If I need further information from her or Lloyd, I'll have the sergeant go through you to get it."

"Thank you." Holt pulled out his card wallet, slid out a business card and handed it to Stanton.

They left Lloyd's office and rejoined the group in the parking lot. A van with Crime Scene Investigation printed on the side doors had arrived, and the investigators, clothed in white jumpsuits, scurried around the scene. A caravan of vintage cars, including a Chevy Bel Air and a Ford Thunderbird, had pulled in and parked in available spaces.

Holt led Stanton to the waitresses, then stood back and let him question the women. Warily, he scanned the crowd of onlookers. Every person here was a potential suspect. Any of them could have returned to the crime scene. He hoped other officers were taking note. His primary duty was to protect Rhonda's identity by making everything seem as normal as possible.

The detective asked questions. Rhonda's voice shook and her look scanned the crowded parking lot as she answered. When she glanced at him, Holt met her look and held it steady, nodding, willing her to calm down.

The other waitress—her name was Jean—was abrupt, no-nonsense. "We came out here to move her friend's SUV before Lloyd had it towed. Saw someone inside, and when Rhonda opened the door and saw the guy was dead, she told me to call 911."

Stanton made a few notes. "I'd like for you both to come down to the office at your convenience tomorrow, so we can get your prints and check them against any on or in the vehicle. You said you were in this SUV earlier today with the owner … Claire Northcutt?" he asked Rhonda as he checked his notes. "Where is Ms. Northcutt now?"

"At the B&B where she is staying. She had an accident at the Round-up Club arena this afternoon and went to the hospital. I drove this Jeep back here to finish my shift." Rhonda had regained control of her voice. It had stopped shaking, but Holt could see her hands were still trembling.

"Okay. I'll check in with Ms. Northcutt. Thank you, ladies. That's all I need for now. I have your contact information."

Rhonda didn't look at Holt as she hurried into the diner with the other waitress, Jean.

Holt rubbed the back of his neck. He didn't like this one bit. Why was there a dead body in Claire's SUV?

He wandered toward the front of the diner, went inside, and sat at a table close to the kitchen. A few minutes passed, but none of the staff entered the dining area. He got up and went through the swinging door into the kitchen.

Lloyd stood outside his office, talking to Rhonda and Jean. He nodded at Holt.

"Excuse me a minute, ladies. I need to speak with this gentleman," Lloyd stepped into his office, and Holt followed, closing the door behind him.

"What's your take on what happened?" Holt asked.

"I have no idea. But I think Rhonda recognized the stiff."

"I need to talk to her, but I need to talk to Jean, too. I've got to tell her who I am."

"She already knows you must be law enforcement after you spoke with the detective," Lloyd said with a smug smile.

"Send her in. I'll be brief, and then I'll talk to Rhonda."

"Okay. I'll grab the paychecks. Today's payday. Might as well brighten the day up for them if I can." Lloyd pulled an envelope from the middle desk drawer and stuffed it into his shirt pocket.

Holt crossed his arms and leaned against Lloyd's desk as the man left the room.

When Jean entered, she squinted at him. "So, who are you? I've seen you in here before, haven't I?"

"You have. I like to eat here. I'm with the DEA, Drug Enforcement Agency, Department of Justice. I was in the area. Heard about the dead body on my scanner. Any idea who he was?"

"Didn't look at him. Didn't want to. And you didn't hear this on your scanner. Rhonda called you, didn't she?"

"Truth is, Rhonda is my sister." He'd decided early on that if anyone connected him and Rhonda, that would be his response. The 'family' angle cleared up a lot of things and got both he and Renee off the hook.

"Your sister? I don't see any family resemblance."
She frowned.

He shrugged. "I was adopted. Doctors told my
parents they couldn't have kids, so they adopted me, and
then, bang, Mom gets pregnant with Rhonda. Guess it
happens a lot."

"Well, okay then. You should talk to your sister."
Jean stepped closer to the door.

"I'm glad you were with her when she found that
body. Sis doesn't hold up well under stressful situations."

"And she already wasn't feeling well today. She left
her shift early, then came back. But maybe you knew that."

He nodded, although he didn't know it. In the
messages she'd left on his phone, she'd sounded stressed.
And scared. "Thank you, Jean. I need to talk to my sister,
and you should probably get back to your customers."

Jean pulled the door open and held it. "I enjoyed
meeting your brother," she said with a wink as Rhonda
stepped past her.

Rhonda faked a smile. Holt saw pain there, and the
same worry and despair he'd been seeing on her face all
week. The door closed behind Jean.

"Holt, the dead man, it's the man who knocked Claire
off the bleachers today. Neve's uncle. Kai," she whispered
hoarsely.

Chapter 42
Rhonda

"I'm sure it was him. And he came into the café this afternoon with the two men I told you about from earlier this week. Now he's dead. Why is his body in Claire's SUV?" Rhonda's ears buzzed and her head pounded. "The men who were with him must have killed him after I left. And then dumped his body."

"Neve's uncle? I'll let the detective know. The coroner will determine how he died and time of death. Someone will speak with known associates."

"Why is he in Claire's Jeep?" Rhonda sputtered. "It looks bad for Claire. He assaulted her this afternoon."

"Could be it was opportunistic. An unlocked SUV, and the killer needed someplace to stash the body. It could have nothing to do with Claire, and certainly not with you."

She shook her head. Holt was trying to calm her, but it wasn't working. He didn't understand. "Or it could be … a warning. They saw me park the SUV earlier, and they know I overheard them in the diner. Kai saw me after the incident at the arena. He spoke to me here when he came in with those other men."

"Rhonda, calm down. You can't let everyone see you this upset."

Why should she care about that now? She'd found a dead man. And two groups could be stalking her, a local gang and the drug dealers. How could she evade both? Her teeth chattered, she pulled at her sweater, wishing it were a thick winter coat.

"Did Claire tell you what Neve's grandmother said?" Rhonda asked.

Holt's eyebrows lifted. "No. After the accident, when we were at the B&B, I told Claire everything I know about Cade's whereabouts. One of the owners came by and offered to stay with her while I looked for him. I talked to a few people and went to my office to review the information."

"Holt, the grandmother thinks that toxic waste from a landfill is oozing onto her property. She told Claire her son Kai was going to take care of it for her. Claire was at that meeting this morning. Could it be that whoever caused the pollution killed Neve's uncle and left him in her SUV to warn Claire not to write anything about it in her article?"

She could see Holt's brain working behind his intelligent blue-gray eyes.

"So, you think the uncle was playing vigilante and the polluters took him out?"

"Maybe," Rhonda chewed at a fingernail. She remembered a conversation she'd overheard. "There's something else, Holt."

"Tell me."

"Earlier this week, I overheard the mayor talking to his cronies when he was having lunch at the diner. I was near the counter where he was sitting."

"And?"

"He said something about getting the reporter out of town before she had a chance to talk to the old Indian woman. I think he was talking about Claire, and about

Neve's grandmother. Maybe it was about the old landfill, and the toxic waste."

"That's a lot of circumstantial supposition, Rhonda."

"It makes sense. Especially after talking with Claire over lunch." She watched his face. It was now, or never. She had to ask. "And I'm wondering something else, Holt. Who is she to you?" Rhonda wasn't interested in dating this man, but she cared about him. And she also cared about his friend, Claire.

Holt shuttered his eyes, making them unreadable.

"And why don't I know anything about you? Have you been married? Do you have children? Why so secret, Holt?"

"How did this suddenly go from all about the dead body to Claire and then me?" His look was not quite a glare. "Get back on track. Anything else about the dead man, Kai?"

Rhonda consciously lowered her shoulders and took a deep breath. "I want relief from the unknowns, Holt. I need facts I can hang on to. I haven't got anything else right now. Could you answer my questions, please?"

Holt tossed her an exasperated look and sighed. "You know I'm with the DEA. Claire doesn't know what my job is. I don't want her to know. I don't want her to worry. I care too much—"

Someone knocked on the office door. He jerked it open. Detective Stanton stood at the threshold.

"Checked with the B&B about your friend, Claire Northcutt. The police are there now. Somebody reported a possible abduction, but it may have been a Halloween prank. Your friend Claire is missing."

Chapter 43
Claire

Claire's throat was raw, her hands and feet ached from reduced blood flow. Her face pressed against the hard floor, her cheek was numb.

She tried, unsuccessfully, to roll over. The effort exhausted her. She took a deep breath and then another, breathing through her nose.

The gag, tied tightly over her mouth, tasted stale, and vaguely of laundry detergent. She tried to swallow. The gag had soaked up any moisture her mouth created.

The silent blackness pressed around her with a nauseating odor of gasoline.

Once again, she tried to roll, and this time, she made it from one side to the other. She peered into the blackness and listened. Something scuttled in the corner of the room, scratching at the floor or the wall. A rat?

The idea of sharing the room with a rat didn't frighten her. But the idea of a hungry rodent, deciding that one of her fingers would make a good lunch, did.

Whatever was in the cage moved again, rustling the material on the bottom of the cage.

She panted as she squirmed, trying to move her hands and create space beneath the binding ropes while at the same time wiggling her feet, hoping to work them out of the binds. The knots were too tight. She was helpless.

Her whole body pounded with her heartbeat. Panic set in. She gulped air. She couldn't breathe.

Claire closed her eyes and willed herself to relax. Someone at the B&B, during the Halloween revelry, could have seen her kidnapping and reported it. Della would have come back to the room and found her gone. She would have called Holt.

Holt would search for her. He'd contact the local police. He would do all he could to find her. He wouldn't give up.

Until he found her, she was on her own. If he found her. The dark consumed her. If … She had to save herself.

Claire peered into the blackness for a hint of daylight. Nothing. If it were night, there would be moonlight peeking in somewhere, she reasoned. There was a full moon outside. Blackout material must cover the windows and doors of the room they'd put her in.

She focused on the smell of dust and mildew in the air. Underneath it, an acrid scent tickled the lining of her nose. Gasoline.

She lay still. Something—the rat? —scratched at the wall again. The thing in the cage rustled.

Darkness pressed onto her like plastic cling wrap. In her head, thoughts swam in rainbow colors. Cade's light swirled green for youth, energy, and the intense love, laced with frustration, that she felt for her son. All the memories. How she'd tried to cover the despair she felt at the divorce; how she'd smile and wave when his dad picked him up for the weekend, a weekend she'd spend alone, either working or riding her horse.

Her nephew, Denver, had saved her from that aloneness when he returned from Afghanistan. Wounded, and suffering from PTSD, he had grabbed her focus, pulled her out of a pool of self-pity. She loved Denver like a son. He had found love, and married, and even though he was still a big brother to Cade, he wasn't living with them like before, he wasn't there to see Cade through these last months before college.

He'd wanted to come with them this weekend, but his family needed him at home. If he had come, this wouldn't have happened.

She imagined Cade to be a typical teen, dealing with his own intense problems of young love and the anxiety that comes with it, and the freedom he would soon experience at college. For her, it meant separation. How will it feel to live alone in the country house they shared? A shadow crept into her mind at the thought of living alone. But she wouldn't be entirely alone. She had Ranger, the big black dog she'd adopted from the mustang ranch. He was always by her side. But he wasn't here now. She'd left him with Denver, a decision she regretted. Ranger never would have let someone grab her like those men had.

Thoughts of Holt swirled blue, a throbbing blue, somehow laced with a pink heartbeat that grew and then receded. Holt had saved her, too. What if she never saw him again? What if HE didn't survive this assignment with Rhonda? Her insides wrenched. He had wormed his way into her life, and she'd taken his presence for granted, gotten used to their odd relationship.

That relationship was like a sword fight between two warriors, one charging in ablaze with energy, the other falling back, biding their time. Then, that second warrior went on the offense, clashing swords, a near miss on the arm before another fall back. With certainty, she didn't want to fight anymore. She wanted him in her life. No swords.

For all the irritations and annoyances, she loved him. He was handsome with his cute dimples and sparkling eyes, but that wasn't what she loved. What set him apart were the annoyances, the way he was so truly himself. His thoughts were obvious to her by the set of his lips, the glint in his eye, the tilt of his head.

What if she never had the chance to tell him? What if it was too late?

What if he was in love with Rhonda? Sadness and despair swelled in her mind. She liked Rhonda, but she didn't want to lose Holt. Claire wasn't sure what she'd seen between the two of them. They had a bond, yes, but was it love? She didn't think so. Even if it weren't, she'd pushed him away for so long. What if it truly was too late for things to work between them?

Claire struggled on the floor, fighting against the bonds on her wrists and feet while the rainbow swirled in her mind. She'd been struggling to get out of the boredom of her life. She'd imagined this news article would be the way. It wasn't. The way out was living right next door. Holt.

Her efforts increased. The knot slipped a bit.

Chapter 44
Holt

Holt and Rhonda raced out of the diner. He pulled up his cell phone and punched in the phone number Detective Stanton had given him. He identified himself.

"I'm headed to the scene now. What can you tell me before I get there? I'm working a case in the area that might have a direct connection with her disappearance."

"A festival was under way and the crowd on the lawn included adults and children in costume. A woman called 911 and reported seeing a couple of costumed men carry a woman to a car. Wondered if it was a prank at first, but the more she thought about it … So, she called. In the B&B, our detective found evidence of a struggle, but no blood. Claire Northcutt rented the room. I understand she had reported her son missing earlier today."

Holt's brain didn't want to accept this information. Why would someone abduct Claire? He blamed himself. He'd been out of touch, absorbed with Rhonda. Had Claire struck a raw nerve with someone she'd interviewed, or with someone who knew about her interviews? She'd talked to the mayor and an older man. And she'd spent time with Neve's grandmother.

"Any idea who might have taken Claire? Or why?" Rhonda's voice was low.

"Has to have something to do with her article, and the interviews."

"Or maybe her son? Could her disappearance be linked with his?"

Holt glanced at Rhonda. He hadn't worried enough about Cade's disappearance. It seemed like typical teenage behavior. The kid thought he was an adult; thought he could do whatever he wanted. And he was having girlfriend problems. If that wasn't a recipe for bad behavior, what was?

He gunned the vehicle and was about to pull out into the street when a fire truck blared its horn and roared past. He waited for the ladder truck to go by and then accelerated into the street behind it. The fire truck blared through several intersections before it turned. Onto Rhonda's street. He took the corner too fast, following the red engine.

Ahead on the next block another fire engine and several emergency vehicles barricaded the street. Smoke billowed in the air, and flames blazed from a house.

Rhonda peered ahead. She grabbed Holt's arm. "That's my neighbor's house. Mrs. P's house is on fire."

Holt braked to a stop behind a police car. They bolted from the truck and ran closer, until a policewoman threw out her hand and stopped them.

"Don't go any closer, ma'am, sir. Dangerous fire. They're still trying to get it under control."

"I live next door. My neighbor, Mrs. Petrovsky. Did she get out? And her dog, a Basset hound, Harry."

The policewoman shouted to a nearby fireman who had removed his headgear and was wiping his soot-covered face. "This woman says a lady and a dog live here. Did they get out?"

"Anyone find a woman or a dog?" the fireman shouted toward the crew fighting the blaze. Several firemen shook their heads. The fireman pulled on his headgear and jogged to the house, ducking as he entered through the front door.

Rhonda grabbed Holt's arm. "She never takes Harry with her when she leaves. He's in there, whether she is or not." She started toward the burning house.

He grabbed her shoulder. "Rhonda, wait. Let the firemen take care of it. If the dog's alive, they'll get him out."

Two ambulances roared up to the scene, sirens screaming, and parked behind the fire trucks.

Holt's mind churned. A bad feeling mushroomed in the pit of his stomach. Was there a connection between the fire and Rhonda?

Smoke billowed from the house as water shot from the plump fire hoses. Another pumper truck arrived. The crew of firemen unrolled a second hose and hooked it onto the hydrant. More water gushed onto the blazing house. The thick smoky air enveloped the gathered crowd, including children in Halloween costumes. People coughed and backed farther into the adjacent yards.

A fireman rushed out of the house through the dense smoke, cradling Harry in his arms. The Basset's ears flopped as the man hurried toward one of the ambulances. A second fireman carried a person out of the house.

"Oh, no," Rhonda whispered.

Holt pushed his way through the crowd toward the two ambulances, with Rhonda close behind.

"Stay back, please," an EMT cautioned as they approached.

"I live next door. Is Mrs. Petrovsky all right? And Harry? Is the dog okay?"

Holt considered pulling out his identification, asserting his authority, but didn't. He didn't need or want to get involved unless it was necessary. Claire was missing. She was his priority. Rhonda was upset, but he was of no use here, except to calm her.

The EMT shook her head. "We have yet to identify the woman. Both she and the dog need medical attention."

"Where will she be taken? And the dog?" Rhonda peered at the EMT.

The woman tucked a blanket around Harry and placed him in a cardboard box on the ambulance floor. "The dog will be taken to the local animal shelter after a veterinarian checks him out. Does your neighbor have family? Do you know her emergency contacts?"

Concern registered on Rhonda's face, but she closed her mouth and remained silent as she shook her head.

Someone shouted. Two firefighters appeared from the house, carrying another body. Rhonda and Holt stepped away from the ambulances as the doors opened. An EMT extended the interior's cot, and the fireman lay a man on it. Face and clothes blackened by smoke and soot; the person was unrecognizable. They quickly covered the entire body with a dark blanket.

"Mrs. P lived alone." Rhonda frowned as the medics shoved the collapsed gurney into the ambulance.

"Any identification?" Holt asked the EMT.

"Sorry sir. I don't have any information." The EMT closed the ambulance doors.

"Mrs. P wanted to talk to me the other night, before I found the dead mouse in the house. She couldn't sleep. Talked about her regrets. I wish she'd told me what she was so anxious about. Maybe I could have helped."

He wanted to get on with the urgent task of finding Claire. But he had a responsibility to Rhonda, too. The fire had upset her. "Was she a widow?"

"I think she was divorced. But I don't know. We hadn't spoken much. I never saw any visitors. No children, no grandchildren." Her ashen face glowed in the bright light from the temporary spotlights the firemen had erected to fight the blaze.

"We've got to go, Rhonda. Claire's been abducted." Holt touched her arm.

"I need to get Samson. He's probably frantic. I can't leave him here alone while this is happening. I'm sure he smells the smoke. And hears the sirens ..." As they watched, another ambulance and a police car screeched up to the scene.

It was a small request that would only take a moment. Holt nodded, and Rhonda trotted off across the yard to her house. He waited outside, watching the firefighters from a distance. The fire cast an eerie flickering light over the crowd. Some of them walked away.

Rhonda hurried up with Samson. The dog strained on his leash. "Samson was ready to get outside."

Holt eyed the dog warily. How was this going to go? Would Samson help or hinder the search for Claire?

Rhonda glanced back at the fire as they walked down the street to the truck. "Wait, Holt. That man. I know him."

"Who?" Holt pulled her further into the shadows as they looked back at the remaining onlookers. Rhonda indicated a figure across the street at the edge of the crowd, an elderly man wearing slacks and a light-colored cardigan sweater.

"The old man there, at the edge of the light. That's Howard Noble. From the diner. Why is he here?"

"Howard Noble," Holt repeated. The man Claire had interviewed yesterday for the Route 66 article.

He asked himself that same question. Why would Howard Noble be *here* at the scene of this fire in Rhonda's neighborhood?

Chapter 45
Rhonda

Rhonda opened the door to Holt's truck and lifted Samson in. A cloud of smoke circled around her. The world spun. She grabbed the strap near the door frame and hauled herself up and into the cab.

Mrs. P's house was gone. Her next-door neighbor and Harry were injured. And someone else was dead. Who?

It could have been her house, with her and Samson inside.

Samson scooted into her lap. She slammed the truck door and fastened her seatbelt., then scratched beneath his collar, and under his chin. What would she have grabbed and taken with her if the fire had been at her house?

A week ago, she'd left everything in her life behind, and not because of a fire.

Except for the clothes she'd worn when she ran from the vet clinic after the drug dealers burst in, nothing in this miserable house was part of her former life. Samson was the only connection to her past. Another dog had been the cause of her tragedy, brought to the vet clinic in great pain, with an internal blockage that turned out to be a bag of drugs.

What if the drug dealers had come after they'd left the clinic for the day? What if she'd been upstairs in the house, and heard them down below, yelling and shooting? Could she have figured a way out, even as their footsteps pounded up the stairs?

What if they'd torched the house? What if smoke had curled under the door of her bedroom and snaked with the air currents toward the ceiling? What would she have grabbed to take with her? What possession did she ache for?

She thought of the photo albums in the cabinet downstairs in her living room. All the memories, a century of memories. Smiles, vacation scenes, Halloween costumes, and stern ancestors staring into the camera, stoic and lifeless. Too much to carry with her. Too many memories. Times forgotten. Her history. Her family's history.

She thought of the small, quilted pillow that belonged to her great-grandmother, the odd little vase her mother had saved from her childhood, the crocheted pieces both her grandmothers had made, her father's humidor, her mother's jewelry, her childhood books, the 1904 sewing machine. There were the flags from two of her great-grandfather's coffins, commemorating their service in World War II, the flags themselves entombed in triangular cases and on display.

Rhonda could picture the items in her mind. They waited in her memory. Would she see them when this was over?

She wasn't sure she wanted to. Last weekend's events had changed her. Those things were distant memories, part of her past, part of who she was then. Familiar. The future was unfamiliar. Would she survive until all the drug dealers were caught and jailed?

As Holt put the truck in gear and Samson wriggled in her lap, she felt the tension of an unknown future. The horrific events of last Saturday had destroyed her life but also given her purpose. With it came an odd sense of peace. She stroked Samson's ears. He lifted his head and stared up at her with wide, trusting, brown eyes.

A siren wailed in the distance. She looked at the firemen who were still shooting water on the smoking remains of the house. How had the fire started? How long had it been blazing before it was reported, and the fire trucks arrived?

"If I'd come home instead of gone to the diner, I might have smelled the smoke and gotten her out of the house," she whispered, mostly to herself.

"It might not have made any difference if you were home. You might not have seen the flames or smelled the smoke. And there's the possibility she died before the fire."

Rhonda wasn't reassured by his words. Dead before the fire? Her neighbor had wanted to tell her about something she regretted. Her thoughts raced down a surprising path. Had regret consumed Mrs. P? Had she lost hope and killed herself?

Another thought blazed in. Had someone murdered her, and set the fire to hide it?

She'd seen Howard Noble lurking in the shadows watching the fire. Why was he there? Had he seen her as well as Holt?

"You okay, Rhonda?"

"Did someone set that fire?"

Holt's face was in shadow. "We'll find out after they've investigated."

Rhonda saw tension in the set of his jaw. "You're worried about Claire."

"Of course, I am," Holt said, voice strained. "Why was she abducted? And where is Cade? And why put a body in her Jeep?"

"Maybe she stumbled onto something during her interviews."

"People with longstanding secrets, when risking exposure, don't take chances. If she stumbled into something, she's dead already."

His words hung in the silence of the truck's cab.

"Don't think that. Maybe it was only someone playing a joke."

Illuminated by streetlights, Rhonda could see his face visibly tighten. He didn't believe that any more than she did.

They passed pockets of trick-or-treaters. She remembered those days with her children. Would she experience it again with grandchildren? She couldn't think about it.

"Halloween was so different when I was a kid," she muttered.

"Was it?" Holt rolled down his window, letting a blast of fresh air replace the smoky air inside the truck. "I wonder. My parents walked along with us when we trick-or-treated until about fourth grade. They never let us out of their sight. Bad things were happening then, too. We were unaware."

"Blessedly unaware. I wish I still were." Recent memories flashed in her mind. She chilled.

"You've had an exceptional experience. Bad enough to make anybody doubt that the world is a decent place to live."

"A world that includes men like those drug dealers is an ugly world to raise children in." She swallowed. A cloud of despair dropped over her again.

"That's true. But we can stop them, one at a time. We're making a difference, Rhonda. We are. You are."

She heard the words and wanted to believe them. If they could get the rest of the drug gang... If they went to trial... If she could testify... At least that small bit of the drug operation would end. Maybe their efforts would spare some lives the horror of addiction.

Holt turned down a dark street and slowed. "According to Google, the grandmother's house is on this street. Long driveway. Do you see any lights behind the trees?"

Rhonda peered into a nighttime landscape full of shadows cast by the full moon. She searched for pinpricks of light. "I think I see houselights at the end of the next driveway."

Holt slowed the truck and pulled off the street, partially into the bar ditch.

"Through there? Sure is dark. Don't think they were expecting any trick-or-treaters." Holt shifted the truck into park and turned off the engine. "We'll park here and walk in."

Chapter 46
Claire

Claire's wrists were raw and bleeding. The ropes weren't going to loosen.

She sucked in a deep breath. Where was she? There was no way to know, but the smells were familiar. Must and mold, sawdust and … gasoline? Was she at Neve's grandmother's?

The room swam around her. She blinked to clear her vision, but it failed. Her brain wasn't working right.

She fought against the fog that had dropped over her and scooted painfully, an inch at a time, first one direction, and then another, avoiding the cage she found earlier. Gradually, the movements caused less pain. Her little scoots took her farther each time until she bumped into something solid. The gasoline smell was stronger here. She bent closer to the object. Rubber. A tire? On a car?

If she was at Neve's grandmother's house, she was in the garage.

She scooted a different direction. When she slammed into something solid again, something fell from above and thudded to the floor behind her.

Fingers extended, she reached for the fallen item. Long handle, smooth. Opposite end made of thick metal, oddly shaped. A hammer. With a claw. And sharp edges on the inside of the claw. She maneuvered the hammer until she was sitting on the handle and the claw was in an upright position. Then she held her roped wrists above the claw and moved her hands back and forth, letting the sharp claw edges bite into the rope. She sawed until her arms ached, rested, and sawed some more. The ropes loosened slightly. She sawed some more.

Finally, the ropes dropped from Claire's wrists. She rubbed her wrists together to get the blood flowing. Once the tingling had stopped, she reached for her ankles. Those knots were also tight, but not so tight that Claire couldn't work the tips of her fingers into them, once her fingers were fully functional. Every few minutes, she closed her eyes and rested. If she could only see what she was doing, and if the room would stop spinning around her … Her head ached, and she was so woozy. It was tempting just to stop, and lean back, and go to sleep.

Her fingers numbed, she was no longer certain that she was loosening the knots, instead, she was just poking at the ropes. She couldn't make any progress.

The rustling started up again in the cage, and so did the scratching in the corners. What creatures did she share the darkness with? She began to imagine her roommates wanted to get out as much as she did, that they were cheering her on. Once she was free, she'd find the light switch. She'd find out what they were, and she'd set them free at the same time that she ran from her prison.

Claire plucked at the ropes again, digging in, and finally, finally, felt the knots loosen. A few more jabs and pulls and the ropes dropped from her ankles. She straightened her legs, wincing at the pain that shot up her calves and into her thighs. She bent her knees and straightened them, feeling the nerves tingling painfully as blood flow returned. Slowly, she shifted to one side, pulled her legs under her, and stood.

She took one wobbly step and sank to the ground as the world curled and pitched. She waited a few seconds, and then pushed up from the floor until she was standing again. She took another step.

Hands outstretched, she moved in the darkness, seeking a wall. A wall could include a window, or even better, a door.

She found the wall. Carefully, she stepped along it, shuffling her feet, avoiding items on the floor, and gingerly touching shelves and pegged wallboards with spades and garden tools hanging from them. She stumbled over the ends of shovels, and stepped around a riding lawnmower, holding onto it with her hands. Finally, she felt the door frame, and then the doorknob.

Claire twisted it and opened the door.

Light from the full moon lit the yard in front of her. She swayed, dizzy with the sudden light, as well as the effort of walking upright to get there. Warily, she surveyed the lawn. Was anyone watching? A structure sat on the other side of the lawn. This was not Neve's grandmother's place. This yard was too orderly, too well kept, and too big. A memory fought to become clear.

Claire scuttled across the lawn away from the house and the garage toward a thick hedge. She brushed against it, moving slowly until she found an opening. It led through the hedge from the yard into an alleyway.

Freedom? Pain wracked her body, and the ground shifted beneath each step. She limped down the narrow, graveled alley, listening for any sound that might tell her that her kidnapper knew she had escaped. He would come after her. Where would she go?

Trash bins and piles of household debris littered the alleyway. She would have to hide in the hedge, behind trash, if they came after her. There was no other choice.

Moonlight revealed her way.

Claire's head pounded. Tears poured from her eyes, so that an aquatic world swam around her. She moved her arms in a swimming motion, stroking the hedges, relying on their substance to keep her upright.

She stumbled into a rut, and crouched there for a minute, letting her breathing even out, closing her eyes to let the watery world dry a little. Then she pushed to her feet again.

The other yards adjoining the alley were dark. Wide lawns separated the houses. Occasionally, moonlight glittered off of the windows of the houses.

Was anyone looking out of those darkened windows? If she crept up to one of the houses, would the resident answer her knock? If she pounded and screamed, would they come?

It was Halloween. At this hour, they might assume it was pranksters.

Her legs quivered. Every muscle complained, telling her to stop moving. Stop. Stop.

A cloud scuttled across the moon, darkening the sky. A putrid scent lingered in the dark underbrush. Who knew what dead things might be rotting there?

In the distance, the horizon glowed. She forged ahead. The glow brightened, outlining the tops of trees and houses.

Claire watched the glow as she stumbled on. Flames licked upward into the night sky. A plume of white smoke rose into the glow. Fifty yards later, as she pushed on, the flames disappeared but white smoke billowed higher into the sky.

In shadowy stretches of the alley, she couldn't see where she was putting her feet. She mis-stepped. Claire's shirt caught on brambles. Greenbriar vine? Blackberry bushes? She tore loose from the thorns and traipsed on. Her arms itched. A damp cold seeped into her bones.

Claire's mind filled with questions. About Neve's grandmother. About her uncle. About her feelings for Cade. The girl was a mystery. But before she could ask her anything, they had to find Cade. Alive and healthy. She refused to even consider he might be dead or injured.

Ahead, a streetlight illuminated pavement. The alley spilled into a street. She paused at the final evergreen, sought the shadows for several minutes before she staggered toward the curb.

Chapter 47
Holt

Holt closed the truck door softly. He motioned for Rhonda to remain seated, but she climbed out anyway, leaving Samson in the truck. Why was it neither she nor Claire would do what he asked? It was such a simple thing. How could he keep them safe when they wouldn't listen?

"Maybe I can help, Holt. You can't go in there by yourself."

"Who says I'm going in? I'm going to check it out. Stay here," he ordered. He knew she wouldn't obey him. He'd been prepared to watch over a frightened, meek woman during this assignment, but Renee Trammel was far from meek, and anger tempered her fear. In the short week he'd known her, she'd shown him determination as well as despair.

He steeled himself to the pumping of his heart, willing the adrenaline to help rather than hinder. Claire and Cade could be in this house, and if they were, he would get them out. His gun was tucked in his shoulder holster. It would remain there until he needed it. This was a residential neighborhood, and he had no reason to believe anyone was in danger. A grandmother lived here, he reminded himself.

Holt moved through the shadows toward the house. Its setting, at least fifty yards off the road, offered opportunities to hide, not only for him, but for others. He paused behind a screen of bushes to peer toward the house's upper windows and the front porch. No signs of movement. A faint putrid smell hung in the air.

As he neared the house, the rocking chair on the front porch moved. A tiny woman wrapped in a Navajo blanket sat in the chair, her head back, her eyes closed.

She lifted her hands upward until her elbows were straight, then, slowly lowered them. Her aged, wrinkled face was emotionless, her mouth and eyes closed. He waited, listening. Nightbirds. A distant owl. A barking dog.

He stepped around the hedge, the soles of his boots slipping on the wet grass as he inched toward the house. One soft light shown in a front window. Was the old woman alone?

The elderly woman began to chant a low, quiet song. He couldn't make out the words. The hackles on his neck rose. Her eerie song continued for a minute before ending as abruptly as it began. Holt stood quietly, hidden by tree shadows. Several yards to his left, a branch snapped.

"What are you doing in my yard?" the grandmother called in a husky voice.

Rhonda moved into a spot cast by the mercury vapor light at the edge of the yard. Her red hair glimmered. "I'm sorry if I startled you. My name's Rhonda, and I'm looking for my friend Claire Northcutt. Is she here?"

Holt reached around to grab the stock of his gun as he scanned the house windows and the surrounding yard. No sign of movement; no sign that anyone else was there. He waited.

"Claire Northcutt," the grandmother repeated. "She's not here."

"She told me she might come out to talk to you again. I can't find her, and I'm worried about her, and about her son, Cade. Maybe Neve knows where Cade is. She showed up at the arena today for the competition. Did she make it into the finals? Is Neve here?"

"My granddaughter is here."

Holt looked toward the house again. If Neve was here, where was she? No other lights shown from the windows. It was a little early for her to already be in bed.

Rhonda crossed the scant grass of the yard and stepped up to the porch. "Claire told me about her interview with you yesterday. She wants to help you find out who's responsible for polluting your property. Have you seen her today? Has Neve? Can I talk to Neve?"

"I expected trick-or-treaters, but no one came. It's too dark and scary out here for the kids. And it stinks." The elderly woman crossed her arms, tucking the blanket around them. "Neve used to come for candy. She's too old for that now."

Rhonda smiled at her. "I bet she used to love to come here. But kids grow up, don't they, and have other interests?"

The Creek woman eyed her. "I don't know you. You say you are Rhonda, but that is not your name. You are an imposter. You should go. Now."

"I'm worried about my friend. Could I please talk with Neve?"

"I haven't seen Claire Northcutt." The old lady unfolded the blanket and lifted a shotgun. She pointed it steadily at Rhonda. "Go."

Rhonda backed away from the porch. "I'm going. I'm sorry I disturbed you."

Holt watched Rhonda until she disappeared into the darkness outside the range of the yard light. He maneuvered back toward the street, passing quietly through the shadows to his truck, where he slipped inside and quietly pulled the door shut. Rhonda already sat in the passenger seat, frowning, Samson in her lap.

He started the truck and backed down the street, watching over his shoulder for the next driveway, where he did a U-turn and then flicked on the headlights.

"That was stupid, Rhonda."

"I found out what you wanted to know, didn't I? Claire isn't there. Neve is. I don't think that old woman could lie if she wanted to. And I distracted her. She was bound to see or hear you any second."

"She had no idea I was there. But you're right. Claire isn't there. But Neve is. We need to talk to her. Why was her grandmother sitting on the porch with her shotgun hidden in the blanket?"

"Waiting for someone? Who? She didn't seem scared."

"She didn't. Maybe she wasn't. Or maybe she was resigned to it happening." His mind traveled to the drug dealer son, Kai. Did she know what had happened at the arena between him and Claire? Did she know her son was dead? If so, who was she expecting to arrive?

"I wish the old woman would have been willing to talk to you. I'm thinking she was sitting there waiting for Kai's killer to arrive. But she wasn't scared. Imagine."

He felt fear every day, faced fear every day. But he couldn't imagine not being scared. Just because it was part of his life didn't mean he didn't wish he could stop feeling it. He had felt it more in the last eight hours than he thought he ever had before. His mind was full of Claire.

Holt started the truck.

Someone tapped at the truck window.

Cade peered in at him.

Chapter 48
Rhonda

Emotions flitted across Holt's face as he and Cade argued outside the truck.

Holt had opened his door and gotten out, leaving her with only snatches of a quiet, but intense conversation. It sounded as if the teenager was standing his ground about something. She peered at them through the window and saw them throw their hands around, cross their arms and scratch their heads. She strained to hear more, unsuccessfully. After a few minutes, Cade vanished into the shadows and Holt slid into the driver's seat.

"Damn it." Holt pulled the truck into the street, thumping one rear tire into the bar ditch as he turned the wheels.

"What did he say? Has he seen his mom? Tell me, Holt." Rhonda exploded. Why was it so difficult for him to talk to her? She needed to know what was happening. Where had Cade been?

"The kid's upset. I asked him to go with us now, to find his mother, but he says he's staying with Neve, to protect her. I told him what happened with Kai and his mom this afternoon. He got quiet, angry, and then concerned when I dropped the news that she was missing. He questioned my ability as a law enforcement professional. The thing is, I've been asking myself that same question the last few hours."

"He's been with Neve all day? Here?"

"Here, and at the arena. He spent the night there and this morning after Neve's time trial he came here with her. Oh, and he 'lost' his phone. According to Cade, they went back to the arena later this afternoon to feed Blaze, and found he'd already been fed. No one mentioned that a woman had fallen off the bleachers, or the fight that preceded it. I got the impression they didn't stay long after her second time trial. Maybe watched the trials for another hour before they picked up some food and came out here, to her grandmother."

"Did he have any idea where Claire might be, or who might have taken her?"

"He thought it was probably Kai, a way to keep Cade from telling me about his drug business. Cade suggested to Neve a few days ago that they tell me what Kai was up to. I gather it caused a big fight between them, and somehow Kai got wind of it."

"But Kai's dead, and his body was left in Claire's car. Was the intention to make Claire look like a murderer? How would that work since she was in the hospital?"

Holt shook his head and peered out the windshield, intent on the increased traffic and costumed teenagers trying to cross the busy street.

"Claire recorded those interviews. And she kept a notebook. I need to go over everything she's heard since she got here, and everything she's written. Her notebook is in her room at the B&B."

Holt kept the speed limit to the next stop light and through the neighborhood as he navigated back to the Bed & Breakfast.

On the lawn at the B&B, the festival booths stood empty, and only a few cars remained parked on the street. Three people were gathering trash while another stacked chairs and folded tables. Holt pulled into the only open parking space in the alley lot reserved for overnight guests.

"Wait here, Rhonda. I want to check something before I take you back to the diner for your car."

Rhonda didn't want to wait. She climbed out of the car and followed a few steps behind Holt. At the door to Claire's room, he flashed his badge and credentials at a bored policeman leaning against the building. "I need to check the scene. Do you know if Ms. Northcutt's work satchel is still here? Did she take it with her? Or did the evidence people grab it?"

The policeman shrugged and glanced at Rhonda. "I know they swept the room, but this isn't officially a crime scene. No blood. Don't know for sure if it was even a kidnapping. I'm here just in case she comes back, so I can notify the chief."

Holt stepped into the room, and Rhonda paused in the doorway, watching Holt walk past the bed to the closet. As he walked, he scanned the room until he saw Claire's laptop on the desk and her satchel on the floor next to it. Holt picked up the satchel, looked inside, then zipped it closed and tucked it under his arm.

"Thanks," Holt said to the policeman. "I'm taking her workbag. I'll see that Claire gets it back once we find her. Do I need to log it somewhere?"

The young policeman shrugged. If he'd been Rhonda's employee, she would have fired him.

Holt rushed back to his truck with Rhonda close on his heels.

* * *

Trick-or-treating activity had ended. Teens roamed the streets, some in costume. It seemed to Rhonda that zombie makeup was trending again this year. There were too many staggering skeletons and limbless monsters roaming about. Most residents had turned off their porch lights. Only the full moon and the streetlights illuminated the scattered pumpkins and spooky decorations in the yards and front windows.

Holt squinted straight ahead, frowning. She knew he was beating himself up. Cade's rebuke would get to him. Claire had disappeared on his watch.

The old Indian woman was psychic. Without a doubt she knew Holt was there in the shadows, and somehow, she knew Rhonda was not who she pretended to be. Older Native Americans had a knack for knowing things. They had a connection to the spiritual realm and used not only the five senses, but the sixth, intuition. Their elders were aware of a spiritual realm most people no longer believed in.

"Think the grandmother was lying about Claire?" Holt interrupted her musing.

"No." Rhonda twisted sideways to study Holt's profile as he drove. Samson panted and sniffed the window. "I think she knows Kai is dead. She's protecting Neve. She's no fool. She's the least of our worries."

Brow creased with worry; a frown pulled down the corners of his mouth. She'd never seen him like this before.

"I haven't been in contact with Claire much these last few days," he confessed. "But you had lunch with her today. What was she thinking? Hopefully, there's a clue in her notes that will tell me who took her and why, and why Kai's body was left in her SUV. It must be because of Kai's activities. He's a drug dealer. And he was acting as a vigilante for his grandmother."

Rhonda remembered her conversation with Claire at lunch. "She's done two interviews for the Route 66 article, the mayor and an older man who's lived here a long time. And she went out to the grandmother's house looking for Neve." Rhonda shook her head at the thought that crept in. "We were both at the environmental meeting about the leaking landfill. Interesting information there, but not really connected to Route 66. She realized that spending time on that issue would pull her article off track." Rhonda searched her memory for anything else, a clue.

"Maybe we need to focus on Neve and her relatives. Who was the uncle, and where did he live?" Holt pushed an autodial number on his dashboard panel. He asked a series of rapid-fire questions, and then punched off the phone.

A muscle worked in his jaw. Rhonda turned her attention back to the town around them and the silvery full moon that hung above it.

Holt's phone rang.

Rhonda stared out the window as he talked and drove, eyeing stragglers, lone trick-or-treaters, and an occasional pair.

"They've positively identified him? Absolutely sure?"

Rhonda turned back to Holt as he clicked off the phone.

"The dead man at your neighbor's house has been identified as Roger Benson. Your friend from the diner."

"What was Roger doing at Mrs. P's house?"

"I don't know, but I'll find out."

Her thoughts tumbled. Was Roger a casualty because of what he'd said aloud at the diner? But why was he at Mrs. Ps? What did she have to do with any of this?

Rhonda rubbed her temple, where a headache had begun to throb.

Holt pulled into the parking lot at the diner, leaving extra room between his truck and the shiny vintage Camaro that was taking up two parking spaces.

"You should go home and lock the doors. Our man is watching the house. And you've got Samson to alert you if anyone gets too close. Call me for any reason, Rhonda. I've got to review Claire's notes and make some calls. You'll be fine. I'll check in tomorrow morning, early. And you'll have a new house."

Neither his smile nor his cheerful tone convinced her that everything was really under control. "Thanks." She pulled the door release and started to get out of the truck. "I know you've got to search for Claire. Do you think the fire crew will still be next door?"

Holt glanced at the dashboard where the clock pulsed. "I'm betting all is quiet for now. Not much more they can do until daylight. An investigator will be there then, and I'm sure they'll want to interview you tomorrow at some point."

"Will the movers come for the furniture?" Not that she wanted the mismatched pieces from the little house. Surely the government could do better than that for witnesses in their protection program.

"The furniture and kitchen things stay. You can throw your luggage in your car whenever you're ready to go and drive over to the new place. Did you look it over today?"

"I drove by. Didn't stop. Remember, that red truck was on my tail." Her stomach turned over as she thought of how frightened she'd been earlier in the afternoon. She'd been so positive those men would find her. She didn't know who they were or why they were after her. But now, she knew Roger Benson was dead. If they killed him because of what he'd said out loud, they would also kill her for what she'd overheard.

"Right. I got your message. For now, I'm going back to the office to read her notebook and wait for some information I requested."

Holt's words registered. Where was Claire? Her disappearance was bizarre. "If she was kidnapped, won't there be a ransom demand?"

"I don't think this is about money."

Rhonda agreed. But if it wasn't about money, it had to be about keeping secrets. Whose?

Rhonda put Samson in the back seat of her Camry and drove slowly back to the bungalow, watching her rearview mirror for any sign of the red truck behind her. She stayed on the main streets, then turned at the corner where the dilapidated motor court sat back from the road. A light glowed in the rear of one of the units.

She pulled over. Was a vagrant living in the abandoned motel? Or was some teenager hosting a spooky Halloween party there? Either way, it was none of her business. Nothing she could do about it anyway, and she didn't have any right to interfere. She could leave the police an anonymous tip, but then they could trace her phone. Hah, forget that. Her phone only made calls to Holt.

She dug it out of her purse and called him. He answered before the second ring.

"Holt, there's a light on in one of the units of that old motor court near my house that I told you about. It's abandoned, but someone's there. Would you call the police?"

"Kids, or a homeless person. I'll give the locals a call. Thanks for the tip. And I'll let you know what I find out about the grandmother's relatives and Neve. So, you know."

"Okay, I'm almost to the house now. Not much activity on the streets, but it's early. A full moon usually brings the mischief out."

"Small town. Not much to do. But I can bet someone is getting into trouble somewhere."

Rhonda pulled back onto the street and drove the last two blocks to her house. As she turned into the driveway, she glanced next door at the blackened ruins of Mrs. Petrovsky's home. The heavy smell of smoke still hung in the air. She parked in the driveway and got out.

In the yard, shadows ruled, with moonlight shining through the limbs of the old trees in odd spots, leaving big gaps where anything, even an elephant, could be lingering. Samson pulled on his leash, wanting to investigate next door, but she pulled him back and urged him toward the house. A few houses away, dogs barked. She glanced over her shoulder. No one there.

Rhonda climbed the porch steps with Samson to unlock the door. As the door opened, a piece of paper on the floor fluttered up and rode the air current into the room.

Samson yipped and dashed into the house, a low growl rumbling in his throat.

Rhonda refilled the dog's water and poured kibble into his food bowl. Then she retrieved the paper from the floor.

Oops, the note said, *wrong house. I'll get it right next time if you don't keep your mouth shut.*

Chapter 49
Claire

Claire watched as headlights approached. Was it her abductors, searching for her?

The world spun slowly around as she sat on the curb. Which way was up? She hadn't felt this way since the last time she'd ridden The Spinner at the state fair. The memory brought back nausea. Claire started to heave, but there was nothing in her stomach to bring up. It had been hours since her last sip of water at the hospital. Hours since the call from the arena had interrupted her lunch with Rhonda.

The lights drew closer, illuminating the pavement yards away.

Chances were slim that it was her kidnapper, but could she risk it? She got to her feet as the headlights neared, then dove into the shadows. The car cruised past.

The evergreen hedge swallowed her, cocooning her body. No one could see her here. No one could find her. Maybe she would die here, beneath this evergreen. The bush would grow taller and bushier, taller, and bushier. Some time, in the distant future, someone would tear these bushes down. They'd find her then, curled into a fetal position. Just a skeleton, with a few scraps of cloth. No identification. She'd be another Jane Doe. Would there be

DNA left for analysis? She'd taken the 23 and Me test last year. Would they finally identify her so that Cade and Denver would, finally, know that she had died here in Persimmon, under an evergreen hedge?

She closed her eyes. Would dying be peaceful? How long would it take? Would it hurt?

Her thoughts swirled. An insect crawled onto her arm. She brushed it off.

Something snuffled in the dirt a few feet away. She remembered the living things that had been in the garage with her, one of them in a cage, the other in the corner, scratching. She'd promised to set them free, but she'd left them without another thought. She should go back.

Claire moved a few inches, pushing aside the evergreen branches. Out on the street, no more than four yards away, a noisy car engine rumbled past. She scooted back into her hideaway.

She couldn't go back to that garage. She couldn't save them. She didn't know what they were, anyway. The thing in the cage could have been a pet. Could have been a rabbit, or even a snake. The thing scratching in the corner was most likely a mouse or a rat. If she went back to set it free, it would find another house or garage to live in. It wasn't desperate to get out of that garage, not like she had been.

She had been desperate. Why? Her thoughts circled. Oh.

She had to find Cade?

Where was her son? Was Holt looking for him? Was Holt looking for her?

Another insect crawled onto her arm, and something else landed in her hair, fluttering at her scalp. She shook her head and evergreen branches rubbed against her, their pungent scent filled her nose. She sneezed and sneezed again.

She heard voices. Someone was coming toward her, walking, laughing as they walked the street. Who?

Claire leaned forward until she could see the street through a screen of evergreen branches.

Kids, just kids. Teenagers, like Cade had been not that long ago. She could yell at them, call for help. Would they get help for her, or would they run screaming down the street, thinking she was a Halloween specter, come to life?

She stayed silent, listened to their chatter as they walked past. She closed her eyes, clasped her knees, and rested her head on them. The world around her continued a slow spin.

Chapter 50
Holt

Holt Braden ran his fingers through his hair and turned back to the front of Claire's notebook. He was on his third read-through. Some of her notes were cryptic. She had initials in the margins, incomplete phrases jotted at the top of the page. They might make sense to Claire, but not to him. And he wasn't sure it could make sense.

It was apparent from the notes that she didn't have her thoughts together. She didn't know where she was going with the story.

She had made notes of Route 66 landmarks, some he'd seen and others he'd heard about. She'd listed the sites in Tulsa:

- The Admiral Twin Drive-In Theater
- The Meadowgold Dairy Sign
- Cain's Ballroom
- Blue Dome Service Station
- Avery Plaza

and then she'd crossed through each of them.

He knew that Claire had wanted the article's emphasis to be on the small towns, the places where Route

66 had made the town, and then broken it years later. She wasn't interested in Tulsa.

Her list for the Persimmon area included the Rock Creek Bridge, an amusement park, the Route 66 Car Museum, a drive-in theater, and an old motor court. She'd noted that the museum was open, and the bridge was still there. Supposedly, the remains of the drive-in were also still standing. Below the list, Claire had doodled a huge question mark with ivy leaves growing along the edges.

Her notes from the environmental meeting at the café followed. She'd printed the names of the speakers and contact information. She'd noted that Howard Noble had attended.

Howard Noble. Rhonda knew him from the café, and he'd been watching the fire that destroyed her neighbor's house. Claire had interviewed him, and he had attended the environmental meeting.

He needed to talk to Howard Noble.

Holt copied down the address and phone number from Claire's notebook, looked up the information on Maps, and headed for his truck.

Chapter 51
Rhonda

Rhonda read the note again and her blood chilled. She crumpled it and tossed it onto the table. She didn't think the drug dealers had written that note. They wouldn't have bothered to torch the wrong house. They would have waited here, and then killed her when she got home. She'd have been dead the second she opened the door. Unless they wanted to have a little fun with her first.

Who had it been, then? The men at the diner? Because of what she'd overheard? Roger Benson was dead, killed in the housefire next door. He would have had to leave the note before setting the fire. It was possible, but it just didn't seem like something Benson would do, unless he'd been told to. It seemed more likely to her that the fire had been an opportunity to eliminate Benson.

First Kai, now Benson. What was the connection? Were both of them drug dealers? Had the competition eliminated them? Maybe she was overthinking this. Roger's death could have been an accident, after he'd set the fire.

Either way, she'd take the fire and the note as fair warning. She wasn't going to hang around to find out the answers to her questions.

She was supposed to move tomorrow. She couldn't wait until then. And she couldn't stay in this town. What difference would moving into a new house make if she went back to work at the diner? They could always follow her home again.

The roaring in her brain drowned out her thoughts. She had to do something. She couldn't wait here, in the dark, for someone to come and kill her.

She'd be safer on her own. She could drive to Arkansas or Missouri, find work, and keep to herself. After a few weeks, she'd contact Holt to let him know where she was in case the trial was moving forward, in case the rest of the drug gang had been caught.

Having a plan calmed her, gave her a sense of purpose. She wouldn't tread water and hope to survive.

Rhonda packed her toiletries into a backpack and zipped her suitcases shut. Her first paycheck was in her purse. She'd go to a branch of the issuing bank and cash it on Monday, wherever she was. Meanwhile, she had tip money to get her by. When he was passing out the paychecks earlier today, Lloyd had pealed an extra fifty off the roll of bills in his wallet and told her to have some fun at his expense. What kind of fun did he expect her to have? He knew she was in witness protection. But as far as she knew, Lloyd didn't know why.

"Come on, Samson. We'll spend the night in the car, someplace safe and secluded. Then tomorrow ... We'll find a better place." She hooked on the leash, grabbed Samson's dog bowls and the bag of kibble, and carried them out to the car. Samson eagerly leaped onto the front seat. She returned to the house and grabbed her suitcases and backpack.

Her pulse pounded. Was she being watched? As she loaded the Camry, she searched the shadows around the house. Wisps of smoke reached up from the ashes of the burnt-out ruin next door.

Wrong house. Could that be true?

Rhonda drove the Camry west on Route 66. She ignored a stabbing headache as she made several turns, always watching the highway signs and staying on 66. She passed a golf course and met up with another wide street. Lights from a Walmart glowed on her left.

The headache blasted like a jackhammer, increasing as each bright headlight passed. She was miles away from her bungalow, and the diner. Would it be safe to pull over and sleep a few hours before getting a head start on the drive in the early morning hours? An insistent thought pounded. Could she really leave without knowing what had happened to Claire? Without saying goodbye to Holt Braden?

A narrow side road hooked to the right. She suspected it might lead to a residential area with large lots, like those in Neve's grandmother's old neighborhood. She'd hardly investigated the town in the week she'd lived there. Route 66 had shaped the area's history, and she had no doubt skeletons of attractions once found on or near the old highway were everywhere, if she'd read up on it and had the desire to explore.

Instead, her brain buzzed with fear. Where would she be safe? It was late, long past dark. She didn't want to drive on the interstate. If someone were looking for her, wouldn't that be the route they'd expect her to take to get away? The better, safer alternative for tonight would be to stay on residential streets and find a parking area somewhere, then take the smaller highways across country tomorrow.

Rhonda turned down the old concrete side road. A tire caught in a rut, and when she accelerated to continue, the steering felt off. Something was wrong. Had she blown a tire or messed up the alignment?

She pulled as far to the right as possible, partly off into the tall grass beside the shoulder-less road. This late in the year, the seed heads of the grasses were well above her head. No one had been mowing this stretch of road over the summer.

Rhonda stepped out of the car and squinted at the rear tire. The ambient light from her taillights and the full moon revealed what she suspected: a flat tire.

Ahead on the road, the night stretched away, unbroken by house or yard lights. The full moon overhead caught the guardrails and arches of an old railroad bridge less than a quarter mile down the road. Something rustled in the tall grass. In the car, Samson barked.

Another sound, a crackling, caught her attention. She turned in a full circle. Off to her left in a field, fifty yards away, stood a tall structure. Too narrow to be a building, a very tall light-colored section of wall stood in a field surrounded by a chain link fence. She crossed the road and a narrow ditch, then peered over the fence. Behind her, in the car, Samson howled.

"Wait a minute, boy, I'll be right back." She took a few steps along the fence, straining to get a better look at the structure. The 'field' on the other side of the fence had once been a big parking lot. Grass grew between broken bits of concrete.

The 'wall' was all that remained of an old drive-in movie theater screen. A small building sat in the center of what had been the parking area. The projection shed? A refreshment stand? The drive-in had not been operational for a long while.

Samson's mournful howl died away into the night, but only for a few seconds. His barking started up again.

She stepped away from the fence and headed toward the car. "Coming," she called.

Round headlights turned onto the road and came toward her. Someone to help her change the flat tire? She hoped so.

Rhonda stepped into the road and waved her arms. The car was a 1956 Chevy Bel Air, like some she frequently saw parked in the Diner's parking lot. The car rolled to a stop.

"Need some help?" a familiar voice asked as the car's passenger door opened.

She pointed at her car and the deflated rear tire. "I do. How in the world did you—"

Something slammed into her head.

Chapter 52
Claire

Claire huddled in the shelter of the evergreen, her head spinning, her stomach heaving despite its emptiness.

Her mind was a blank. How had she gotten here? Where was Cade? Where was Holt? What time was it?

Her body began to shake.

What had they given her? A fatal dose of ... what? Some drug. Something she wouldn't wake up from. Her life was over.

She didn't want to die.

Cade would go back to his father. What kind of life would that be? The man was abusive, angry and a drunk. Cade was old enough that his father's lifestyle wouldn't alter him, but who was to say?

Cade would still have Denver. But could Denver stand up to Tom? Would Cade spend as much time with Denver as he did with Tom? Would Cade go to college? Would he move away and forget all about her and his childhood and their five acres in the country?

It wouldn't take long for Manny to find someone to replace her at the newspaper. He liked her work, but she hadn't been anything special. She'd tried to be, tried to come up with news articles of interest to the community.

Tried to write unbiased, informative pieces. She had really tried.

Holt would go on, living his adventurous life. He'd solve crimes and help people. He'd find someone who returned his love willingly. Someone without bad memories, someone who was able to give him the love he craved.

Her eyelids were heavy, too heavy, but she didn't want to sleep, didn't want to give in to the dark. She was afraid she might never wake up.

She pushed out of the sheltering evergreens and crawled across the grass toward the street, unable to pull herself to standing, unable to walk.

Headlights shone down the alleyway. Someone was coming, driving from the garage where she'd been left to die. Slowly, the vehicle moved forward, a search light illuminating the bushes first on one side, and then the other.

A sob exploded from her throat.

The lights—big, bright headlight beams—caught her before she could dive into the shadows.

The vehicle jerked to a stop.

She fell back against the grass. She didn't have the energy or the will to fight whoever had come to return her to captivity.

Chapter 53
Holt

Holt drove past Howard's house again. A black Harley sat out front, but there were no lights on. If the old man were home, he'd already gone to bed.

He parked a few houses down on the street and climbed out of his truck. With the full moon above, it might as well be daylight. Anyone looking out a window would see him. With any luck, they'd call the local police, and cops would flood the neighborhood. He could talk them into doing a house-to-house search for a 'suspicious person' he had seen while on a short stroll.

Holt walked back to Howard Noble's house, keeping to the shadows of the huge trees on the property line. He watched for signs of life in the windows as he eased through the side gate and into the back yard. The place was well kept, with a manicured lawn, neat flower beds. A large workshop/garage sat in the back corner of the lot. Most likely, a riding lawnmower was parked in there next to his car and an assortment of lawn tools and boxes full of Christmas decorations.

At the garage, he tried the doorknob and found it unlocked. He peeked inside. There was the lawnmower as expected, and next to it, a pile of ropes and a claw hammer.

A blanket, and a kerchief rolled into a gag lay on the floor a few feet away.

"Claire?" His harsh whisper cut through the quiet. She'd been here. Was she still here?

He used the small flashlight from his gun holster to look into every corner, under and around every object in the garage. "Claire? Honey, are you here?"

Finally, he was absolutely certain the large garage was empty of living things, except for a few vermin, and the flop-eared rabbit that inhabited the cage in the corner.

Holt left the shed, closing the door behind him. He walked the perimeter of the yard, searching the bushes. A back gate led to an alley. He stepped through it and looked each direction down the narrow, graveled way.

Claire had been in that garage, he was certain. If not Claire, then someone else who had been bound and gagged, and left on the cold concrete floor with only a thin blanket. The air had chilled after a nice fall afternoon. Claire was out here, somewhere. Hurt. Cold. He had to find her.

Holt raced back through the yard and down the street to his truck, no longer concerned if anyone saw him, or if anyone called the police.

He revved the engine and drove to the end of the block, turned right, and found the alleyway that stretched behind the row of houses. He pulled his auxiliary spotlight from under the seat and, driving slowly, shone the light first on one side of the alley and then the other, searching the hedges for any sign that Claire had been there.

He was nearing the end of the alley. Only two more houses, and then the street.

His headlights caught something in front of him. No, someone. At the end of the alley. Near the street.

He slammed the truck into park and threw the door open.

Chapter 54
Rhonda

Slowly, Rhonda became aware of sounds. A cricket chirping, a plane flying overhead. The rustling of fabric against fabric. Someone breathing.

She stretched her fingers, shifted her back. Her head ached. She moaned and moved one arm. When she opened her eyes, lamp light increased the ache in her head. She closed her eyes and tried to sit up.

"Easy, Rhonda. I'm sure your head really hurts. Didn't mean to hit you that hard."

This time, she opened her eyes slowly, and turned her head toward the voice. "Where am I? Who are …?"

But she recognized the owner of the voice. It couldn't be.

"Rhonda, I wish this had ended differently. Why couldn't you leave it alone? You were at that meeting, and you talked to that reporter. Had lunch with her! She's stuck her nose in where it's not wanted and the two of you won't let it be. You and your friend must pay the consequences. I don't intend to spend the next twenty years in a jail cell."

Rhonda rubbed her forehead, and gingerly touched the back of her head. She squinted at the person who bent over her. "I don't know anything. And Claire was researching Route 66 …"

"That's what she said she was investigating. But that wasn't all. She went out to the Indian's house. And she fought with her son, Kai."

Rhonda pulled herself straighter and glanced around the room. She was on a sofa, in a sparsely decorated room. Stained white roller shades covered the windows, and a single lamp sat on a side table next to the sofa. The walls were barren of pictures, and there were no knick-knacks or decorations anywhere in the room. A sour smell hung in the air.

The Indian? Neve's grandmother? Was that what this was about?

"This is crazy. I have no idea what I'm doing here, or what you think I know or saw. My neighbor's house burned down a few hours ago. I didn't want to stay home. I've been out driving around." Her heart pounded. "I'm not an investigator. I'm a waitress. I don't care anything about the landfill. I only heard about it at that meeting."

"I know who you really are," the man snickered. His familiar face hovered over her. "And you know I'm not going to let you go. My life, and everything I've worked for, depends on it."

Chapter 55
Claire

"Claire?"

She opened her eyes. A bright light flicked over her and someone took hold of her arms and pulled her into an embrace.

She was hallucinating.

"You're all right. I found you. Everything's going to be okay."

"Holt?" she pulled away slightly and studied him. His face wouldn't stay still, instead it moved in front of her, blurring and expanding, his eyes mere slits, his mouth just a smear.

"Claire, let's get you into the truck and out of the cold. Hang on to my neck."

She tried to grasp him as he lifted her, but her hands slipped, and finally Holt scooped her up in his arms and carried her to the truck. He tried to get her to stand while he opened the door, but she slumped to the ground as soon as he released her. She had no strength in her legs.

When the door was open, he spooned her up again and set her in the front passenger seat.

After Holt got in the truck, he adjusted the heater so that it blew full force on her. The hot air was soothing. He took both her hands in his and rubbed them, peering at her from where he sat behind the wheel. The shivering stopped.

He handed her a bottle of water and watched as she took a few swallows. Then he took the bottle away.

"That's enough for now. It may upset your stomach." He reached into the center console and pulled out a package of peanut butter crackers. "You must be hungry. Eat these."

Claire struggled to tear open the package, her fingers unable to grasp the end of the plastic. Holt took them from her and swiftly pulled the end open before he handed it back to her.

"Do you remember what happened? Did you recognize the people who kidnapped you?"

Claire gazed at the unfamiliar neighborhood, opening her eyes wide to make sense of the swirling trees and houses illuminated by streetlights and moonlight. She moved her shoulders in a tiny shrug.

"I don't know where I am," she whispered. "Did you find Cade?" She focused all her strength on Holt's face. His answer was the most important thing in her life right now.

His smile meant everything.

"Yes, I found Cade. Actually, he found me. He's with Neve at her grandmother's house. Everything's okay."

"Thank you, oh, thank you, Holt." She turned her face to him, and he kissed her, softly, on the lips. He pulled away. She wanted him to keep kissing her, wanted him to wrap her in his arms and take her somewhere private. Wanted him to hold her as she slept.

But Holt put the truck in gear and turned onto the street. A half block later he turned again and drove slowly down a street of ranch-style homes.

Even with the odd swirling colors, it seemed familiar.

He stopped in front of a house and shifted the truck into park, letting the engine idle. Holt handed her the bottle of water. She took a drink.

With a foggy mind, she registered the house, and the lawn, and the front porch with the table and chairs at one end. She'd come here to talk to someone. A man. His name balanced on the tip of her tongue.

"This is Howard Noble's house."

Her lips formed the name. *Howard Noble.* She remembered him from the interview. "I don't understand. I interviewed him, but I didn't come here again. He was at the meeting at the diner, but I didn't see him after."

"I think you were kidnapped and placed in his garage."

"Why do you think I was here?"

"I found ropes and a gag inside. And minutes later I found you at the end of the alley behind this row of houses." Holt brushed her cheek with one finger.

"I don't remember. My brain is so muddled."

"You've probably been drugged. On top of whatever you were given at the hospital earlier today. I'm taking you back there."

She wouldn't argue. She wanted the world to stop spinning.

Claire screwed the lid back onto the top of the water bottle, closed her eyes and leaned back into the plush seat.

Cade was safe, and she was so tired.

Chapter 56
Holt

Outside the exam room, Holt paced the hallway. He'd tried three times to contact Rhonda. She wasn't answering her phone.

Holt scrolled through his contacts to the duty crew member who was supposed to be watching her house, or at the minimum checking on Rhonda every thirty minutes.

"Hey, boss," the man answered.

"I'm trying to get hold of Rhonda. She's not answering her phone. Is her car at the house?"

"Nope. When she and the dog came back, I was parked down the street as usual. They went inside. I waited a bit, then went to take a leak. When I got back, her car was gone again. I wasn't gone ten minutes. I've been sitting here since, but she hasn't come home."

Holt glanced at his watch. It was nearly midnight. "Hasn't come home? You've no idea where she went?"

"No. She didn't leave any lights on. I tried the front door. Locked up tight. And the dog isn't there either."

Holt swallowed the saliva that flooded his mouth. His mind buzzed. Where would Rhonda have gone? The new house? Back to the café for someone to talk to?

Neither place felt right. His stomach churned. He had lost control of the situation. First, he'd lost control of Claire. Now, he'd lost control of Rhonda. Was she 'in the wind?'

"Mr. Braden. Step in, please." The doctor wore blue scrubs under her white coat. She led him into the cubicle and pulled the curtain closed.

Claire lay on the bed, eyes closed, with an IV stand and apparatus near the bed, the needle inserted in the bend of her left elbow.

"How is she?" Holt whispered.

"I see from her chart that she was here yesterday afternoon following a fall. She left with you. Now, she's severely dehydrated, and obviously drugged with an unknown substance. We are isolating and analyzing that substance now. Hopefully, it will wear off, but we'll be prepared to administer an anecdote if the tests identify the drug and show it to be necessary. She'll be spending the rest of the weekend here. I've ordered her a room." The doctor glared at Holt.

Holt registered the doctor's ire, but shifted his look to study Claire's face, the pinched look of her eyes, her wrinkled brow. He'd done this. He'd not taken care of her and look what had happened. His hands fisted.

"I'll let you get her settled in. And I'll be back tomorrow." He started to add, 'keep her safe,' but didn't. She would be safe here, certainly safer than she'd been when she was in his care.

He closed his eyes, shifted gears in his mind. It did no good to feel guilty about what had happened. It didn't change anything. He'd allowed someone to kidnap Claire. He'd allowed someone to hurt her. He couldn't change that.

But he could change the future. He had to find Rhonda.

Chapter 57– SUNDAY
Rhonda

Rhonda circled the now dark room, feeling the walls and windows. Beneath the roller shades, plywood securely covered the windows from the outside. Boards also covered the door in the center of the back wall. An adjacent room?

She felt her way around what was probably a kitchenette. She opened each drawer, each cabinet, carefully feeling for anything that had been left behind. No tools. No silverware or utensils. Nothing except a chair and a small table against one wall, not to mention the crispy roach carcasses and mouse pellets in the drawers.

Sweat trickled down the back of her neck. Her head pounded.

Rhonda sat in the single chair and stared into the dark. Her eye lids grew heavy. She blinked once, and then again. Each time, her eyes stayed closed a little longer. After a while, it became impossible to keep her eyes open.

* * *

Slowly, Rhonda lifted her head. Her neck ached. She opened her eyes. The darkness spun around her. Her mind was spinning too. Where was she? Who had put her here? Why?

Gradually, she remembered the drive-in, and the vintage car. She remembered the driver. He'd shot her up with something. Why hadn't he just killed her?

She shifted her body, tried to get up, but a headache pounded. She closed her eyes, had to sit again. Wanted to sleep.

Where was Samson? What had happened to him? A sob erupted out of her mouth. The dog was all she had left of her former life, and now he was gone, too. Images of the dead animals she'd found in the grass around the old motor court came to mind. Was Samson lying there with more dead animals? Had she led him to that fate?

It was all her fault. She'd made a stupid, impulsive decision, and now here she was, stuck in some awful place.

Her eyes grew heavier. She closed them. Slept.

Chapter 58
Holt

Holt Braden drove from the hospital to Rhonda's house at 4 a.m. Sunday morning. He parked in the driveway and jogged to the porch. Using his key, he entered the house, then flicked on the light and quickly surveyed the room. He marched across it to the bedroom, and then the bathroom.

All her things were gone.

He tried her cell phone number again. She didn't answer.

Two obvious questions filled his mind: had she left voluntarily or had someone taken her?

Holt went to the back door and opened it. He stared at the yard, and then scanned the porch. In the corner, where the torn screen hung, swinging slightly in the breeze, a man lay still.

In two strides he reached the body, checked the man's neck for a pulse, and found none. He stepped away, aware that he had unknowingly entered, and tampered with, a crime scene.

Back in the house, he checked the room once more, looking for something, anything, that would explain where Rhonda had gone, and why a dead man lay on her back porch. All that remained besides the crappy old furniture was a crumpled yellow paper ball on the table.

He read the words on the paper and exhaled deeply. This note had spooked her. She was gone.

As Holt locked the house, his mind churned. He had to report the body. Somebody had staged it to look like Rhonda had killed someone. And not just anyone. Howard Noble.

What did the man have to do with all of this?

He climbed into his truck and mentally reviewed the facts.

From Cade, he knew that Kai had been cooking meth somewhere in the vicinity. And Kai was dead, found in Claire's car, after an argument at the arena.

Mrs. Petrovsky's home was a pile of blackened timbers and bricks. She was dead, and so was Roger Benson. Rhonda had overheard Benson talking with two men in the café about a dead woman. Had Benson set the fire? Had someone killed him before he did it, or after? Was their intent in setting the fire to cover that crime, or to frighten Rhonda? Did they want to frighten her because of what she'd overheard? Or did they know who she really was?

He was certain that Rhonda had wondered that same things after reading the note. She had packed up and left.

None of that explained who had kidnapped Claire. Yes, she'd interviewed Kai's grandmother and Howard Noble. What had she learned that called for kidnapping? And what had Howard Noble done that got him killed?

Everything Cade had told him concerned Kai's drug involvement. He was a hothead and had been pushing his niece Neve around. Kai had learned that Cade knew a DEA agent. Claire's kidnapping could have been an attempt to keep Cade from talking. But it had backfired. Cade hadn't even known his mother had been kidnapped.

Della Munoz. The name popped into his head. One of the owners of the B&B. And Rhonda had found her dead cat at the old motor court. Carbon monoxide poisoning. Drugs and leaking pollutants. Mrs. Petrovsky's fire. Kai dead. Roger Benson dead. Howard Noble dead. Rhonda missing.

Could Della Munoz fill in any missing pieces?

He backed the truck into the street and drove toward the B&B.

* * *

Holt rang the front bell of the beautiful old home. A minute later, footsteps sounded inside the house and the porch light flicked on. Someone pulled the curtain aside in the door's window and peeked out at him.

It wasn't the woman he'd met yesterday in Claire's suite. Most likely, it was her sister, Betsy Spoon. He pulled out his badge and identification document and held them up so she could see them. The door opened a crack, the security chain still secured.

"I'm sorry to bother you so early. I'm Agent Braden. DEA. I need to talk with you and your sister about recent events."

"Have you found that dear lady, Ms. Northcutt? And her son? Della told me he was missing and then someone nabbed her right out from under our noses."

"Yes, to both those questions. And they are both doing well. Is your sister here? I need to speak with both of you."

The door closed and the security chain was removed.

"Come in," she said when the door opened again. "We're in the kitchen preparing breakfast. Early hours for us on weekends, when we offer a full breakfast as early as 7 a.m."

Holt followed her into the home, noting the wood banisters on the grand stairway, and the thick carpets on polished oak floors. Tiffany lamps sparkled from side tables in the hallway.

Holt stepped into the kitchen and was engulfed in the aroma of fresh-brewed coffee and the scent of rising bread dough and cinnamon. He staggered. When was the last time he ate or slept? He didn't remember.

"Oh, Agent Braden." Della Munoz turned toward him from the counter. She rubbed her flour-covered hands on a paper towel. "You're up early. I'm making cinnamon rolls. Need a cup of coffee?"

"That would be wonderful." Holt looked around the kitchen, where breakfast was definitely in progress.

Betsy Spoon took a white porcelain mug from an open shelf of dinnerware and filled it with steaming brew from the tall metal coffee pot. "Here you go. We've got leftover cookies from yesterday. Getting today's goodies ready for the oven right now." She poured a cup of coffee and slid it and a crystal cookie jar across the island to where he stood. "Sit down. What can we help you with?"

Holt perched on a stool next to the island, taking in the many mixing bowls and utensils spread across the counters and islands, each area staging a different dish for the morning's breakfast.

"Have either of you remembered anything else about yesterday afternoon, when Claire Northcutt was kidnapped from your property?" Holt pulled a lemon cookie from the jar and took a bite. He could have crammed the whole thing into his mouth, as well as several more, but he didn't think these women would approve.

The sisters exchanged a glance. "We've both talked to the police. And no. Nothing new," Betsy said.

"The community's festival was under way on our lawn. People had parked cars all up and down the street. Kids in costume were running everywhere. It was a melee," Della added.

Holt chewed another bite of cookie as he pulled his phone from the pocket of his jacket and opened the Notes function. "Nothing out of the ordinary that caught your attention?"

"There was this sweet little girl in a pink fairy costume. She was flicking glitter everywhere. Extremely cute." Betsy grinned.

"But nothing that made you suspicious of anyone?"

"No. Is there anything else?" Della turned back to the counter and pressed the ball of dough with the heels of her hands.

"Mrs. Munoz, have you recently lost a cat?"

Della straightened, and turned around to peer at Holt. "Misty. My gray cat. She disappeared last week. How did you know?"

Betsy stepped around the island and went to stand beside her sister. She stroked her arm.

"I have news about your cat. Several dead animals were found next to the old motor court off Route 66. Your cat was among them. We identified her by the microchip."

Della closed her eyes. When she opened them, they were full of tears. Her sister patted her shoulder. "I was afraid something bad had happened to her."

"Did your cat leave the house often?"

"No. Mostly a house kitty. But a guest let her outside, not realizing she wasn't to go out. Cats kill birds, you know, and we enjoy the songbirds in our yard so much."

"If you'd like to pick up your cat's remains, you can call the animal shelter. They are holding them for you."

Della sniffed and looked at Holt. "I don't think you came here at 5 in the morning just to tell me about my cat."

"No, ma'am. I'm working several cases with the local authorities, including Ms. Northcutt's kidnapping. Do you know Howard Noble?"

Betsy Spoon reacted first, with a wide-eyed look.

Mrs. Munoz leaned against the counter. Her eyes grew big in a stony face.

This news seemed to affect her more than the news of her cat's death.

"Howard Noble was my first husband," Della said. "We were married for seven long years. Has something happened to Howard?"

"He is deceased. Sometime last night."

"Did someone finally kill him?"

"That's your first thought? That someone killed him? Why? Who would want him dead?" Holt knew never to be surprised by anything, but this surprised him. Della Munoz and Howard Noble? He couldn't imagine a more unlikely pair.

Della turned back to the dough and punched it several times before smoothing it flat with her hands. "I was married to the man briefly, in the scheme of things, and once we were divorced, we both made our lives with other people. He married Claudia and had a life here. I didn't see much of him, even after my Jerry died and I moved back to our parent's house. We didn't have children together. No reason to stay in touch."

"Did he have any enemies?"

She glanced at him over her shoulder. "He could be cruel. He fooled people with that polite way he had. Fooled me for a good while. Howard wanted what he wanted when he wanted it. If you got in his way, watch out."

"I'd appreciate your help with this. It could be connected to a fire. Someone torched Mrs. Sally Petrovsky's home last night. A dead man was found there, Roger Benson. Do either of those names ring a bell?"

"Petrovsky, you say?" Della spread a mixture of brown sugar and cinnamon over the dough and rolled it up. She grabbed a butcher knife from a drawer and sliced the roll into even segments. "Sally was married to one of Howard's business partners. He was as crooked as they come. The two couples were inseparable, until things fell apart. I don't know the details. Don't know Benson."

Holt glanced over at Betsy Spoon, who had been at the sink, washing bowls and utensils. Betsy dried her hands. "Roger was a no-good. Meth head. People talk in this town, and he's one they talk about. Runs with a bad bunch. Sells drugs to kids. Somehow manages to never get caught. Friends in high places, you know?"

Holt typed a note into his phone. "Anything else about Howard? Other family members, or people he's gotten crosswise with?"

"His sister's boy and he have stayed close, I think. Vince Matheson is his name. He stops in to see him a couple of times a year. Lives south of Fort Worth somewhere. Hill country." Della used a spatula to place the slices of the roll onto a baking sheet.

Holt's finger punched too many periods into the notes app. Vince Matheson again. "Did Matheson know anyone else in town? Like the Petrovskys?"

"Likely. Vince would have been in his twenties, going to college, when his mother died, and he got really friendly with Howard. Same time Howard was partnered with Petrovsky."

His mind worked as he jotted more notes into his phone. "Interesting. Can you think of anything else that might help the investigation?"

The sisters exchanged a glance; both women shook their heads. "If anything comes to mind, we'll let you know."

"Here's my card. You can reach me at this number any time."

"If you're anywhere near here about 7 a.m., stop by for one of these cinnamon rolls. They'll be ready then." Della covered the baking dish with a cloth and set it on the cook top above the oven.

* * *

Back in the truck, Holt punched in a number and fired off several questions.

Vince, Howard, Roger, Kai.

Connections.

Chapter 59
Rhonda

Rhonda woke up with a start. The rancid air in the room carried a new scent. Men's cologne. And she heard breathing that was not hers. She was no longer alone in the lightless room.

"Hello, Rhonda. Or should I say Renee." The man chuckled. A beam of light flicked on, spotlighting her where she sat on the sagging sofa. "Such a waste. I've been watching you sleep. I want to get to know you better. But I guess there's no time for that. I've got my orders, and I'm a good soldier. The best. This production operation should be mine, and before long, it will be."

The light came from a blinding light attached to the top of the helmet he wore.

She couldn't see his face and didn't recognize the voice.

The man crossed the room and reached for her. She summoned every ounce of strength she had and pulled away, but he put his hands on both sides of her head and held her there. He bent close and licked her cheek. At the same time, one of his hands reached inside his front shirt pocket. Seconds later, something pricked her neck.

"Noooo," she brought her hands up to push him away, but the powerful drug quickly took her down, down, down. The room and everything in it made a slow turn and she felt herself falling. Without his hands there, holding her upright by her head, she would fall to the floor.

"Oh. Such a shame. No one will find you for days. And we'll be long gone. If you're still alive, and you talk, it won't matter at that point." He tilted his head. "One quick kiss before I go."

She struggled, but his lips were on hers. She tried again to pull away, fighting the man's grip on her head.

The air around her fogged. She fought to keep the room in focus.

The man let her sink into the cushions.

"Sleep tight." The beam of light clicked off, leaving the room black, and everything in it vanished. A door, opened and closed.

* * *

Something small ran across her cheek. Her eyes opened, and liquid dripped into one eye. She blinked and struggled to sit up. Despite the sharp headache, she managed to sit, open her eyes, and peer around the room.

Skinny shafts of light squeezed through the window coverings. A small sack sat by the door. The sensation of the floor tilting beneath her nauseated her as she crawled across the filthy floor to the sack. Inside it, she found two Lunchables, and a bottle of water. Her stomach growled. She didn't remember the last time she had eaten.

She took a drink and ate a bite of cheese, savoring the sharp flavor of cheddar. She immediately felt stronger, revived.

Rhonda got to her feet using the wall for support. The effort exhausted her. When her heartbeat slowed, she made her way around the small room, feeling the walls. Was there anything she could use as a weapon against her captors when they came back? If they came back?

They were feeding her. Why? Surely, they wanted her dead. She was quite certain the drug gang had found her. They'd never let her out of this room.

She inched around the room to the windowless wall. She felt a doorframe, and another door. She tried the doorknob. Locked. She shook it and then kicked weakly at the flimsy panel. She kicked again, and again, using all her strength. Finally, the wood split. A few more kicks and the door splintered apart. It opened into blackness.

Rhonda stepped through, and into rank air. She coughed, nauseated by the smell of decomposition in the room. Gradually, her eyes adjusted, and the blackness turned to grayness, splintered by dim light squeezing through the gaps in two boarded windows.

Small bodies littered the floor. Cats, dogs, a furry something that was probably a rabbit. And something else, in the corner of the room, a bundle of rags.

She stumbled, stepped closer. Not rags.

She bent down, saw dark hair, leathery skin, and a hand, fingers bent like a claw and a wrist, with a charm bracelet still clasped around it.

Dizziness overtook her. She fell to her knees, the dead body inches away.

The room swam, bile rose in her throat.

The world blackened.

Chapter 60
Claire

"Holt. It's about time you got here. I'm going crazy lying in this bed. I want to see Cade. Have you talked to him today?" Claire winced as she sat up. Earlier, she'd spent some time in the small bathroom, washing her face, brushing her teeth, trying to look normal again. Her hair was flat against her head, but it was relatively clean, despite the hour she'd spent in the evergreens last night. She summoned up enough strength to smile at Holt.

"I haven't talked to Cade today. But he was safe at the grandmother's last night, Claire. Kai isn't a threat to either of the kids anymore. It's a long story. I'm not sure you—."

"I'm not an invalid. The drugs are out of my system and I'm thinking clearly. What's happened? You haven't slept. And I don't think you've showered either." He smelled like sweat. What had he been doing for the last twelve hours?

"Kai's dead. Rhonda found his body in your Jeep at the diner. For a short while, you were a suspect in his murder. But I think we've cleared all that up. He was a small-town drug dealer who got a little too big for his britches—as the saying goes."

"Cade said he was into drugs. Was he cooking meth?"

"Yes. We're still searching the area for his lab."

Claire studied the face she knew so well. "What else? I see it on your face. You need to tell me. Stop keeping things from me." She wouldn't let their relationship continue as it had been. The walls between them were coming down, one way or another.

"Rhonda is missing."

"What?" Claire pushed back into the pillow and crossed her arms. Her brow furrowed. "Because you were looking for me." She threw the covers off. "We've got to find her. This is my fault."

She grimaced with pain as she got out of bed and charged across the room.

"Claire, you can't . . ."

"Yes, I can, and I will." She dug in the closet for her belongings, feeling air on her bare bottom. She glanced back at him. "Oh, you. It's not like you haven't seen it before. And you better get used to it." She hurried into the small bathroom with the bag of clothes but left the door ajar. "I've been lying here thinking for the past few hours. I'm making some changes. One of them has to do with you."

"Oh? How do you mean?" His voice was low.

Claire shoved the door farther open and crossed the room, pulling a turtleneck sweater down over her hips. "I mean this." She threw her arms around him and kissed him. As his arms tightened around her, she pushed him away.

"But that's for later. We've got to find Rhonda. Do you have any leads?"

The grin faded from Holt's face. He cleared his throat. "Yes. I had an interesting conversation with the sisters at the B&B. Della Munoz was the owner of one of the dead cats Rhonda found by that deserted motor court. And it turns out that Della used to be married to Howard Noble. I found his body last night at Rhonda's house."

Claire slipped into her shoes and kept her eyes on Holt. "Sounds like a busy night. Where do we start?"

"I'm doing background checks on people Della Munoz and Betsy Spoon mentioned. Rhonda overheard a man named Roger Benson talking at the diner about someone being dead. Benson turned up, in the house next to Rhonda's, where someone set a fire. He's also dead."

"Coincidence?"

"I don't think so. I think Benson set the fire. He, or someone, left a note at Rhonda's saying he meant to burn her house down, probably because she overheard him at the diner. Or it could be because she's in the witness protection program, hiding from a drug ring."

A lot of things suddenly made sense. "Witness Protection? Her name's not Rhonda? You're protecting her, not working with her?" Relief flooded her heart.

Holt nodded. "And not doing a very good job."

Claire perched on the edge of the hospital bed. "I complicated things by showing up here, didn't I?"

"I should have told you about my job. I was going to. No excuses."

"Things will be different from here on out. Anyone else you've been running background checks on I should know about?"

Holt took a deep breath and lifted his chin. "Actually, yes. Neve's uncle Kai. Turns out he cooks meth, sells it, ships it. He quit a job in the Dallas area and moved here a few years ago. With a lot of money."

"Great. By bringing Neve and Cade here, I brought them right into the middle of a meth ring."

"You had no way of knowing. But that's not all. I've also been investigating your old friend Vince Matheson."

"Oh? Jealous, maybe? And?"

"He's been on the DEA radar for several years, working from Fort Worth to Springfield. Has a nice cover set up; the biker group he travels with in a tri-state area is not part of his drug ring. We've been working to uncover who his boss is. The latest information is that he's part of the Mendosa ring working in Texas, Oklahoma, and southern Missouri. It seems they're looking to expand."

Claire's brain felt ready to explode. Her hands shook. "Drug deals! He's connected to what happened to Rhonda. Did you dangle her like fish bait here, knowing who he was and that he'd find her?"

"We didn't dangle her. We didn't know his uncle lived here."

Anger rose like boiling steam in her throat. "You knew he was dangerous?"

"Calm down, Claire. I had firm control on the situation."

"Firm control? Rhonda is missing."

Holt cleared his throat. "It won't be long before Vince is in custody. Everything is under control. If we haven't found her by the time we have him, he'll tell us where Rhonda is, and we'll go get her. Easy enough."

But Holt didn't look relaxed. If anything, his face was tenser that she'd ever seen it, his gray-blue eyes dark and troubled.

Claire ran her fingers through her tangled hair and glanced in the reflection from the room's window. Outside, the hospital's parking lot lights were still on. Her image reflected an exhausted woman, her face etched with pain.

Holt shook his head. "There's something I'm forgetting. Something Rhonda said. Something about Route

66." His mind raced. What had she said yesterday? What had she told him?

He pulled out his phone and went to voice mail messages where he clicked through the recordings. He hit 'play' and listened, but it wasn't there. The conversation must have been in person. What had she said? His mind clicked.

Rhonda had told him about a light at the old motor court. He hadn't called it in.

"That old motor court on Route 66. I read your notes. Is that the place that Howard owned? The one he told you about?"

"Most likely. There aren't too many of those old motels around. Could it have something to do with the drug ring?"

"We'll soon find out. For now, I need you to stay here, safe." He glanced at his watch. "I'll be back in about an hour. There's something I have to take care of, but I promise I'll come back, and, if she hasn't turned up yet, you and I will find Rhonda."

Chapter 61
Holt

A black Harley Davidson sat in front of Howard Noble's house. Holt pulled into the driveway and sat for a moment. He doubted the old man had a motorcycle; Claire had said Noble was a car collector. But he knew who this motorcycle probably belonged to.

The front door opened, and a man came down the steps and started walking toward the Harley. Straightening his Ray Ban sunglasses, he noticed Holt's truck, and headed toward it instead.

"Can I help you?" he asked, sizing up the truck and Holt.

"I'm looking for Howard Noble. Is he here?" Holt watched the man's reaction as he slid out of his truck, taking in the man's leather jacket, and motorcycle chaps. Most women would be attracted to him, because he had the ever-popular bad boy look about him. Women would take notice.

"Who's looking?"

Holt pulled out his identification and held it out. The man peered at it and smiled nonchalantly.

"DEA. What do you want with my uncle?"

Holt felt a check in his gut. The relaxed man was more at ease than he should have been when a DEA agent flashed his credentials. "Noble is your uncle? Is he here?" He watched the man's face.

"He went out last night and didn't come back. I was going to look for him. Want me to have him call you?"

Holt handed him one of his business cards. "I saw him last night. At the scene of a house fire. I'd like to ask him a few questions."

The confident man blinked. His forehead creased. "A house fire? Whose house?"

"Mrs. Sally Petrovsky. Do you know her?"

"Only by name. She was married to my uncle's business partner. I haven't thought of her in years."

"Any idea why Mr. Noble would have been at the fire?"

"Is Sally okay?"

"No."

The man processed the information with guarded eyes. "Sorry to hear that," he said. "She was a nice person. Surely you're not insinuating that Uncle Howard had anything to do with the fire."

Holt's phone buzzed in his pocket. He glanced at the Caller ID. "Excuse me, I need to take this." He stepped a few feet away and turned his back to the man. "Yes. You sure it's Howard Noble? I'll meet you in the parking lot, behind the café." Holt clicked off the phone and turned back to the man.

Noble's nephew squinted at Holt. "Did someone find my uncle? I should have known. He's at Tiny's Diner, isn't he? He eats breakfast there every day."

"What did you say your name was?"

"Vince Matheson."

"Do you live with Mr. Noble?" Holt asked the question although he already knew the answer to that question as well as where Howard actually was.

"I'm from Fort Worth. Drove up for the weekend with some of my biker buddies."

Holt nodded. Matheson acted like a man in charge. Confident. Smooth. Holt had chased down and arrested enough drug dealers to know one when he saw one, although their disguises ran the full gamut. Teachers, doctors, lawyers, bus drivers, waiters.

"Mind if I follow you there?" Matheson straightened his sunglasses. "I need to talk to my uncle. Staying out all night isn't something he would usually do, especially when I'm in town."

"No problem. I'm headed there now." Holt stepped back to his truck as Vince climbed onto his motorcycle. Holt backed into the street. As he drove toward the café, Vince's bike rumbled along a few yards behind his rear bumper.

He wasn't impressed with Matheson. He'd known who he was the instant the man walked out of Howard Noble's house. From the hospital, he'd called his crew and sent one of them to Noble's house, to see if Matheson were there. They'd confirmed it.

He'd sent another agent to Tiny's Route 66 Diner and asked them to call him in 10 minutes.

Adrenaline raced through his system. He hoped what was about to happen didn't become a blood bath. As usual, he wore bulletproof Kevlar under his clothes.

A bead of sweat popped out on his forehead and ran down the side of his face. He should have put it together faster. The likelihood that the gang would find Rhonda so quickly had been miniscule. It was a matter of coincidence more than anything, nothing the drug dealers had done on their own.

They had literally stumbled onto her. He prayed he would get to her in time to save her life.

* * *

Holt pulled into the diner's parking lot and drove to the employee's section. A half dozen cars were parked there, and a few customers had already entered the café for an early Sunday breakfast. As he parked, Vince pulled up beside his truck. Holt slid out, and Vince got off his bike.

"He's probably inside," Vince said, nodding at the diner. They walked toward the front door.

A black BMW sedan roared into the parking lot. Holt watched five men pile out of the vehicle. In formation, like geese flying, they headed across the asphalt toward Holt. He glanced at Vince, knowing he would signal these men—his men—to open fire if necessary.

Vince lifted a hand to pull off his sunglasses.

A white van pulled in off the street. Seconds later, cackling laughter filled the air as a group of middle-aged women, wearing athletic shoes, sweatshirts, and sweatpants, slowly climbed out of the van.

Immediately after, another van entered the parking lot, this one advertising a local Methodist church. It angled across two parking spaces and stopped.

When the sliding door opened, uniformed men jumped from the van, guns drawn. The SWAT team surrounded Matheson and his gang.

The middle-aged women near the white van pulled off their sweatshirts to reveal SWAT flak jackets and guns.

Vince and his men had drawn their guns, but quickly lowered them to the ground, obviously outnumbered.

Holt entered the café through the employees' back entrance.

Jean, the waitress he'd met the day before with Rhonda, was preparing a tray cluttered with several dinner plates and side dishes.

"Employees only back here, sir." She did a double-take and then nodded. "Your sister's not here. She has the day off."

"I'm looking for Lloyd. He in his office?"

"I don't think so. He left about ten minutes ago. Probably went home to pick up his wife and bring her back with the daily special. That's his usual routine."

"Do you have his home address?"

Jean blinked. "Nope. Never been there. Might ask Vivian. I'll send her back here when I take this tray out."

Holt fidgeted as Jean finished adding the garnishes to the plates and moved through the swinging doors to the dining room.

Another minute passed before a different waitress sauntered into the kitchen, scowling.

"Who are you and what the hell do you want? We're busy here, taking care of customers. Lloyd doesn't allow anyone else in the kitchen. You gotta go." The nametag stitched on her uniform read *Vivian.*

Holt pulled out his credentials and held them up.

Vivian's face blanched. She whirled and dashed through the swinging doors back into the dining room. Something crashed.

Only a step behind her, Holt almost tripped over the waitress and the young man who'd been carrying a bin full of dirty dishes into the kitchen. Both were on their hands and knees trying to get up. Swiftly, Holt grabbed the waitress's arm and twisted it behind her.

"Not so fast. I need to talk to you."

She glared and struggled to get away.

"Let's take this somewhere more private." Holt pulled the waitress back into the kitchen and down the hallway toward Lloyd's office.

Chapter 62
Claire

Claire put on a little makeup after Holt left the hospital room. She was in the tiny bathroom, fluffing her hair. She pulled it into a high ponytail as someone knocked on the doorframe.

Cade stepped into the room.

"Mom? Are you okay?"

She flew across the room and threw her arms around him. "I was so worried about you. Where have you been?" She peered up into his face.

"Didn't Holt tell you?" Cade took a step back.

"Of course, he did, but I need to hear it from you. What were you thinking? Didn't you know how worried I'd be? You should have called me or left a message."

"Stop thinking of me as a little kid, Mom. I was with Neve, helping her get through this thing with her uncle. When we heard what he'd done to you at the arena, Neve was so scared. Her uncle is a ticking time bomb, and we had to do something."

"He's dead. Did Holt tell you?"

Cade nodded. "Neve called the police late yesterday. The detective came out to talk to us this morning. He told us that a rival drug gang was in the area and had probably killed him."

Claire shivered. "I never would have brought you here if I'd had any idea ..."

"Mom, wake up. People make meth and sell drugs everywhere. It's part of life. You've got to trust me, Mom. I have a brain."

Claire studied her son's intense look. "I believe you. And I'm proud that you stayed with Neve to protect her. But I would have appreciated a call or a message. Something other than TTYL."

He grinned. "Neve had my phone. She typed that in. Neither of us had been responding to messages in case Kai was tracing her phone, or mine, to find out where we were. We hid in the storm cellar. Creepy down there, and no cell signal. Exciting, but Neve was scared."

Claire lifted her eyebrows. "Romantic?"

Cade reddened. "I didn't say that. We're both glad it's over. So, we're good, right? I'm not in trouble?"

"We're good. I'm being released, and Holt will be back to get me in a few minutes." She glanced at the wall clock. "We should go downstairs."

"I'll wait with you. Everything packed?"

* * *

Claire and Cade sat on a bench at the main entrance to the hospital. They sat in a comfortable silence, waiting. She wanted to talk to him, but there would be time later, as they drove home to Stillwater. It was nice to have him here, beside her, safe. Minutes clicked past on the wall clock above the information desk.

Holt's truck pulled up to the portico. He jumped out and hurried to them. She felt the warmth in her face as he kissed her cheek.

"Meet you back at the B&B, Cade?" Holt patted Cade's shoulder. "Your mom and I have something to take care of first."

Cade extended his hand to shake Holt's, then walked toward a white Honda parked not far from the hospital entrance. Someone sat inside, waiting for Cade. Neve. Claire wanted to talk to her to get a feel for her relationship with Cade now. It could wait until another time.

Holt took her elbow and helped Claire climb into the truck's front seat. "Are you okay? Not feeling faint? Is anything hurting?" He rested one hand on her leg.

"I'm so relieved Cade's okay. Did you know that he and Neve called the police about Kai yesterday?" She tried to ignore the throbbing pain.

"So, I heard. Too bad it was after he'd been to the arena. Wish we could have avoided that whole episode."

"Do you think my kidnapping had anything to do with Kai?"

"I think it had to do with your friend Vince. He wanted to keep you quiet, keep you from investigating while he wrapped up his enterprise work here, which was taking over Kai's operation."

"Vince is the head of that drug ring?"

"No. He's not the head. We're searching for the boss. Worse case scenario, he's skipped town and taken Rhonda with him." Holt remained silent as he pulled out of the hospital area and onto the city street.

Claire watched his face, the set of his chin, the grim look around his eyes. Rhonda meant something to him. If the drug cartel took Rhonda, she could be dead, or worse— trafficked or sold. She could be anywhere in the world.

* * *

Holt's truck bounced over the curb and onto the crumbling driveway that once led into the motor court parking area. One wheel dropped into a rut. He gunned the engine and drove closer to the line of cottages. "If she's not here, I have no idea where she is. We may be too late."

He parked, bailed out of the truck, and jogged toward the duplex cabin at the left rear of the complex. Claire followed. She rubbed her clammy hands together. The saliva in her mouth dried up. What would they find? She hoped they didn't find anything dead.

Claire stumbled over a buckled brick sidewalk concealed by the grass. Roof shingles and boards poked up through the overgrowth. On one derelict cabin, the door hung by a single hinge. Broken screens leaned against the weathered siding beneath boarded-up windows.

"Careful. This old motor court should be torn down." Holt tried the doorknob, and then pounded on the wood. "Rhonda? Are you in there? Anybody?"

He continued to pound, and when no one responded, he kicked at the door. The wood splintered. He threw his weight against the boards, and then again.

"Get back from the door. I'm going to shoot the lock."

Holt fired a round into the lock. It fell apart and the door swung open. When he stepped inside, Claire was right behind him.

Chapter 63
Holt

The scent of decay and mildew, as well as the stink of something dead, hung in the air of the room. Underneath it all, another acidic scent, like a urine-soaked box of cat litter, permeated the room. He flicked the flashlight up at the ceiling, and then into the dark corners of the room. Something fluttered.

Holt put his arm out to stop Claire from advancing into the room with him. As he took a step, the floor crunched.

"Wait. Let your eyes adjust. There may be boards with nails poking out on the floor, rat traps or who knows what." He scooted his feet along, kicking things out of the way.

"Holt–"

Behind him, Claire's voice broke. Holt whirled, his gun ready. His light caught Claire, and the man holding her.

"Put the gun down, Holt. No time for that, anyway. Claire will be dead even if you do manage to get a shot off at me," the man said.

Holt swallowed. The familiar voice was not completely unexpected. The man had been at the bottom of his suspect list, almost above suspicion, but not quite. Adrenaline raced through his veins. He laid the gun on the floor.

"Never thought it would come to this." The man's voice was a growl. "Now it's clear what has to happen. The three of you, rotting here in this old building until they demolish it next month. Four bodies, counting Tatia. I was so close."

"We've got Vince, you know. It's all over, Lloyd." Holt spoke politely to the man he'd long considered a friend.

"Not quite over. I can start again someplace else. I'm still the boss, I've still got my men. Minus a few. Nothing has changed. I'm the one with the gun. And two hostages. You're all alone. Where's your backup?"

Holt's mind raced. Backup was on the way, but could he put Lloyd off long enough for them to arrive silently?

"Let's talk this through, Lloyd. How'd you manage it? The DEA did a thorough background check and you were squeaky clean. A former SEAL?"

"I've got friends. It's easy enough when you know the right people," Lloyd snickered. "Pad a pocket here and there. I can pass any background check. Little did I know that after years of this, I'd end up providing a safe haven for the very person whose testimony would put my top men in jail and threaten my entire operation."

"Once you run, the DEA will know who you are. Your face will be plastered everywhere. You're only going to make it worse if you add more murders to your list of crimes." Holt's voice was smooth, calm.

"You don't believe that, and neither do I. I'll be dying in that jail cell anyway. But killing you will buy me a little time. Curious, how did you know to come here? What tipped you off?"

"Actually, it was Rhonda. She saw a light on here last night, thought some kids might be partying it up. Guess you snatched her sometime after that."

"Yeah. She freaked, and I followed her. Caught her at the old Route 66 Drive-in with a flat tire. And for the record, my guys didn't burn down her neighbor's house. That was Roger Benson, working on the Mayor's directive to throw Rhonda off the scent, get her to keep quiet about Roger's loose lips. 'Loose lips sink ships.' And the Mayor's pollution coverup was headed for the Deep Six the minute Roger was brought on board. I tried to tell him as much, but he didn't listen to me." Lloyd shifted a few feet back toward the door, pulling Claire with him.

"Wait," Holt said. He needed to stall for time, had to hope that backup was nearly here.

A sharp bark cut through the silence.

The small room exploded with screeching and the flapping of wings.

Chapter 64
Claire

When his arm dropped from her neck, Claire darted away into the dark chaos. The air was alive with wings.

"Argh! Keep them away from me," Lloyd screamed.

Samson raced into the room barking sharply, waking up any bats still slumbering in the darkness. Claire protected her head as she crouched near the floor.

Holt swung his flashlight around the room, catching sight of a few remaining bats as they dropped down and swooped over Lloyd's tall frame before flying through the open doorway and out into the night. The man's mouth gaped open in a soundless scream. He'd dropped his gun, and Claire kicked it across the room. Holt grabbed Lloyd, twisted him around, arms behind, then pulled out a pair of handcuffs and secured Lloyd's wrists.

"It's over Lloyd. Where's Rhonda? Tell me."

Sirens blared outside, and blue and white lights strobed through the moonlit night. One last bat swooped over them and out the door.

Samson barked furiously at Lloyd.

"Tell me, now."

Lloyd clamped his mouth shut and swayed. Beads of sweat coated his forehead. "Damn bats," he said through gritted teeth. "Damn dog."

Several men in uniform stormed into the room. Holt spoke to them, and they hustled Lloyd outside.

Holt bent down, petting Samson. Claire went to him, put her arms around him and patted his back.

"I've got to find her. She's counting on me," he said as he stood. The dog barked again.

"Then we'll find her." Claire watched the dog race around the room, sniffing the floor. He barked at another door on the far side of the room. "Where does that door go?" Claire motioned toward it. "A closet? Or an adjoining room?"

Holt strode across the room to the door and tried the knob. It turned easily. Holt pushed it open. Samson dashed in.

Light fell through the doorway of the dark room. Claire stepped up to the threshold. Inside, she could make out a table and chair, but the rest of the room was hidden in shadow.

She coughed. The putrid smell from Neve's grandmother's house and the sickeningly sweet smell of death hung in the stale air.

"Damn." Holt took one step into the room, flashing his light onto the floor. The beam reflected off an empty water bottle, and an empty plastic carton. His face fell. "She's not here."

"But someone was," Claire said. She pinched her nose shut, breathed through her mouth, and stepped into the room. Then, she crossed the room to another connecting doorway, where broken boards had once sealed the entrance to an adjacent room.

Inside the room, Samson barked again.

Claire peered in. Her eyes adjusted to the dimness as she scanned the room. "Holt? Here."

Chapter 65
Rhonda

The room was so bright, Rhonda squinted when she opened her eyes. Blinds at the windows did little to block the light. Machines beeped around her. White sheets, light green walls, and Holt sitting in the chair next to the bed, elbows on his knees, eyes closed. It hurt to smile, so she didn't. She relaxed muscles that had tensed at the brightness, muscles that had been tense for more than a week now.

"Rhonda," a soft voice said.

She turned her head. "Claire."

The attractive journalist sat in another chair next to the bed on her other side. Makeup had smeared below her eyes, and exhaustion hung on her face.

Rhonda reached for her hand.

"Claire, my name is Renee. Renee Trammel. I'm a veterinarian, in the Witness Protection Program. And Holt—your Holt—is the agent who is my 'keeper.'"

Claire nodded. "I should have known it was something like that."

She glanced at Holt. He shifted, stretched one arm, and opened his eyes.

"You're awake. Thank God." He touched Renee's other hand.

"What happened?" Renee blinked and glanced around the room, but her vision blurred. "This is a hospital."

"Yes. They drugged you, but otherwise, no injuries. How do you feel, other than lightheaded?"

Renee thought about that. She could feel her toes, her fingers, and when she flexed her leg and arm muscles everything seemed to work. Her head was another matter. The headache pounded. "I think I'm okay." She searched Holt's eyes, wondering if he was keeping something from her. "What happened?" she asked again.

"Claire and I found you. The police arrested Lloyd and several others. They're being interviewed now. I'll know more in a few hours. The immediate threat against you is over. We're closer to going to trial, closer to putting them away."

"So, I can contact my family? I can go home?" Renee sat up in the bed, and then lay back, dizzy.

"Let's see what the rest of the day brings. They want to keep you overnight for observation."

She closed her eyes. Could it really be over?

"Renee?" Holt cleared his throat. "I should have never let you go back to that bungalow alone after the fire. I didn't—"

"Don't, Holt. You were doing what you had to do, finding Claire. It all turned out for the best. I'm alive. The trial will happen soon, and I'll get part of my life back."

"You'll get all of your life back."

"Not quite," she bit her lip to keep from crying. Just over a week had passed since that horrible day at her vet clinic. She closed her eyes, instantly reliving the sounds of the men storming into the clinic, and the gunfire. Her throat clogged, and she sobbed.

"That's where you're wrong. And now's when I have to apologize for not telling you something."

"What?" She peered at him, but Holt wasn't looking at her. He was staring at the doorway to her hospital room.

Chapter 66
Holt

An orderly wheeled someone into the room. Gauze bandages swathed the patient's head, covering some of the bruises that had purpled his eyes and his cheeks. Both legs were heavily bandaged.

Holt watched Renee's face, and glanced at Claire. Both women stared at the figure in the doorway.

Renee blinked, her eyes already full of tears.

"Truthfully, we didn't think he would survive. But he did." Holt spoke slowly, in a low voice. He had so much respect for Renee. He'd almost failed at his mission to keep her safe. This case had reminded him, more than any other, that there are unseen forces at work. Daniel shouldn't have survived, and truth be known, it was only coincidence that had allowed him to find Claire, or Rhonda. He could have lost them both. Holt cleared his throat.

"He regained consciousness Thursday. I was at your house to tell you the new place was ready when I got word. He would have been there on Sunday, waiting for you."

Renee's eyes widened and a cry broke from her. She tried to get up, but the various lines attached to her body stopped her from moving more than a few inches.

Claire grabbed her, helped her sit up, patted her arm.

"Daniel?" Renee's voice broke.

The man in the wheelchair held his arms out to Renee as the orderly wheeled him across the room. He grinned, and his beautiful eyes gleamed as he rolled up next to his wife and grabbed her hand.

Holt moved around the bed to stand at Claire's side, his arm snug around her waist.

He smiled at her. Claire had said she wanted things to be different between them. He intended to make sure that they were.

The End

More About THE MOTHER ROAD – Route 66

Nearly 400 miles of Route 66 passes through Oklahoma, perhaps thanks to Cyrus Avery, a Tulsan, and a prominent member and president of the National US Highway 66 Association in 1927. In Oklahoma, the route followed former unimproved Oklahoma roads numbered 39, 7 and 3, which mostly followed a branch of the former Ozark Trail in eastern Oklahoma, overlapped the Postal Route and followed the railroad. Most of Route 66 through Oklahoma, a two-lane highway, was completely paved by 1937.

Additional Resources:

Dunaway, David King editor. A Route 66 Companion. University of Texas Press: Austin, TX. 2012.

Knowles, Drew. Quick Reference Encyclopedia. Santa Monica Press: Santa Monica, CA. 2008.

Ross, Jim. Oklahoma: Route 66. Ghost Town Press: Arcadia, OK. 2001.

Wagner, Don. Route 66: The Oklahoma Experience. Oklahoma Tourist Guides, Inc/Tulsa Books: Tulsa, OK 2010.

Wagner, Don. Route 66: The Tulsa Experience: Where Route 66 Intersects Art Deco. Oklahoma Tourist Guides, Inc/Tulsa Books: Tulsa, OK. 2009.

Wallace, Michael. Route 66: The Mother Road. St. Martin's Press: New York, NY. 1990.

Other Books by MARY COLEY

Fiction:

The Family Secret Series

Cobwebs: A Suspense Novel. Wheatmark. 2013.

Ant Dens: A Suspense Novel. Wheatmark. 2014.

Beehives: A Suspense Novel. Wheatmark. 2015.

Chrysalis: A Suspense Novel. Moonglow Books. 2018.

The Oklahoma Series

Blood on the Cimarron: No Motive for Murder. Moonglow Books. 2017.
Blood on the Mother Road: No Place to Hide. Moonglow Books. 2021.

The Ravine. Wild Rose Press. 2016

Crystalline Crypt. Moonglow Books. 2019

Nonfiction:

Environmentalism: How You Can Make a Difference. Capstone Press: Mankato, MN. 2009.

Short Stories by ML Coley:
Naked Ladies: Seasons of the Heart. ML Coley and CreateSpace, 2013
Beneath A Wild Sky: Forest Cat and Other Stories. ML Coley and CreateSpace, 2013

What Others Are Saying About Mary Coley Mysteries (taken from certified reviews on Amazon.com)

COBWEBS (Book 1 of the Family Secret Series) Winner of the DELTA KAPPA GAMMA Creative Women of Oklahoma award for Young Adult Fiction, 2015. Set in Pawhuska, OK with ties to the Osage Indian Murders. Readers say: engrossing…characters and plot are finely drawn…lots of little details…twists and turns kept the pages flying…true facts inspired this story…great quick read…love her books and the history she includes n the story line…well-written…intriguing and atmospheric.

ANT DENS (Book 2 of the Family Secret Series) Finalist in the OKLAHOMA BOOK AWARDS and the NEW MEXICO/ARIZONA BOOK AWARDS, Winner of the DELTA KAPPA GAMMA Creative Women of Oklahoma award for Young Adult Fiction, 2016. Set in Las Vegas, NM. Readers say: very suspenseful…surprised by the ending…atmospheric…creeping suspense…well crafted…an excellent suspense story…research into aspects of the story to make it realistic…a scenic, beautifully described location.

BEEHIVES (Book 3 of the Family Secret Series) Set in Osage Hills State Park, Oklahoma.
Readers say: Never a dull moment…a master of location research and description…kept me guessing…excellent writer…weaves history around her fictional characters…great read with great suspense…paints beautiful pictures with her words…fast paced…emotionally deep…immensely satisfying.

CHRYSALIS (Book 4 of the Family Secret Series) Set in Ponca City, Oklahoma. Readers say: Great read...captures your attention from the beginning and keeps it through the end...intricate relationships...enjoyed the whole book...good mother/daughter twist...kept me guessing...didn't see the ending coming...creepy.

THE RAVINE (Book 1 of the Black Dog series) Set in Tulsa, Oklahoma. Readers say: Five stars...an emotional journey...suspense and sympathetic characters...captures both the ennui and quiet desperation of suburban life...skillfully woven narratives...twists and turns...hard to put down...very well-developed story line...good solid stories of relationships, expectations, and life and death.

BLOOD ON THE CIMARRON (Book 1 of the Oklahoma Series). Winner of the HILLERMAN AWARD from New Mexico/Arizona Book Awards, 2019. Finalist in the OKLAHOMA BOOK AWARDS 2019. Set in Stillwater, Oklahoma. Readers say: Entertaining...great ending...good action and suspense...intriguing characters...full of suspense and surprises...riveting...greed vs. integrity...hard to put down...never saw the ending coming...highly recommended.

CRYSTALLINE CRYPT (stand-alone mystery). Set in Oklahoma locations (Tulsa to Medicine Park). From readers: A thriller from beginning to end...amazing...carefully crafted...explosive unpredictable ending...deftly drawn characters...vivid descriptions...highly recommended...fast paced...thrilling...a masterpiece.

About the Author:

Thank you for reading this Mary Coley Mystery.

A native Oklahoman, Coley has worked professionally as a naturalist, a park planner, a journalist, an outreach director, a communications officer, and an adjunct professor focusing on environmental education before pursuing her life-long passion for writing as a mystery/suspense author. Her writing reflects a devotion to mystery and her love of nature, animals, and the study of relationships.

Mary Coley has traveled widely in the United States, as well as Ireland and Scotland. Coley and her husband have five children, five grandchildren, three step-grandchildren, and their dog, Trixie. She lives part-time in northern New Mexico but has been a resident of the Tulsa area for 25 years. Currently, she is working on a book of short stories, roughly based on personal experiences.

Blood on the Mother Road: No Place to Hide is her eighth mystery.

Learn more about Mary and her books on her website/store: https://marycoley.com. Additional social media accounts:
www.facebook.com/MaryColeyAuthor
https://www.goodreads.com/author/show/3004195.Mary_C
oley?from_search=true&from_srp=true
www.amazon.com/Mary+Coley+Books
www.pinterest.com/MaryColeyMysteries
https://www.youtube.com/results?search_query=Mary+Col
ey+Book+Trailers

CPSIA information can be obtained
at www.ICGtesting.com
Printed in the USA
LVHW011117190222
711485LV00008B/301